THE TIME THAT TRAVELED

Copyright © 2013 by Kyle Todd

Table of Contents

Part I – Ancient Rome

Part II – Feudal Japan

Part III – Ancient Greece

Part IV – The Future

THE TIME THAT TRAVELED
PART I
ANCIENT ROME

This story begins in the modern era with a boy named Todd who has just turned eighteen years old. He has a family who loves him and he just recently graduated from high school. He was not like most kids his age, not that he was really different, but he did not drink, smoke, or do any drugs. Even though some of his friends did, he just accepted them for themselves. He also played for his school's varsity soccer team and worked out on a regular basis.

Todd often felt like he was going to do something great with his life, but he didn't really have an idea as to what that great thing would be. He would recall that several times his teachers and friends would say things like, "I have a feeling you're going to become someone really famous." or "I just know you're going to have an amazing future, Todd."

A few weeks after Todd graduated from high school, he was at home sitting at the dining room table and had got to talking with his parents. His mom said, "Now that you have finished school, what do you want to do with your life? College, technical school, a job?" His dad firmly stated, "I think you should join the Army."

Todd thought for a minute and replied, "I still don't know what I want to do just yet. Let me think about it some more and I'll get back to you."

Todd's mom said, "Okay, don't worry about it, but try to come up with something soon." His dad insisted, "He doesn't have that long to think about it, he needs to have a future now."

Todd said, "I know dad, I get it. I need to do something soon." Todd went downstairs to his bedroom to sleep for the night.

Todd's room was in the basement down a steep set of stairs. He opened the door to his room, which had a few stickers stuck on it. One of the stickers was the American flag and the rest were sports teams he liked.

His room had an oriental theme, because he liked the Asian culture and history, as well as many others. History was one of his favorite school subjects. The room was a little bit of a mess. Todd had a few stacks of clothes around the room, movies and video games on the floor, and dishes he'd been meaning to take up to the kitchen.

As Todd made his way over to the window to look at the stars, he glanced at his bed and thought, 'How am I going to sleep tonight?'

Staring out into space at the stars, he said to himself out loud, "Man, I wish I could just go back in time and live in ancient Rome. Back then, things like planning your future didn't matter so much."

After Todd made his wish to the night sky, he looked out into his backyard with a slight sadness, feeling as though he missed the past and ancient times. Deep inside Todd had always dreamed of what it would have been like to live in ancient Rome. He loved the stories of the Roman Empire in his history class and thought it would be incredible to live in that time period.

Todd's digital clock's glowing green numbers read 11:11pm. Todd thought to himself, 'Well, I might as well get to bed.' Since it was June and summertime, he knew it was rather early for him to call it a night. But Todd was too depressed thinking about his conversation with his parents, so he didn't even bother to see what was going on with his friends. He didn't feel like going out, even though it was a Friday night.

Todd got into his bed and looked around his room. The TV was against the wall by his bed. His bookshelf was at the foot of his bed across the room. The desk was near the entrance to the room.

Todd had a sword in his room as a decoration following the oriental theme. Todd's sword was a samurai's sword, the katana, which had an attractive black case with a golden sun dragon. The case and dragon would shine very brightly in the light, which made it look very beautiful. The sword was a real and very sharp one, and Todd knew how to use it.

Todd had researched and practiced Kenjutsu training and planned to find a sensi (teacher) for further guidance. Todd always thought, 'At least now if the world ends, I have my sword.'

Before closing his eyes, Todd looked back at the clock, which still read 11:11pm as it had when he made his wish at the window. He didn't think anything of it, as his thoughts turned back to his conversation with his parents. When he began thinking again about his options for the future, he found his way back to considering, 'What if I lived in ancient Rome?' Then as Todd thought about this enticing option, he fell into a deep sleep.

The following day when Todd woke up, it was really hot in his room and he wondered why. He guessed it was because his mom had not turned on the A/C the night before.

Todd lifted his head and looked at his clock, finding it not on but plugged into the wall. Now he knew why it was so hot in his room. It was because the power was out.

Without looking out his window, Todd sat up and got out of bed. Still dressed in what he wore to bed, which was just his boxers, he made his way to the door and as he twisted the knob and pulled the door towards him, a rush of warmth came over him from the other side. Much to his surprise there was no family room and no stairs.

As Todd's eyes adjusted to the bright light from opening the door, he noticed what was on the other side. Todd saw only trees and grass with rays of sunlight coming at him through the trees' leaves. His face was warmed by the sun as he looked out his doorway. He thought, 'This is crazy. I must be dreaming.' Todd shut the door and went to his bed, got in, and fell back to sleep.

When Todd woke again, his room was even hotter. He remembered his crazy dream and quickly jumped out of bed. As he ran towards the door, he kicked a pile of clothes that were near the foot of his bed and flung open the door.

When the door opened, there was a breeze of hot air. As Todd looked out his open door, he could see the trees and grass were still there. Only now, there was more light shining through the trees and a small deer, which ran away as soon as it noticed Todd's movement.

Todd hit himself in the leg with his right hand to make sure this was not some kind of dream. It hurt when Todd hit himself, so he knew he wasn't dreaming. This was all very real.

Todd backed up into his room and shut the door. He put on a plain, red tee and some black basketball shorts. He put on some clean white socks and his Jordan sneakers. He took his sword down off the wall and tied it around his waist. When Todd had finished getting dressed and was ready to go, he thought about his family. What might have happened to them or did this thing only happen to him? He thought about his sister, mom, and dad, then he left his room.

As he opened his door again, Todd looked up into the trees for the sun. When he saw it bright, high in the sky right above him, he noticed that it was at its highest. 'Well it must be noon, since the sun is straight above me,' he thought. Once Todd had figured out what time it was, he walked in a straight line from his bedroom door through the woods.

After Todd had been walking for some time, without making any turns left or right, he started to hear some voices. He ran closer to where the voices were and hid behind a tree, kneeling in the shadows.

Todd noticed the voices he heard had come from troops in a Roman camp. Todd was now in shock. He thought, 'Somehow I must have traveled back in time to ancient Rome. This is so awesome.' He got up from the ground and started to head towards the Roman camp, now thinking he would be safer with them than in the woods by himself.

As Todd came out of the woods into the little clearing, two Roman soldiers came out from behind some bushes and seized him. They brought Todd to their captain. They stated, "We found this spy in the woods."

Todd was thrown on the ground in front of the Roman commander. He looked at the commander's feet then picked himself up. He didn't pull out his sword. He knew that if he did, he would surely die and fast.

The two Roman guards that seized him stood close by. The one on Todd's left was about his height and well-built, like Todd, but the one on his right was a lot bigger than him and very muscular. He reminded Todd of how a bodybuilder would look in his time.

The Roman commander looked much older than the two guards, who both looked to be in their early twenties. Todd guessed the commander was in his late thirties or early forties. He had a few grey hairs but was pretty well-built too. Todd also noticed the commander's armor was of a much finer quality than the Roman guards.

The commander looked at Todd strangely and said, "What are you doing here? Where did you come from? Why were you spying on us? Are you with the Gauls or the Carthaginians?"

Todd was puzzled and said to the commander, "What?! I am no spy and I'm not with any army! I don't know what I'm doing here."

The guard on Todd's left said, "We know he is a spy, sir. We found him out lurking around the camp in the woods." The other guard on Todd's right said, "Yes, sir, Lord Quintius, he was out in the woods and he was trying to hide as well."

Todd replied, "I was only hiding because...," when Quintius put his hand up to silence him. "What is your name, young man?" "Well my name is Todd, sir."

Quintius looked at Todd strangely, because that name was very unusual for his time and he had never heard anything like it before. "Well, that is an odd name I have never heard before. I will be calling you Toddacis. I know you are no spy, even though you are dressed very strangely. But you wear our colors, which lets me know that you are no spy."

Todd looked down at his plain, red tee shirt and noticed that under the Roman guard's armor their shirts were red and that their flag banners were red as well. He put two and two together and remembered, 'Duh, the Romans wore red as a symbol of power.'

Quintius asked, "So tell me, Toddacis, what are you doing here?" Todd replied, "I don't know, sir. And to tell you the truth, I don't know how I got here either."

The commander replied, "Very well, but for now…" He was interrupted by the war cries of the Gauls, as they came running out of the woods towards the Roman camp.

Quintius yelled loudly, "Men, quickly to your positions and arm yourselves now, for there is going to be a glorious battle today!" The guards left Todd and ran to go do battle with the Gauls and help the other soldiers.

As Todd stood there next to Quintius, he noticed a Roman shield on the ground reflecting the sun's rays. He picked it up with both hands and put it on his left arm. It was very heavy. Todd knew he wouldn't have been able to pick it up if he was too weak. He was very thankful he had taken weight lifting in high school for three years and that he was on the school varsity soccer team. These activities had made him strong enough to pick up the shield. It was very large, the shield's length ran from his shoulder to his knee, and it was as wide as his body from shoulder to shoulder.

As Todd got the shield situated, he heard running from behind and turned around to see a Gaul charging right at him. Todd quickly raised the shield and blocked the Gaul's attack. The slashing sword stroke bounced right off the shield.

As the Gaul backed up from the recoil of hitting the shield, Todd took out his katana and swung it at the Gaul's neck cutting off his head with ease. Todd was surprised and shocked that he'd just done that to another person, and was even more surprised at how sharp his katana actually was. He knew he had to defend himself or he would have been killed. Todd was now shaking from the shocking encounter.

Quintius and a few Roman soldiers had seen all that Todd had done and came running over to him. Quintius said, "Thank you Toddacis, for you have saved my life and in doing so, I will not harm you or punish you for the earlier misunderstanding."

Todd looked confused and then realized he had actually kept a Gaul from coming up behind Quintius and killing him. He said, "Thank you, Quintius."

Quintius replied, "If you do not know where you are, I will at least tell you. You are in the Spaniard countryside, off the edge of the wilderness. I am willing to have you join my legion of men here today, if you find that is what you want to do?"

Todd thought about it and considered that he wouldn't survive for long out in the middle of the wilderness alone. He said, "Sure, why not, I'll join your legion."

Once Todd answered, Quintius smiled as if knowing Todd would agree. "Men, go and get me some of the best newly made armor, shield, and sword for this man here," he ordered his soldiers.

When the soldiers came back with the equipment for Todd, he received a shiny helmet with a red feather on top, a newly made and extremely strong chest plate that came with a chain mail shirt to go underneath it. There were also leather bracers with two very shiny shin guards.

Todd decided to keep his Jordans for his shoes, as well as his black basketball shorts and plain red tee. He dressed in his new Roman armor – chain mail shirt, chest plate, shin guards, and leather bracers. Then Todd put on the final touch, his new Roman helmet.

After Todd was fully armored, he tied his own katana around his waist, so he did not take the Roman sword that was offered to him. He then picked up the shield he had used at the ambush from the Gauls.   After seeing Todd with all his new gear and armor on, Quintius remarked, "Toddacis, you look like a true Roman." Todd guessed this was a compliment and said, "Thank you, Quintius."

Quintius then yelled to the legions, "Now men, we move out to the Spaniard coast. We make for the Roman Lake to go over to the Africa and take down the Carthaginians for what they tried to do to Rome and our families!"

Todd thought this was a strange way to speak, 'the Africa' but figured it was just Quintius' way.

They headed out towards Spain's coastline, so they could make way to Africa and the city Carthage. The Spanish coastline was not a far distance. On their way there, they only had to camp once. The campsite was pretty safe. It was in a good clearing, so they could see all around and no one could sneak up on them.

When they camped, Quintius had Todd stay with him in his tent. As they sat at a fire out in front of Quintius' tent, Quintius said, "Toddacis, I have a question for you."

Todd answered him, "Yes, sir. What is your question?" Quintius asked, "I was wondering if you have a woman where you come from?"

Todd laughed for a second and smiled, because he hadn't had a girlfriend in a whole year. He replied, "No, sir. Why do you ask?"

Quintius stated, "I was curious to know. And when we get back to Rome, I believe you may find one, for the women of Rome are very beautiful and strong spirited."

Todd was surprised to hear that he would be going to Rome and asked, "We are headed to Africa. We will be going to Rome when we are done there?"

Quintius now laughed and said, "Yes. Did you think we were going to stay at the place the god Mars demands be conquered and destroyed?!"

Todd was confused for a minute and then remembered the god of Mars in Roman times was the god of war. Todd was very excited to hear he was going to see

Rome. He replied, "Well yes, but if we are going to be heading to Rome, then I am very happy and cannot wait to get there."

Quintius laughed again saying, "Ah, yes, Rome is a magnificent place and when you get there, I would like to show you my daughter, Natilia. She is very beautiful and all the men of Rome wish for me to give her to them, but I am very particular when it comes to choosing a suitable man for my daughter."

Todd recalled how women were treated in ancient times. He knew they did not get to do much freely and could not even choose the man they wanted to be with. At first Todd doubted he would even be interested, not having met or seen her. He also remembered that back then men often had more than one wife. But he didn't want to be rude to Quintius, so he said, "Well, I should let you know Quintius that I am a one-woman type of guy. There will be no other women besides the one I pick and ask to marry me."

Quintius laughed with joy for what Todd had said. He stated, "Yes, aren't we all?! I knew you would say that, for it pleases my heart to know that you would never leave the woman you are with for another. That is why I want you to meet my Natilia."

Todd smiled at Quintius and was glad to know that he hadn't insulted him in any way. He was also pleased at the thought of meeting Natilia. At least, he might get to meet a pretty girl out of this wild adventure. However, he didn't want to make any promises to Quintius yet.

Todd was also wondering how Quintius had known that he was a one-woman type of guy and said, "I would very much like to meet her when we get to Rome. Also, how did you know that I am a one-woman type of guy, Quintius?"

Looking away from the fire, and back at Todd, he said, "Because you are a lot like me in character. You are loyal, honest, trustworthy, and even kind. All the things a man should be."

Todd could sort of see how he figured him out, since they were alike, but he was shocked to know that Quintius was fond of him. He said, "Well...wow...I didn't know all of that, thank you, Quintius."

Smiling at Todd Quintius said, "You are welcome, Toddacis. And if there is anything you need in the future or have problems with, just let me know about it. I will help you as much as I can."

Todd thanked Quintius again and then they ate their evening meal. It was just bread, grapes, ham, and some water for Todd. When Todd finished his cup of water, he went to bed in Quintius' tent.

When morning came it was a little foggy, the grass was moist, and the sun was shining a little light over the top of the trees at the edge of the clearing. The soldiers packed up everything and as they were getting ready to head out, Quintius said to Todd, "Today we will cross the Roman Lake and head to the Africa."

Todd thought that was rather quick but was excited to be crossing over the Mediterranean Sea to go to Africa. He smiled at Quintius and said, "Sounds like today is going to be a fun day."

Quintius replied, "Yes, it will be if by the gods all goes well." As they headed out and the legion of troops started marching towards the Spanish coastline, Todd tried getting on his horse, which was an action he was still trying to master. After a few attempts, he finally made it onto his horse.

The soldiers marched on. As they neared the coast, Todd could hear the surf splashing on the shore. They continued forward and as they arrived at the top of a hill, the harbor and sea came into view.

Quintius said, "Well Toddacis, you are about to see the magnificent Roman Navy and her fleets. They are the most superb ships out in the Roman Lake and no other ships can best ours."

Todd said eagerly, "I am very much looking forward to seeing the Navy." Quintius replied, "I know you will enjoy it, Toddacis."

Todd recalled what he had learned in his history class and knew that at this point in time, the Roman Navy was the finest in the whole Mediterranean Sea. Quintius had called it the "Roman Lake." Todd knew why he had used this name. Rome ruled almost all of the lands around the Mediterranean Sea, so it had come to be known as the Roman Lake.

Once the soldiers arrived at the harbor, Todd saw fleets and fleets of galley ships and legion after legion of Roman soldiers arriving at the same location. The ships were much bigger than he had imagined them to be and the number of legions gathering there was more than he could have pictured. He was even more impressed with how all of the legions stayed in perfect formation, as they all grouped together and came to this one area. Each legion stayed totally organized with disciplined soldiers standing at attention.

Quintius said to Todd, "Feast your eyes on the magnificent Roman Navy in all her glory!" Todd was amazed to see the numerous ships and legions and replied, "Wow! There are so many of them!"

With a grin, Quintius said, "I told you Toddacis, we have the greatest navy in the whole world. And now we are going to avenge ourselves of those barbarians."

As they made their way through the harbor, many of the soldiers saluted Quintius. And many of the legion soldiers stared at Todd. One of the soldiers who was short, stocky, and had a long scar across his cheek said, "Hey you! What are those on your legs? And why do you wear such a thing?"

Todd looked down at his pants, which needed to be washed, and realized the solider was asking about his black basketball shorts. He said, not thinking of the words he was using as he spoke, "What, these? They are just my Nike basketball shorts."

The soldier looked puzzled for a moment then replied, "So they are your victory shorts. That is very odd, but I do hope they work."

Now Todd was the one puzzled, until he realized he had said Nike and back in ancient Greece 'Nike' meant victory. Todd laughed a little to himself and was glad to see that other soldiers were laughing too.

Todd answered, "They will, soldier, don't you worry about that." Todd decided from now on he better just call them his basketball shorts instead of 'Nike basketball shorts'.

Upon arriving at their ship, Quintius said to Todd, "There she is Toddacis. Is she not a thing of beauty? One of the best ships in the whole of Rome."

Todd thought of the modern day carriers and how big they were, as he looked at the smaller galley ship with all its oars and sails. He didn't realize how far technology had come, until he saw the Roman ship and the huge difference there was between a wooden ship and a metal one. Not wanting to disappoint Quintius, he said, "Oh yes, it's great, truly great, sir. A thing of wonder."

Quintius replied, "Yes, it took a lot to build this ship." Todd thought to himself, 'If you think that takes a lot, try making a full steel carrier.' Quintius took a deep breath, "Come aboard with me, Toddacis, and have a view of this glorious navy warship for yourself."

They proceeded up the galley's ramp that was connected to the docks and onto the ship's deck. Once onboard, a man ran right past Todd and gave a letter to Quintius. The man was breathing hard and looked very tired, like he had run a long way.

After Quintius finished reading the letter, Todd said, "I hope all is well, sir." Quintius replied, "Yes, it is just a letter from my dear friend, Julius Caesar."

Todd's mouth dropped open in shock at what he'd just heard, "From the Julius Caesar?!" Quintius looked at him puzzled. Todd's shocked reaction and comment sounded like he thought the letter was from the ruler of Rome.

Quintius replied, "Yes, Toddacis, from my good friend Julius. After all, he is the General."

Todd was still surprised to hear that it was from the actual Julius Caesar from his history books. He wondered if he would get to meet him and what he would look like.

Todd said, "Well, I mean I know of him. That's why I was...umm...shocked."

Quintius said, "I thought as much. Everyone has at least heard of my old friend. When I write him back, I know he will be pleased to hear he is renowned, as well as the story of how you saved my life." He smiled at Todd.

Todd was now even more surprised and very pleased to know that someone famous from history was going to hear about him. Now he could tell people that Julius Caesar knows his name. Excitedly he said, "Me, you would put in a good word to Julius about me?!"

Quintius replied, "Yes, would I not? You did save my life so I must tell my dear friend all about it." Quintius laughed and said, "You are a strange one, Toddacis, but that is why I like you so."

Todd was still dazzled by the thought that a famous person would learn of him. After all, back in his time no one famous had ever heard of him. He said, "Thank you very much, Quintius. You really are a good man."

Quintius replied, "Well, by the gods, I try to be. Now if you will excuse me, I must write back to my friend."

Anxious for him to respond to Julius' letter, Todd said, "Of course, I understand. Don't let me hold you up. Tell Julius I said hello."

Quintius smiled and said, "Thank you, Toddacis. I will be a few hours, but I will be back nonetheless." He turned and walked away.

Todd thought to himself, 'What should I do now? Maybe I should go and get to know some of the soldiers.'

Todd walked back down the galley's ramp and away from the ship. Once back on the roadway, he headed towards a soldiers' tent. Todd was still dressed in his newly made Roman armor.

When Todd entered the tent, it was brightly lit in most areas and also very warm. Most of the soldiers were sitting around, laughing and drinking, having a good time. Some of them were arm wrestling and others were actually wrestling on the ground.

As Todd made his way through the tent, one of the soldiers noticed him and shouted, "Hey you, captain's boy! I challenge you to a wrestling match!"

The tent immediately got quiet. Everyone was staring in shock at the soldier who had shouted. It seemed they couldn't believe he had just called Todd out.

Another soldier spoke, "Hey Bruteeni, you do not need to mess with that man. He is not worth it."

The soldier Bruteeni sneered at Todd, "Or is he worth it? I want to see just how strong you are, captain's boy. Then we will see who truly should wear that shiny new armor."

Todd looked at the man and realized he was the same big soldier who had seized him, when he found the Roman campsite. He was also pretty sure he would lose to this big guy if they fought. Todd asked, "And why do you want to wrestle me?"

Bruteeni replied, "Because you are weak and I know I will win. Then I will have some nice new armor to fight in and kill those barbaric Carthaginians!"

Todd thought to himself, 'Obviously this Bruteeni guy has had a bit too much to drink. I think I know just how to handle this.' He said, "And I know that you are drunk, Bruteeni."

The other soldier who'd spoken up also said to Bruteeni, "Come on, he is not worth it." "What? Of course he is worth it. And now he has insulted me!" screamed Bruteeni.

As Bruteeni weaved back and forth because of how drunk he was, he almost fell down but caught himself on a nearby table. Todd stated, "It's no insult to say a drunk man is drunk."

Bruteeni shouted, "Look, there he goes again making fun of me!" Bruteeni sprinted at Todd, almost falling over a stool.

When Bruteeni got close, Todd just moved out of the way by stepping to his right. Bruteeni ran past Todd and slammed into a table. Bruteeni fell backwards to the ground and passed out. It was probably a combination of both hitting the table and ground, as well as all the Roman ale and wine he had imbibed.

The soldier who had been trying to talk Brureeni out of it said to Todd, "Sorry, he always gets like that when he drinks."

Todd looked at the soldier and recognized him as the other guard who had seized him, when he found the Roman encampment. Todd recalled he was about his height and well-built, like himself, but it was hard to tell since he was sitting down. He then noticed that all of the other soldiers in the tent had already gone back to their drinks and conversations.

The soldier said, "It is alright, nothing to worry about. So what is your name, good sir?"

Still feeling on edge from all that had occurred with Bruteeni, Todd slowly replied, "My name is Todd." "Yes, now I recall you telling Quintius, such a strange name. I will just call you Toddacis. Is that fine?"

Todd was still trying to figure out why everyone kept calling him Toddacis and thought maybe it was just how you would say Todd in Latin. He answered, "Yeah, its fine. So what's your name, if I may ask?"

The soldier answered, "My name is Starpius. I am one of the captain's guards."

Todd had already figured that much out, because he recognized him from when the soldiers had seized him. He had also noticed Starpius with Quintius every now and then. Todd said, "I thought you looked familiar. I've seen you walking beside me and Quintius on occasion."

Starpius looked at him in surprise. He was shocked to hear that Todd had even noticed him. "Yes, I am just making sure that both of you are safe, that is all."

Todd knew that's what he was doing because that was his job. Todd replied, "Thank you, Starpius, for watching out for me."

Starpius quickly stated, "No, please, you do not have to thank me. I am just doing my duty. Come here. Sit down so we can talk."

Todd was feeling a little more relaxed but still looked around to make sure this wasn't some kind of set up. He wasn't about to get jumped. He proceeded over to the table where Starpius was seated and joined him.

Todd glanced over at the tent entrance and noticed it was starting to get dark out. He figured he better head back shortly. He wanted to return to Quintius before he could think anything was wrong. Todd was also anxious to hear what Starpius had to say to him. He asked, "So Starpius, what is it you want to tell me?"

Starpius thought for a moment then raised his brow and said, "Well, where should I start? Oh I know! Do you like the captain, Quintius?"

Todd thinking this could be a trick question to see if he was loyal or not, said quickly, "Yes! Why?"

Smiling Starpius said, "Good, good, I thought it to be true. Quintius has no sons, only a daughter. And I know she is very beautiful, but that is beside the point. I believe Quintius is treating you as if you are his son. He is very taken with you, Toddacis. And I thought you would like to know this. Also, I think he wants to make you into a great man. He has said that you are very skilled with your sword, and it is like no other sword he has seen before. Since you do not know how you came to be here, he sees this as another sign. Quintius truly believes you to be the son he has been asking the gods for."

Todd thought about how Quintius had been behaving towards him since they met. He realized that Quintius was treating him very good, and perhaps even sort of like a son. He said, "Wow! I never looked at it like that... I mean...I knew he was treating me very well, but now I understand why."

Starpius replied, "You are fortunate. Quintius is a very smart and brave man, and kind as well. Many of these men here would kill for a chance to learn from Quintius. They know he could teach them much about fighting skills and battle strategy."

Todd considered this for a moment then remembered the setting sun. Now that he knew Quintius was treating him like a son, Todd figured he was probably wondering where he'd got off to. He didn't want Quintius worrying about him so he stood up from the table and said, "Thank you for that insight, but now I should be getting back. I don't want Quintius to be concerned. I will see you tomorrow. Good night, Starpius."

As Todd turned towards the entrance of the tent and started to walk away, Starpius said, "Hey! You be good to him, Toddacis, for he is a very honorable man."

Todd turned back and smiled. He said to Starpius in confirmation, "I will!" Todd headed out of the soldiers tent entrance and back to Quintius' galley ship.

As Todd walked the path back to the galley ship, he could feel the temperature had already dropped a little bit. The night air was warm and the heat from the day was starting to subside. He noticed the bright light of the moon in the clear night sky. He thought the moon was much bigger in ancient times than in his own time. He stopped walking for a moment to admire its beauty. As he gazed at the moon, he felt a great sense of warmth in his heart. He smiled as he started to walk again towards the ship.

As Todd came up to the ship, he noticed that Quintius was standing at the top of the ship's ramp. Todd headed up the ramp and met Quintius.

Quintius smiled and asked, "So, how did you like the soldiers in the army tent?"

Todd thought of how Bruteeni had tried to fight him for his armor. However, he didn't mention this to Quintius. Since Starpius had apologized for his friend, Todd didn't want to get one of Quintius' own bodyguards in trouble. He also considered Starpius' efforts to be sure Todd's intentions were honorable and that he wasn't a threat to their captain, Quintius. Todd replied, "You have some really good men. They are very loyal to you."

Quintius knew immediately who Todd was talking about and said, "Oh, you must have spoken with my guard, Starpius. He is a very loyal soldier. I couldn't have picked a better man to protect and defend me."

Todd was a little surprised Quintius knew it was Starpius he had talked to. He started to ask about it but then remembered the letter Quintius had received from Julius Caesar. Todd thought it would be so awesome if he were able to read it. He asked, "So, what did the General say in his letter, Quintius, sir?"

Quintius replied, "Julius wants us to move out to the Africa at first sunlight."

Todd was now anxious to get to bed so they could head out in the morning, and maybe he'd get to meet Julius Caesar. He asked excitedly, "Do you want me to go tell the soldiers?! I mean...I can do that for you, sir...if you'd like."

Quintius laughed and was pleased that Todd was eager and wanted to help. He said, "No, I will go inform the men and give the orders. You should board the ship and get your rest. When you wake up, we may already be out to sea."

Todd thought it wouldn't be possible for him to sleep through the ship leaving port...if he could even get to sleep. He replied, "Ok, I will go to bed. Once again, thank you for everything you have done for me, Quintius, sir."

Quintius was gratified to hear Todd's thanks but responded, "No thanks are needed. Now go and sleep. We may have to do battle soon." Todd said, "Good night. See you in the morning."

Quintius headed down the ship's ramp and then proceeded towards the army tent to give the soldiers their orders.

After watching Quintius depart, Todd looked at the stairs leading down into the galley ship. They were dimly lit by a few oil lamps. He proceeded down the steps into the hull of the ship to his quarters. Surprisingly, he was sound asleep shortly after lying down.

The next day when Todd woke up, he found himself again on the galley ship and knew he was still back in time in ancient Rome. He dressed in his basketball shorts and tee shirt and then slipped on his Jordans. He left his quarters and headed to the stairs to walk up out of the hull. As he proceeded up the steps, he felt blinded by the bright sunlight.

Todd reached the galley deck and his eyes adjusted to the light. He looked around and found that they had already left port. The Mediterranean Sea was beautiful, blue and sparkling in the sunshine. He noticed the sound of a beating drum and saw all the soldiers rowing in synchronization. They were first stroking right, then left, to the beat of the large drum.

Quintius spotted Todd on the deck and walked over to him. He was happy to see him finally up and about. "Ah, at last, you are awake. I was beginning to wonder how long you would stay abed."

Todd answered laughing, "I didn't think I slept that long." Quintius, guessing he must be in need of rest, said, "Well, I know the last few days have been very demanding for you. After all, you are accustoming yourself to being a Roman now."

Smiling at each other, Todd replied, "Yeah, it's been very exciting." He thought to himself, 'Exciting to be a Roman and to have traveled back in time!' Todd decided he was curious to know how old Quintius was and asked him.

Quintius, with a slight grin on his face, replied, "Well I'm now 39 years and still fighting strong. If the gods are willing, I believe I may reach my 60's." As he gazed out at the beautiful blue sea, Quintius asked, "How do you fair at fishing?"

Todd was a little surprised by this question. He answered, "Well, I'm pretty good at it. Why do you ask?"

Quintius replied, "I was just thinking we could do some fishing and try to give our hard working soldiers something good to eat for dinner. What do you say to that, Toddacis?"

Todd was pleased to think about doing something he knew well and enjoyed. He said, "I think that's a great idea. Let's get to it."

Todd recalled his many visits to his aunt and uncle in Florida. He enjoyed these trips and especially the time they spent fishing. They would fish from the pier or the ocean surf, and one time they took a boat out into the bay. It was always a lot of fun.

Quintius had gathered up the fishing gear. He came back to Todd and asked, "Shall we get started?"

Todd smiled at his fond memories and the thought of making new ones with Quintius. He very happily replied, "Yeah, let's do this!"

While fishing that day, Todd caught several average-sized fish and a nice large one. Quintius, on the other hand, caught himself a big fish, two large fish, and many average-sized fish.

Once Quintius and Todd had plenty to feed the men, they both worked on skinning and gutting their haul. Quintius loaded up the fire bowl on the deck of the ship and started a fire. The oarsmen continued rowing steadily to the beat of the drum.

Once the fish had finished cooking, Quintius ordered half of the men to stop rowing and these soldiers received their dinner ration. When they finished eating, they returned to rowing and the rest of the crew enjoyed their fish dinner.

Quintius had enjoyed the day fishing and shared with Todd, "Well, that was a pleasant day and a delicious meal." Todd agreed.

Quintius stated, "Now I believe our journey to the Africa will not be much longer."

Todd asked, "So what are we looking for when we reach Africa?" Quintius answered, "There will be a messenger there from Julius to give us orders on how we should proceed."

Todd hoped he meant "the Julius Caesar" but said nothing of it. He inquired, "What if the messenger is not there when we arrive?" Quintius appreciated Todd's interest and efforts to understand their plans. He advised him, "Then we head out for the Carthage to destroy it and kill all those barbarians inside the city."

Todd was glad to hear there was a back-up plan. He said, "Good, that sounds better than just waiting around for a message."

"Yes it is," Quintius said smiling. "We will go to the Carthage if we do not get a message. That is what we will do."

Todd made his way to the back end of the ship to watch the other galleys following them. As he looked around, he saw what appeared to be hundreds of ships stretching into the distance. It seemed to him that there was no end to the number of galley ships following them. Todd thought, 'I wonder how all of this will go down when we get there.'

A short while later, Todd heard Quintius yell, "Alright men, get ready to land at the Africa! Get your armor on and be ready for anything!" At once, the soldiers went and got ready. They had to be prepared for the possibility of a battle on the coast.

Once Todd heard Quintius' command, he turned around and proceeded to the front of the ship. From there he saw the coastline of Africa.

Starpius came up to Todd and said, "Do not worry. I will not leave your side now. I have orders to stay with you and keep you safe from any harm."

Todd figured this was a command from Quintius. He told Starpius, "It's ok, man, you don't have to."

Starpius appreciated the gesture but told him, "Yes, I do. Quintius has ordered me to. But I know you can well care for yourself in a battle."

Todd smiling slightly replied, "Thanks, Starpius. I'm going to go get my armor on."

Starpius looked around at everyone else rushing to gear up and stated, "That is a very good idea."

Todd quickly headed below deck and made his way to his room. He hurriedly dressed in his armor and tied on his katana. When he rushed back up on deck, he ran right past Starpius.

Starpius followed Todd as he made his way across the ship to Quintius. Todd noticed Bruteeni standing next to Quintius. Bruteeni eyed him warily. He was concerned Todd might say something about their confrontation last night. Todd knew better than to mention Bruteeni's efforts to pick a fight with him.

Quintius said, "Toddacis, I would like to introduce you to my bodyguard, Bruteeni. And, I believe you know my other faithful guard, Starpius. I am giving Starpius to you. He will now be your guard. His orders are to protect you and keep you safe from harm on our journey to the Carthage."

Todd answered, "Thank you, sir. I have already met both of your guards back at the army tent in Spain. They both seem to be loyal, honorable men."

Quintius was pleased to hear this and stated, "Yes, they indeed are!"

Quintius turned and yelled out, "Prepare to land!" as the galley ship hit the beach sands of Africa and came to a stop. The other galleys landed and the soldiers began to disembark. Quintius had disembarked and was looking for Julius' messenger. No messenger was found and Quintius knew this could mean trouble. He ordered the men, "I want all the supplies unloaded immediately and then we make for the Carthage at once!"

Todd left the galley ship with Starpius by his side and continued scanning the distance for an approaching messenger. He said to Starpius, "No messenger is not a good sign for us."

Starpius, who was looking around cautiously, answered, "I know, keep on your guard, Toddacis."

Todd gave Starpius a look of confirmation and lifted up his Roman shield for protection. His other hand was on his katana hilt ready to draw out his sword at any moment.

A short time later, Quintius yelled, "Alright men, once everything is packed up and ready, we march to the barbarian city of Carthage!" Starpius turned to Todd and said, "Well, it is good that we will be moving out at any moment now."

Todd, anxious to leave the beach and start their journey, said, "Yeah, you're right." Todd stood staring over at the hills for a few minutes.

Starpius noticed him and asked, "What's wrong Toddacis?"

Todd snapping out of a small daze said, "Oh, I thought I saw someone over there at the top of the hill."

Starpius looked for a moment then replied, "I do not see anything. It was probably nothing. Hopefully we will soon be on our way."

Todd answered, still sure he'd seen something, "Yeah, man, you may be right. Let's get ready to go." As they prepared to march towards Carthage, Todd kept his eye on that hilltop.

When Quintius saw that everyone was ready, he yelled, "Now men, let us move out. We make way to the Carthage!" When the legions started marching, Quintius came over to Todd with an extra horse and said, "Here Toddacis. Take this horse to ride with me on our march to the Carthage."

Todd thinking of all the other soldiers that had to march, answered, "Thank you, sir. But I would like to walk with the legions whenever I get tired of riding. Is that ok?"

Quintius was pleased to realize Todd's consideration of the soldiers. He smiled and said, "Of course, Toddacis. To march with the men is a grand thing. But for now we ride."

Todd wondered about their journey and asked, "Quintius, sir, how long do you think until we get to Carthage?"

Quintius replied, "Three days at most, if there is no trouble. Now let us be on our way."

Todd answered, "Yes, sir!" Todd started to mount the horse, which was difficult to do with all his armor on. He decided it would be easier without his shield, so he tied it onto the horse's side. He then mounted the horse and almost fell off. Fortunately, he caught himself and was able to get upright.

Quintius laughed and said, "Are you having a little trouble? It seems as though you have never mounted a horse."

Todd answered, "No, I've never mounted or rode a horse before, but I'm going to learn very quickly, right now." Todd smiled at Quintius and added, "This should be interesting." He wanted to reassure him that he was up to the challenge.

Quintius replied happily, "Good, that is the spirit."

Once Todd was finally situated on the horse, they all started to head out towards Carthage. As they began their three-day journey, Todd thought of how it would only take a few hours to get to Carthage if he was in a car. At least he had the horse. He then reflected on how many of the activities and undertakings done in ancient times took a considerable amount of time.

Later in the day as the sun was going down, Quintius yelled, "Halt! We rest here for the night. As soon as there is sunlight, we make towards the Carthage!"

As the long day's journey came to an end, the legions set up camp. They took the supplies off of the carts, unharnessed the horses, and set up their tents.

Once the camp was organized, Quintius announced, "Good work, men! Now enjoy some rest and relaxation tonight, for as soon as there is sunlight we head out."

The soldiers gave a hearty cheer. Soon the air was filled with music, conversation, and laughter.

Quintius made his way over to a group of legion soldiers and said to them, "You men will be the first watch." The soldiers immediately got up and moved out to patrol around the camp. Then Quintius headed over to Todd and said, "Toddacis, you can again rest in my tent for the night, if you would like."

Todd glad to hear he had somewhere to sleep, smiled and answered, "Thank you, Quintius, I will."

Quintius replied, "Good, I am pleased." Quintius turned and started to walk away towards his large tent.

Todd quickly asked, before he got too far away, "Quintius, sir. What are you going to go do now?"

Quintius responded, "I am going to write Julius and tell him how far we are from the Carthage. And let him know there was no messenger when we arrived at the Africa."

Todd still amazed that Quintius was actually friends with Julius Cesar asked, "Will you tell Julius I said hello?"

Quintius laughed and said, "Very well, I will, Toddacis."

Quintius proceeded to his tent and Todd moved towards a campfire with a group of soldiers. As Todd approached the campfire, he noticed Starpius was with the soldiers.

Starpius saw Todd coming and yelled to him, "Toddacis! Come, we are just about to start a story of how the Spartans of Greece were conquered and laid waste by the Roman legions. Also, we have good wine and ales for all. Come, join us!"

Todd joined the soldiers at the campfire and observed that it was Bruteeni beginning to share the story. Todd also noticed that he was already slightly drunk.

Bruteeni said, "Well men, I will tell you of how the gay Greeks were brought to their doom!"

Todd thought to himself amused, 'Oh this should be good.' Bruteeni continued, "The colossal legions of the great Roman empire were amassed in front of all the Spartans of Greece. Mars, the God of War, came charging across the sky in his war chariot led by four horses. With his sword, Mars killed more than half of the Spartans alone. The great legions of Rome marched over top of all the Spartans and destroyed the rest of them, one by one, with ease!"

All the soldiers around the campfire clapped and cheered for that long ago victory. Starpius looked over at Todd and said, "So Toddacis, what did you think of the story of the victory over the gay Greeks?" Todd thought it was a crazy story, but said, "I think it was a great victory for Rome."

Starpius smiling answered, "Yes, thanks be to the gods, it was a great victory." Todd nodded in agreement and smiled at Starpius.

Todd looked up to see the big Bruteeni making his way over to them. Bruteeni stopped in front of Todd and said, "Toddacis, I just want to say sorry about the day I met you in the soldiers' tent, for I was very drunk on fine Roman ale and wine. I would also like to thank you for not sharing it with Quintius."

Todd knowing that Bruteeni was already slightly drunk, told him, "Bruteeni, it's fine. I thought perhaps you had been enjoying some ale or wine and supposed that was all there was to it."

Bruteeni was pleased to hear that Todd understood and accepted his apology. He said, "I thank you, Toddacis. And ask of you to have a drink with me." Bruteeni presented Todd a cup of wine.

Todd replied, "No thank you. I don't drink wine, only water." Bruteeni and Starpius both looked at him in shock. Bruteeni stated, "That is very odd. Here then, have this cup of water. Let us drink to this fine victorious story and to you, for being so merciful to me."

Smiling, Todd took the cup of water and said, "Ok, cheers to a great victory for Rome and for the goodness of kindness!"

Before they could drink, Bruteeni quickly interjected, "You mean your kindness, right?"

Todd replied, "No, I mean kindness in general, since you were also kind by apologizing to me."

Bruteeni stood dumbfounded for a few seconds, then he broke into a wide grin. Starpius looked at Todd with great admiration and stated, "Yes, to kindness by all!" They all drank and finished their cheers. The other soldiers also looked at Todd with great esteem. They all now said he was an honorable man.

Later that evening, Todd stood up and announced to the group at the campfire, "I'm going to go to bed now, since we will be heading out early."

Bruteeni seeing the wise choice in getting some rest, said, "Very well, that sounds about right for this time of the night."

Starpius, still following orders from Quintius, stated, "I will head back with you, Toddacis."

Todd replied, "Ok. Well, good night, Bruteeni. I will see you in the morning."

"Alright Toddacis, good night," replied Bruteeni.

Todd then headed towards Quintius' tent for the night. When Todd reached the tent, he said, "Thank you for escorting me, Starpius. I will see you in the morning, good night, man."

Starpius answered him, "It is my duty, Toddacis. A good night to you and may the gods watch over you." Starpius left for his tent.

Todd turned around and pushed open the tent flaps and went into Quintius' tent. When he entered the tent, he noticed Quintius was already asleep, so Todd made his way quickly and quietly to the other bed Quintius had set up for him to use. Todd took off all his armor, got in bed, and went to sleep.

Not so long after he had gone to sleep, Quintius shook him to wake him. When Todd opened his eyes, he saw Quintius already in his armor and ready to leave. Quintius told Todd, "Do not worry. We are not leaving just yet. I am waking you now, so you will have time to get all your armor on. I am going to wake the soldiers, so you may wish to hurry."

Todd jumped up and hurried to start getting his gear on. He said to Quintius, "I will be ready as quickly as I can, sir."

Quintius replied, "Very well, I will go rouse the men." He then headed out of the tent.

Once Todd was ready, he walked outside of the tent to see all the soldiers packing everything up. The men quickly started taking down Quintius' tent as soon as Todd exited it.

When all the camp gear was packed up, Starpius came over to Todd. He said, "Good morning, Toddacis."

Todd shivered from the cold chill of the morning air. As he rubbed both his arms, he answered, "Good morning, man. Boy, it sure is cold out here right now!"

Starpius knew the cold would not last too long. He told Todd, "I would enjoy it while it lasts, for it is going to be a very hot day. We will be marching on the edge of the desert today."

Todd smiled thinking about the heat of the desert. He answered, "Oh cool! That sounds like it's going to be a fun day."

Starpius said with a confused smile on his face, "If you say so, Toddacis."

When Quintius saw that Todd was ready and the camp gear was stored and ready for transport, he yelled out, "Men! Let us move out, and today we get close to that damned city!"

At once, all of the men cheered and started to march towards Carthage. Todd, realizing that everyone was moving out at this moment, quickly tied his shield to the horse and jumped up on it. Fortunately, this time he didn't have as much difficulty.

As the march began, Todd started thinking, 'What have I gotten myself into?' He was again wondering how he could have come back in time and why was he still there. He knew for sure this wasn't a dream, because he had been here for two days, maybe three now. He thought about all the time traveling movies he had watched back home. In all of them, the person who was going back in time or to the future used a machine or some type of device to make it happen. All Todd knew was that he had no way to travel back and no time machine either, but somehow he was back in ancient Rome. He couldn't figure it out, so he just accepted it for what it was, for now.

As Todd was thinking of these things, Quintius rode his horse up beside him and asked, "So how do you like these marches, Toddacis?"   Todd coming out his deep thoughts, which was more like a day dream, looked up at the sun and noticed that it was already the middle of the day. He answered Quintius' question, "I love them. It's fun to go to new places, where you have never been before. And conquer them. It's great!"

Quintius, smiling with joy to hear such an answer, replied, "Yes, we Romans do great things for our people and the gods." Todd said with a slight laugh, as he was still distracted with his thoughts, "Yeah, that's the good things."

Before Quintius could respond, a band of Nubian raiders came over the sand dunes on their camels. Quintius quickly rode his horse up to the frontline of the men and drew out his gladius. This was his short steel sword. He held it up high in the air and yelled, "Stand guard!! Form lines, forward ranks in front! Shield walls now!"

As Quintius yelled, the men split into groups of lines and put their shields together side by side with their swords drawn and ready. Todd, who was still on his horse, drew out his katana. He quickly untied his shield and strapped it to his left arm.

The Nubian raiders yelled out their war cry, put their spears out in front of them and charged down the sand dunes from both the right and the left. It appeared as though the Nubian raiders were riding very fast, as their robes whipped in the air. As they collided with the Romans, their war cry seemed even louder, as it was being carried across the winds.

When the camels collided with the Roman soldiers on the front line, a few of the men were knocked down but not killed. The Roman soldiers seemed to be cutting down the raiders with ease.

Out of nowhere a camel raider came at Todd with his spear. Todd quickly cut the spear in half with his katana and then swiftly cut off one of the raider's arms with ease. With a follow through swing, he managed to slice off the raider's head as he rode by.

As he turned around, Todd noticed Starpius had just killed a raider, which was coming from behind to strike him. Once seeing he almost got attacked from behind, Todd jumped off his horse and took up his shield. As he did this, he saw a raider running towards him. Todd charged at him with his shield and katana. When they ran into one another, Todd blocked the raider's sword and fiercely cut him in half with his katana. Once he had defeated the Nubian, Todd looked over at Quintius, who was starting to get surrounded by the raiders. He speedily ran over to Quintius' side. Coming up behind two raiders, Todd cut them in half with his katana. Todd, now slightly winded, said to Quintius, "I thought you could use some backup."

Quintius with a small sigh of relief, which also showed on his face answered, "Thank you for this great deed. I was starting to be overwhelmed."

Todd and Quintius then went back to back and Todd held up his shield. Every time a raider would hit his shield, he would then move it aside and strike the raider with his katana. Quintius was doing the same with his shield and sword.

Now that the battle was nearing an end, all that remained were the raiders left hurt and dying on the ground and the ones fleeing away from the fight in obvious fear. Fortunately, there were only a few casualties and injuries among Quintius' men. He ordered, "Bind the wounded and then on to the Carthage! For the god Mars is on our side today!"

After attending to the wounded, the soldiers quickly reformed into marching formation and prepared to leave. Once all of the men were in their positions, Quintius yelled, "March!! To the Carthage!!"

Todd ran back to his horse and quickly mounted it. He had also tied his shield back on the horse.

Quintius came over to Todd and said, "You did very well, Toddacis. Now we need to hurry and resume our march to the Carthage to take the barbaric city and crush them."

Todd, wondering why they were in such a hurry now after a battle, asked, "Ok. But why do we need to hurry?"

With a serious look, Quintius replied, "For there was no messenger here when we arrived at the Africa. And now we were attacked by raiders. It seems to be the Carthaginians' doing. We need to take the city Carthage straightaway before they receive word of our coming and have time to give us a good fight when we arrive. For we are trying to take the city without them being aware of our coming."

Todd now realizing the strategy responded, "Oh I see, then let's hurry." Quintius, happy to see he understood, said, "Yes, let us move out with haste."

The troops were now marching faster than before. They were anxious to get to Carthage, so they could overthrow the city and burn it to the ground.

As they marched more rapidly towards Carthage, Todd was still trying to figure out how he had traveled back to this time period. While they marched on the rest of the day, he came up with three ideas as to how he got there. His ideas were: one, God brought him back in time. Or two, the Roman gods had brought him back in time to be the son Quintius had longed for. Or last, but not least, something had transported him back to this time period. Todd was still unsure which one it was but decided he would just have to make the best of being here in Roman times. For some reason, he felt that he would not be going back home anytime soon.

After the long day's march, the troops were ordered to halt and set-up camp. As Todd looked at the setting sun from the top of a hill, he realized he could see the city of Carthage in the distance. They were setting up camp on the other side of the hill, obviously, to stay out of sight of the city.

Starpius came over to Todd and said, "We are very close now, Toddacis. Tomorrow we will take Carthage and burn it to the ground." Todd responded, "I didn't realize we were so close to Carthage." Starpius agreed, "I am pleased. We made good time in our march today."

Todd, thrilled that they were so close to Carthage, ran down the hill to Quintius. Todd asked him, "Quintius, sir, did you know how close we are to Carthage?"

Quintius laughed at hearing such a question. He replied, "Yes, I do. And we will rest tonight behind this hill. So they will not see what is coming at them."

Todd wondered about their hurried journey to Carthage and asked, "So why did we have to make it here within three days?"

Quintius revealed a part of the plan to him. He stated, "For this reason, if I or Julius did not receive each other's messages, we were not to wait, just proceed to the Carthage."

Todd thought for a second then figured out Quintius' intentions. He answered, "Oh, I see. So if something happened to the messenger, it wouldn't really matter because both of you would still arrive at the same time and place."

Quintius was pleased to hear that Todd understood and said, "Yes, Toddacis! You truly are very bright." Smiling, Quintius headed to his tent where Bruteeni was standing guard outside the entrance.

Todd walked over to Bruteeni and asked him, "So are you ready for the big day tomorrow, Bruteeni?"

Bruteeni was very happy he had been asked. "Yes! We are going to crush the Carthaginians until none of them are left standing."

Todd, realizing how eager he was to fight the Carthaginians, said, "Alright, sounds good. I'll see you in the morning then."

Bruteeni, wondering why Todd had not had a drink yet, said to him, "Wait! Are you not going to drink for the fallen soldiers that died on the way here?"

Todd then paused for a moment, thinking of what else he could do instead of drinking and answered, "No. But I will pray for them."

This pleased Bruteeni greatly. "You truly are a great man. And I almost forgot that you do not drink!"

Todd, seeing he had chosen the right answer and knowing that Bruteeni loved to drink his Roman ale and wines, said, "That's right and you can go ahead and drink for me. How's that sound?"

Bruteeni answered him in a proud voice saying, "Do not worry, Toddacis. I will drink for you in your absence." Todd thanked Bruteeni.

Starpius came over to Todd and asked, "Sir, will you be going back out from your tent later this evening?"

Todd knew why Starpius had asked the question, so he answered, "Starpius, you don't have to call me sir, just Todd or Toddacis will do. And no, I will not be going out again later on. You can go enjoy yourself, don't worry about me, really."

Starpius appreciated Todd's understanding and replied smiling, "Thank you, Toddacis. I did want a few drinks with the men. Have a good night." Starpius then turned around and walked away toward the campfire.

Todd went inside Quintius' tent. He took off all of his armor but left his shirt and shorts on. He also took off his shoes and socks, and tucked his socks in his shoes.

As Todd was sitting on the edge of his bed, Quintius came over and stood in front of him. "Toddacis, there is something I want to tell you and it is what I have been thinking about lately."

Todd, wondering what he was about to say, asked him, "What have you been thinking about, Quintius?"

Quintius answered, "I would like to give you my daughter as a wife, for I have been treating you like a son and you are now like a son to me. Therefore, I would like to make you my son in some way, so you would therefore be able to call me your father."

Todd knew the seriousness of Quintius' statements and didn't want to cause any offence. He replied, "Quintius, you are truly a good man and I will accept this offer, but only if she loves me. You see, I can't marry someone who doesn't love me."

Quintius responded happily, "Well, I know my daughter best of all people and I know that she will love you, for you are a noble and honorable man and truly good hearted. It seems as if you were given to me from the goddess Venus herself."

Todd, pleased to see he hadn't offended Quintius in any way, told him, "You're welcome, Quintius, sir. And I promise you if your daughter does love me, then I will do right by her. I will treat her better than any man could."

Quintius' heart was filled with joy and happiness. He hugged Todd and said, "Thank you, Toddacis! May the gods bless you in everything that you do."

Todd, not sure what to say while Quintius hugged him, simply replied, "Your welcome, sir."

Quintius released him from the hug and declared, "Tomorrow after we burn the Carthage, we will have a feast of victory and a celebration for you and my daughter, Natilia."

Todd responded, "That sounds like a great plan, sir, and it should be a fun day tomorrow."

Quintius said, "Yes it shall, but for now let us sleep, for tomorrow we do great battle with the Carthage people."

Todd, reminded of the upcoming battle, agreed and said, "Very well, sir. I will see you in the morning before we go to battle." Todd quickly made up his bed and laid down.

Quintius said, "Good night, Toddacis. Tomorrow will be a great day." Quintius left Todd's area of the tent and headed over to his own bed.

Todd tried to go to sleep but he had so much on his mind, it wasn't coming easily. He thought of how he got to this time period and how his family was doing without him at home. He also thought about the battle tomorrow and if he would even live through it. Then he thought about how Quintius' daughter might look and what she would be like as well. With all these things stirring through his head, Todd got little sleep that night but he did finally fall asleep.

A little while after Todd had fallen asleep, Quintius woke him up and said, "Wake up Toddacis, for today is the day we attack the Carthage."

Todd sprang up and started to get his armor on quickly and said, "I will be dressed shortly, Quintius sir. And I will be ready to help destroy the Carthaginians."

Quintius, happy to see how eager Todd was for battle, said, "Good, for I am waking the men now. So do hurry and I will be back soon to get you."

"Don't worry, I'll be ready," Todd replied as he rushed to get dressed in his armor. Quintius then turned and walked out of the tent to go wake all the men.

Todd had gotten on his socks and shoes and was already dressed in his shirt and shorts. He went over to where he had left all his armor. He put on his steel shin guards and next his chain mail shirt over top of his regular shirt. Todd then put on his steel body plate and the leather bracers around his wrists. After that, he tied his katana to his waist and put on his Roman helmet. Todd then picked up his shield and walked out of the tent. Now that he was fully dressed and armored, Todd was ready for the battle ahead.

Outside of the tent, Todd noticed how quickly everyone was packing up the campsite. Starpius spotted Todd and walked over to him. He asked, "Toddacis, are you ready for the great battle?"

Todd, trying to imagine how the battle was going to be today, answered him, "Well, if it's going to be as easy as those raiders were, then yes."

Starpius laughing at such an answer, responded, "Yes, let us hope so. But I would not count on it. The Carthage people are rather strong."

Todd, remembering what he had learned in his history class...that the Romans take the city of Carthage, said, "I know for a fact that we will take this city."

Starpius, not having the luxury of knowing the future like Todd, replied, "I hope you are right, Toddacis."

Quintius, seeing Todd and Starpius talking, came over and said, "Toddacis, we will move out shortly. You need to go and get your horse ready now."

Todd replied, "Ok, Quintius. I will go get on my horse and be ready to leave whenever you are."

Quintius was proud to see how eager Todd was to do battle. He advised, "No, you do not need to mount your horse yet. Right now, we are going to build a ram and a ladder, so we can gain access to the city."

Todd, realizing he had more time, said, "Oh, okay. Thank you, Quintius sir."

Todd was pleased not to have to rush. He went to get his horse geared up with the help of Starpius.

When they reached the horse, Todd noticed his horse's saddle on the ground nearby. He picked it up and started working on getting the horse ready to go. Todd said to Starpius, "So Quintius wants to give me his daughter's hand in marriage."

Starpius was shocked and stood stunned for a few seconds. He replied, "Toddacis, do you tell the truth!?"

Todd, now a little embarrassed that he had brought it up, answered, "Yes, I am. Why do you ask?"

Starpius realized Todd didn't understand why he was so shocked. He explained, "Quintius has never thought any man to be worthy of his very beautiful daughter. Yet, in a matter of days, he sees you fit enough to have his daughter. Not that I do not agree, for I am sure you would treat her well. The Captain must hold you in very high regard. This is magnificent, Toddacis!"

Todd was a little surprised to hear Starpius' comments. He said, "I told Quintius I would not force her to marry me if she did not love me."

Starpius was shocked again but proud to hear such an answer. He responded, "Toddacis, you truly are a noble and honorable man! More so than any man I have ever met. And I have met many men in my travels."

Todd replied, "Well, thanks. But I just told him the truth."

Starpius stopped working on getting the horse ready. He said, "And this is why he sees you fit for his daughter, Toddacis. For you are a good man inside and fair looking on the outside, if I do say."

Todd was a little embarrassed by Starpius' comments but also pleased to hear someone speaking so well of him. He thought of Quintius' daughter and told Starpius, "I do hope she likes me."

Starpius responded with a smile, "I believe she will favor you greatly."

The horse was now ready to go so Todd said, "We shall see. Now that we've finished here, let's get back to Quintius and see if any other preparations are needed."

Todd and Starpius headed over to Quintius. He was overseeing the building of the siege equipment. When they reached Quintius, Todd asked if they were ready to head out yet.

Quintius advised, "The ladder is finished and we are almost done with the ram. We shall proceed with the attack on the Carthage soon." Todd inquired, "So should I go mount my horse?"

Quintius checked on the ram's progress. He determined it was nearly complete and answered, "Yes, for we are now putting on the last wheel."

Todd quickly went and mounted his horse. He was ready to head out and go attack Carthage with the whole legion.

Seeing the ram complete and Todd ready on his horse, Quintius mounted his own horse. He yelled out, "Men, we make for the Carthage to burn it to the ground!"

Upon hearing their captain's command, all the soldiers yelled and cheered loudly, each one ready to do battle. They all started to move the siege works and marched out towards the city of Carthage.

As they neared the city, Quintius yelled, "Halt! Do not go any further near the city walls! We are out of their archers' range here!"

All the legionaries came to a sudden stop and stood perfectly still in their ranks. Quintius lifted up his sword and yelled out, "We take this city for Rome!! Burn the Carthage to the ground!"

The soldiers let out a large cheer. Quintius then ordered the soldiers with the ram, "Move forward with the ram! To the city gates! Break them down!"

At Quintius' orders, the men started to push forward the ram they had built. It was a good one, large and sturdy. The ram had eight men working it and roofing to protect them while they pushed it.

Todd could hear the men groaning as they pushed the ram. It was very heavy. He could also see the hard effort each man was putting into moving it forward. As the soldiers pushed the ram towards the gate, Todd asked, "So what are we supposed to do, Quintius, sir?"

Quintius still staring straight at Carthage's walls answered, "We wait until the men are through the gates of the city."

Todd replied, "Oh, I see." He watched as the soldiers started the siege on Carthage. He didn't like sitting back and waiting while other men were doing all the work and might die trying to ram the gate open. Once they reached the gate, the soldiers started to hit it with the ram. The Carthaginian soldiers threw down large rocks and shot tons of arrows. They also poured burning hot tar onto the ramming soldiers. Luckily, the roofing that was built on top of the ram apparatus protected them from most of the assaults. Only a few arrows had taken down some of the men pushing the ram. When they fell, another soldier ran up and took his place.

After seeing several men fall to the arrow attacks, Quintius yelled, "Men, Testudo form!" All the soldiers immediately went into that defensive form. Each legion bunched together and locked their shields together facing front, side to side. The men in the middle held their shields over top of their heads to protect them from any arrows that might rain down on top of them.

Once each legion was in their Testudo form, they all looked like they were in large square boxes that were well protected from any long range attacks. With the legions in formation and ready, Quintius yelled, "Move out, men!" The legions moved forward slowly, holding their Testudo form.

As the men marched further away from Todd, he became upset seeing them all being attacked by the archers while they held their defensive form. He said to Starpius, who was beside him on his horse, "Starpius, I can't just sit here doing nothing and watch our men die." Todd jumped down off his horse, untied his shield from the horse's side, and quickly ran towards the legions of men.

Starpius, reacting to Todd's swift departure, yelled, "Wait, Toddacis, for I will come with you!" Starpius dismounted his horse, grabbed his shield and ran after

Todd. Once Starpius reached Todd, he said, "This is either very brave or very unwise, Toddacis."

Todd, with a slight smile, responded, "Well, let's hope it's brave."

As they got closer to the archer's firing range, Todd and Starpius both raised their shields up above their heads to protect them from the flying arrows. When they reached one of the legions that were still in Testudo form and slowly marching towards the gate, they marched beside them while continuing to hold their shields up for protection from the rocks and arrows raining down on them.

As Todd was marching forward, he happened to look over at the coastline and saw the Roman navy arriving. He yelled out, "The Roman navy is here!"

When Todd had run off towards the legions into battle, Quintius said to his guard Bruteeni, "What is Toddacis doing?"

Bruteeni was unsure of Todd's motives but proud to see him taking action. He responded, "I do not know, sir, but he is very brave." Quintius, shaking his head in acknowledgment, said, "Yes, he is a valiant man, is he not?" They then heard Todd yelling that the Roman navy had arrived to help aid in the battle.

Quintius peered over at the coastline and confirmed that the Roman navy had landed. As Quintius focused in on the activity on the coastline, he spotted his dear friend Julius Caesar approaching on horseback accompanied by six bodyguards.

Bruteeni decided he better get a hold of Todd's and Starpius' horses, which they had left behind when they went to go join the fighting. He gathered their reins and returned to Quintius' side as Julius rode up with his escort.

Julius addressed Quintius, "Quintius, my friend! It has been a long time since I have seen you."

Quintius was happy to see his friend but curious to know if Julius had received his communications. He asked, "Yes, it has been too long. But hopefully you have been receiving my letters?"

Julius responded, "I only had one letter from you. You were still in Spain and told me about a Toddacis you found in the woods around your camp."

Quintius, acknowledging that their plan had worked, said, "Well then, it would seem we both arrived when needed, even if we never heard from each other."

Julius agreed their plan had succeeded but was curious to meet Quintius' stranger. He replied, "Yes, it would seem as though we did. Now, where is this Toddacis? I would very much like to meet him."

Quintius was pleased to tell Julius about Todd's brave action. He replied, "Well you just missed him. He jumped off his horse and ran to aid the legions attacking the city gates."

Julius, surprised to hear this, said, "Well done. He is a courageous man, Quintius."

Quintius answered, "Yes, this I know. And it is why I asked him if he would take my daughter for marriage. But can you guess what he said to me after I asked him this?"

Julius was curious to know what Todd had stated. He responded, "No, what did he say to you, Quintius?"

Quintius advised, "He told me only if she will love him, then he would marry her."

Julius was surprised to hear such a thing. He responded, "You have the most beautiful daughter in all of Rome and you have not given her to any man. Now you find the right man and he says only if she will love him. This Toddacis is not only a valiant man, but he is an honorable one as well. I would very much like to meet him, once we have burned down this city of Carthage."

Quintius smiled at hearing Julius' request. He responded, "Very well. Thank you, my friend."

Julius and Quintius turned their attention to the city gate and were excited to see that the ram had just broken through the gates of Carthage.

Todd glanced back at Quintius and saw him on his horse talking to Julius. Behind Julius were his many legions of Roman soldiers at the ready. They seemed to stretch as far as the eye could see. The legions also appeared very eager to do battle and anxious to charge at any order. Todd returned his focus to taking the city walls and stopping the archers from the constant stream of arrows raining down on them. He knew they needed to act swiftly to try to save Roman lives.

One of the legions of soldiers fought their way into the city. The legion Todd was with moved quickly behind and into the city as well. They trampled over a few dead Roman soldiers as they made their way in. Todd could see they had been killed by the arrows from the archers on top of the city's walls.

As Todd came through the gates, he saw the first Roman legion of soldiers fighting with the Carthaginian soldiers. Todd noticed that the Carthaginian soldiers had long square shields like that of the Romans and their short swords were made from iron instead of steel. They also weren't as fully armored as the Romans. All they wore were leather chest guards.

Todd was looking for a way to get up the wall and take out the archers when he noticed a door. He pointed at it and said to Starpius, who was still by his side, "Let's try that door to see if we can get up on the wall. We need to stop the archers that are giving us a hell of a hard time."

Starpius looked over at the doorway and agreed that it would probably take them to the top of the wall. He replied, "Good idea, Toddacis. Let us send them all to Pluto himself!"

Todd and Starpius both moved quickly towards the door and through it to get to the top of the wall. They ran up the stairs and when they reached the top, Todd pulled up his shield to protect himself from any arrows that might be coming his way.

Todd charged at a group of archers. He slashed them with his katana, cutting their arms, legs, and heads off. He even sliced a few in half.

Starpius was also cutting down archers with ease. The archers only had their bows and arrows to defend themselves. They had no swords or shields for close combat.

One of the archers got a lucky shot off. Todd was struck in the right forearm with an arrow as he was swinging his katana cutting down archers. Even though he was injured, Todd steadied his wounded arm with his left hand and kept slashing away to cut down the last of the archers.

When the archers had all been killed, Todd pulled the arrow out of his forearm. He heard Julius yell out the order to his legions, "Men, go now into the city Carthage and send their soldiers to Pluto!"

Todd went over to the edge of the wall and looked out from where the archers used to be. He saw all of Julius' legions storming through the city's gates. He turned to see the soldiers spreading out through all of Carthage and destroying everyone in their path.

A short time later, no Carthaginian soldiers remained standing. The legions had finished storming the city and they had extinguished all Carthage's inhabitants.

The legions had worked their way through the entire city. They had been through the palace and raided it of all its gold, silver, weapons, and food. The soldiers lit the palace on fire as well as several other buildings. The fire spread quickly and easily. It wasn't long before the whole city was covered in fire and burning to the ground.

As the city started burning, Todd walked back into the stairway and down from the walls of Carthage. He left the city and made his way towards Quintius.

When Todd reached Quintius, he was thrilled to see the famous Julius Caesar by his side. Julius Caesar looked like a hardened soldier who had seen many battles. Although Todd could not see any battle scars on him. He had a nearly shaved head like that of a military haircut. He appeared to be about the same age as Quintius. He had on the best body armor Todd had seen yet. It had a design of the god Jupiter on the chest and golden trimmings on the outlines of the armor. Julius also looked very strong and well-built. Even if you didn't know who he was, he seemed to be someone you wouldn't want to mess with or have to fight.

Julius looked at Todd with a slight grin on his face. He said, "You are a very brave and valiant man, Toddacis. It is an honor to meet you. I have heard much about you from my dear friend, Quintius. I am pleased to see this day that you hold up to your reputation."

Todd stood shocked. He couldn't believe that the Julius Caesar was speaking to him. He was amazed that Julius knew of him and wondered what reputation he could have. He didn't think he had any to speak of. 'What had Julius heard of him?' he thought to himself. He took a deep breath and tried to calm his nerves. He was so awestruck. He answered, "Thank you, sir. I do my best to keep to what I say."

Julius acknowledged Todd's heroic actions by stating, "I can tell. And you saved many Roman soldiers from dying by slaying those archers on the wall. Just you and your faithful guard Starpius, I believe."

Todd answered honestly, "Yes sir. It was Starpius and I that killed the archers."

Julius was impressed to meet a noble man like his friend, Quintius. He told Todd, "You are truly an impressive soldier, Toddacis. Tonight we will eat and drink to this great victory, as well as to your heroic deeds and for saving so many good Roman lives today."

Todd was grateful to hear a noteworthy figure from history speak so highly of him. He replied, "Thank you, sir. I'm truly honored."

Todd turned to Quintius and was about to speak to him, when a messenger came galloping up on a brown horse and shared news with Julius. As Julius read the report a troubled look came over his face. Todd could tell it was bad news. Julius advised them, "There is trouble in Egypt that needs our attention. We must depart at once for the city of Alexandria. We are a four-day sail away."

Quintius was curious to understand what was happening in Egypt. He asked, "What has happened, Julius. Are we under attack at the Alexandria?"

Julius turned to Quintus and replied, "No, there is rioting in the city. We must go and put an end to it."

Todd recalled what he had learned about this point in time in his World History class. He remembered that the people in Alexandria revolted and were in the midst of taking over the city. Julius arrived in time to stop it. From his galley ships, he shot flaming arrows into the city and put an end to the revolt.

Unfortunately, the flaming arrows caused an inferno of the Great Library. Todd recalled his teachers' comments about the Great Library. He thought that if it had not been burned to the ground, we would be a thousand years more advanced than we were in Todd's time.

Todd was anxious to go with Julius and help stop the revolt. And maybe, if he could figure out a way, get inside the Great Library and try to save some of the scrolls. Todd was surprised and thrilled to hear Julius' request, "I will need your help Quintius. And bring Toddacis as well, for he is a great soldier. We need someone like him to aid in our battles."

Quintius nodded in agreement and responded, "Very well, Julius. Toddacis, once we are done here, we will head out to the Egypt and put an end to these riots."

Todd was overjoyed. He said, "Alright, let's do it!" Todd went over to Bruteeni, to retrieve and mount his horse. Starpius followed and mounted his horse as well.

Bruteeni told both of them, "Let me know the next time you two decide to go running off to fight. For your horses could have run away or wandered off."

Todd realized his mistake and apologized. "I'm sorry, Bruteeni. I was so anxious to join the battle. I didn't think about anything else." Bruteeni was pleased

Todd appreciated his concern. He said, "Oh, it is all well. I was just telling you what may have happened. I thought it best to take hold of your horses for you."

Todd was still feeling slightly guilty about having Bruteeni watch after the horses. He said, "Thank you, Bruteeni. We appreciate you looking after the horses for us while we were gone."

Bruteeni could tell that Todd felt bad for what he had done. He quickly reassured him by stating, "Do not be concerned. It was no trouble, Toddacis."

Todd wanted to be sure that Bruteeni knew he was sorry for the mistake. He stated, "Well, still thank you for looking out for us."

Bruteeni was pleased to hear Todd's appreciation. He replied, "You are welcome, Toddacis." Bruteeni turned and rode his horse back over to Quintius' side.

Todd asked Starpius, "What should we do now, Starpius? Should we head over to the harbor?"

After thinking for a moment, Starpius answered, "Yes, let us go show them we are ready and eager to help put an end to this riot in Egypt."

Todd smiled and replied, "Sounds good. Let's go."

As Todd and Starpius started towards the harbor full of Roman navy ships, they heard Julius give orders to the legionaries. He commanded, "Men, once you have set fire to the whole city, put salt into their ground so nothing may grow here for years to come!"

Todd looked back towards the city. He saw that the whole city was in flames and the soldiers were already spreading salt on the ground all around the entire city and into the fields where the crops grow. These actions made Todd remember how much the Romans hated the Carthaginians. He also recalled that there had been three wars before the Romans finally killed all of the Carthaginians.

Remembering these things he'd learned in his history class back in his time period made Todd wonder again about how he could have come back to this time period. He had no idea how it had happened or what had caused it. His bedroom had seemed completely normal. He hadn't noticed anything strange. Before he could give the problem anymore thought, they had finished making their way to the galley ships.

Starpius said, "Well, I guess we should just wait. Julius or Quintius will need to let us know which ship we are to board."

Todd agreed, "Yes, you're right, Starpius. How long do you think it will take for them to finish with Carthage?"

Starpius replied, "I do not believe it will be much longer. Starpius then wondered if Julius and Quintius had anything else in mind for Carthage.

Todd looked back to focus on what was happening near the city and noticed that Julius and Quintius were already heading towards them with all of the legions. Behind them, the city of Carthage was ablaze with the sun beginning to set into the desert sands. This view of the sun setting behind the desert sand dunes and the Romans marching out of the burning ashes of what remained of their victory over Carthage, symbolized for Todd the final fall of the Carthaginian peoples and their empire.

As Julius neared Todd and Starpius, he called out to them, "Board the galley behind you, for it is my ship and we make leave immediately." Without saying a word, Todd and Starpius rode their horses up the ramp and boarded Julius' ship. The soldiers, Julius, and Quintius boarded the ship as well. Todd and Starpius put up their horses for the trip to Egypt.

Julius looked around at his men slowly getting things ready. He yelled out orders, "Men, quickly get into your rowing positions and make ready to leave without delay!"

The soldiers stopped what they were doing. Putting their shields and swords down beside them, they took seats in their rowing positions. They all waited for the order to leave and for the drums to begin beating. It was as if they were like a computer and very quickly got everything ready to move within seconds of Julius' command.

When all the ships were ready to leave, Julius yelled to them, "Now we make way and go to Egypt to settle this riot!"

Once Julius spoke, the drummers started beating their drums. Then the men started rowing to match the drum beat. The rowing men and beating drums became a synchronized pattern.

Julius came over to Todd and said, "It is a four-days journey to Egypt. Tonight we will celebrate our victory and your brave actions today, Toddacis."

The men rowed all day at a steady pace. Once it became too dark to see, Julius ordered, "Stop rowing, men! Drop the anchors. We feast to our victory and rest for the night." The soldiers immediately stopped rowing and anchored the ships.

The whole fleet was lined up side by side. Then wooden boards were laid across to each ship to form a small link. This made it possible for the soldiers to travel from one ship to the next with some ease.

Next the soldiers on each ship got a large stone bowl out and started a fire in it. With the bowls set up near the center of each ship, they started their feast of victory around the fires.

After Todd had witnessed how they set up for their camp at sea overnight, he walked down into the ship where Julius and Quintius were dining. As Todd was about to enter the hull of the ship, he told Starpius, "You can go enjoy yourself, man."

Starpius, relieved to hear these words, said, "Thank you, Toddacis, I will see you in the morning." And without Todd having to say anything else, Starpius joined Bruteeni for some drinks with the other soldiers around the fire.

Todd continued down into the ship to join Julius and Quintius for dinner. Just before he was about to enter the dining room, he heard a noise come from the storage room area of the galley. Todd looked down the dimly lit hall but didn't see or hear any movement. He then felt a twinge in his right forearm and recalled being hit by the arrow. It had really hurt him. His arm was wrapped up in a bandage to keep it clean and help it heal properly. He hesitated trying to decide whether he should go and check out the noise. He thought about getting injured and that he now knew for certain after everything that had happened today that all of this was very real. It was definitely not a dream.

Todd snapped out of this reverie and headed towards the noise he'd heard. He made his way down the hall very carefully, staying in the darker areas against the walls, and made sure that he was ready to pull his katana from his side.

When Todd got to the storage room door, he opened it very slowly and saw nothing but crates and barrels with a few candles hanging from the ceiling. The room was not well lit. It would be very difficult to make out any movement with all the shadows. The darkness in the room seemed to be playing tricks on him as he tried to focus on the many dark corners.

Todd heard yet another slight noise and went towards a barrel, from where he thought the noise had come. He drew his katana out and was ready. He quickly removed the lid of the barrel and all of a sudden a girl yelled out, "No, don't!"

As soon as Todd heard these words and her voice, he stopped himself before he had even raised his katana to strike. Todd demanded, "Who are you and how did you get here?"

The girl stood up and got out of the barrel. He noticed right away that she was a very beautiful girl. She had long, black hair that fell a little past her shoulders. She had a light olive skin tone and hazel eyes that were a stunning light green with a hint of brown in them. Her figure was a beautiful hourglass shape. She looked to be around his age. Her height was just a little shorter than him.

Once the girl was out of the barrel, she explained to him why she was hiding. "My name is Natilia and I always follow my father when he leaves Rome. I follow him, for I am afraid when I am in Rome without my father there to protect me. With only my mother there, the men of Rome will try and take advantage of me. You see, a lot of them wish to have me, but my father sees them all unfit for me."

Natilia had been looking at the ground the whole time she was telling her story to Todd. She had not looked him in the eyes or even glanced at him at all.

Todd thought she would be in even more danger out of Rome. He asked, "Did you really think you would be safer following your father into the dangerous places he goes?"

Natilia, eyes still towards the ground, answered, "Yes, I figured I would have a less likely chance of being taken advantage of, at least."

Todd understood but thought it would probably be best for her father to know that she was aboard. He asked her, "Who is your father, so I may let him know you are her?"

Natilia answered without hesitation, "My father is Captain Quintius. Perhaps you have heard of him?"

Todd stood silent, remembering that her name was familiar. Of course it was, because Quintius had talked about her before.

Still looking at the ground to avoid eye contact, Natilia asked, "Will you please not tell him I am here, sir? I promise that I will not be a problem. I will hide myself better."

Hoping to get a glimpse of her face, Todd said, "Look at me. I have a question for you and I need to know the truth from you, please." As Natilia lifted her head and looked up, their eyes locked. As their eyes met, Todd felt as if he had been hit hard and had the wind knocked out of him. He had, of course, met many girls in his time, but no one he had ever laid eyes on had ever made him feel this way before. There was something about her. When their eyes met an overwhelming sensation came over him. He knew it wasn't his mind playing tricks on him. He just knew instinctively that being near her, with her, felt very right to him.

As Todd and Natilia stared into each other's eyes, it seemed as if time stood still. They gazed silently for a few more seconds, as if they were talking to each other in their heads.

Natilia recovered first and inquired, "What is your name, soldier?"

Todd shook his head a little as if coming out of a day dream and answered, "Umm, Todd. Why do you ask?"

Natilia replied with a smile and a gentle voice, "I was just wondering."

Todd and Natilia stood silently again, but both continued to seem mesmerized, smiling and holding each other's gaze. Suddenly Todd asked, "Natilia, was that you I saw sitting on a horse at the top of the hill, when we landed in Africa from Spain?"

Natilia, surprised Todd asked or even remembered, answered, "Yes, it was me."

Todd now wondered how Natilia could have gotten there. He inquired, "But how? I mean how did you get there so quickly and without being noticed?"

For some reason Natilia felt she could trust Todd and that he was a good person. She answered, "Well, to tell you the truth, my cousin Starpius has been helping me the whole time."

Todd was shocked to hear this answer. He said, "What?! Starpius, I would have never guessed. So that explains why he said he saw nothing on the hill when I saw you."

Natilia said, "Yes, I have been following my father for some time now. Also, Starpius is how I got on this ship. Well, I almost did not make it onto the ship, for I almost did not get the signal from my cousin. There was a lot of commotion when that very brave soldier got off his horse and ran to help the other soldiers instead of just watching. Fortunately, as Starpius got off his horse to aid this soldier, he was able to signal to me to go and get on Julius' ship."

Todd, realizing that it was him she was talking about, said, "Well, to tell you the truth, the soldier Starpius was protecting was me. And I was that person who ran to go and fight with the men to help them. That is why I have this wound on my arm, because I got hit by one of the arrows, when Starpius and I were taking out all those archers."

Natilia, amazed to hear this and a little happy to meet the one who put his life on the line for the whole army, said, "What? That was you? Todd, you are very brave. You saved many lives by risking your own."

Todd was very happy to hear that she thought of him in a good way. He replied modestly, "That is what I was trying to do. Save lives and make sure we won with few losses."

Natilia was so pleased to hear such a response. She knew Todd was different than most and told him, "You are a very honorable and kind man. You are not like most men I meet, for they are very rude and only think of themselves."

Todd enjoyed hearing that Natilia thought he was a better and different man than the usual guy. He said with a smile, "And that is why I will not tell your father you are here, because I am a kind and honorable person."

Natilia was shocked by Todd's answer. She had been sure he was going to tell Quintius that she was onboard. She responded, "Thank you. I was certain you would have told my father."

Todd said, "No, I won't tell. And I will keep you safe myself. When I see Starpius, I will let him know that I am aware you are here."

Natilia happily replied, "Thank you, so very much, Todd." She smiled at him and then gave him a big hug. She was so very grateful that he would keep her secret and help keep her safe.

Todd was shocked by the hug but very happy to finally hear someone call him by his real name. Natilia felt good in his arms. He liked her more every minute. He thought she was smart, kind, and very attractive. He told her, "You are very loyal to your father. And since you called me by my real name, I am happy to do this for you. Also, I think you are a very nice and beautiful woman."

Natilia blushed and realized she was still holding onto Todd. She let go of him and said, "Thank you, Todd." She smiled saying, "I will try to hide better. I hope to see you soon."

Todd smiled back at her and thought, 'She's right. I better leave before someone comes looking for me.' He scanned the room and noticed the shelf lined with breads. He grabbed a loaf, saying, "Just in case someone sees me leave here." He then gave her a wink to show a sign of trust. As Todd made his way out of the storage room, Natilia picked a new spot to hide.

Once Todd had exited Julius' supply room, he realized why she was hiding there. It was because only Julius, her father, Starpius, Bruteeni, and himself could enter that room in the ship. It would be off limits to everyone else.

As Todd started to move away from the supply room, he noticed a soldier standing in the hallway. Todd addressed him, "What is your name, soldier, and what are you doing just standing there?"

The soldier replied with an attitude and a tone of suspicion, "My name is Scipiio. It does not matter as to why I am standing here, for who were you talking to, Toddacis?"

Todd answered as he gave him a small glare and with a slight tone of anger and annoyance, "Myself and why does it matter to you, Scipiio?"

Scipiio replied rudely, "Only for the reason that you were in there a long while."

Todd kept eye contact with the soldier and slowly moved his right hand onto the hilt of his sword. He said, "For your information, Scipiio, I was in there talking to myself about which loaf of bread would be most suitable for Julius' and Quintius' meal. Now, go back and enjoy this victory meal with the other soldiers."

Scipiio glanced at Todd's hand on his sword, then returned to eye contact with him. Scipiio replied, "Fine. I was only wondering why you were in there so long." Scipiio backed away slowly, turned, and moved down the hall. He went back up on to the ship's deck to enjoy the rest of the night.

Todd was relieved the soldier had left the storage areas. He thought to himself, 'Wow! That was a close one.' He found himself starting to wonder if Natilia would be ok, since that soldier was suspicious of him and to whom he was speaking. Todd thought again about her beauty, her lovely eyes, her attractive smile, and the way she felt in his arms. He also smiled thinking about her shyness, kind words, and caring demeanor. He knew he'd just met an incredible person. And she took his breath away.

Todd slowly made his way to Julius' dining room to make sure the soldier didn't try to come back to the supply room. Luckily, he didn't.

As Todd opened the door to Julius' dining room, he saw both Julius and Quintius seated and talking. They were enjoying their meal together.

Todd entered the room and came over to them. When Julius saw him, he said, "Ah! The great hero Toddacis, come! Have a seat. We were just starting to talk about what our next plan should be on how to stop these rioters in Alexandria."

Quintius reassured Todd that it was fine for him to be there by stating, "Toddacis, you are very much welcome in this conversation of our plans."

Todd didn't want to intrude on their discussion. He answered, "Thank you, Julius and Quintius. I just came to bring you both this loaf of bread as an offering of thanks for all you have done for me."

Quintius appreciated Todd's humble gesture and advised, "Toddacis, we require no thanks. You have done so much for us. And you have saved my life two times already."

Julius recalled Todd's brave actions from the day. He stated, "You also saved many countless Roman lives from the arrows of those archers today. There are no thanks that you are required to give us. But we did need some bread, for we just ran out." They all laughed at this happy occurrence. Todd was delighted to learn how much they appreciated his help. He smiled and said, "Well, then it's the least I could do."

As Todd sat down next to Quintius, he began to wonder if Natilia was going to be ok. Quintius restarted the conversation they had begun before Todd entered the room. He said, "Now where were we? Oh yes, our plans to stop the riots in Egypt."

Julius, very at ease with this problem, responded, "Yes, the rioters... I think we should just handle them from the ships."

Quintius was surprised by this comment. He asked, "How do you suppose we go about doing that, Julius?"

Julius, with a smirk on his face, answered, "With ease, my dear friend. We shoot flaming arrows at them from our ships at sea."

Todd remembered this story and knew what would happen to the Great Library if Julius took this course of action. He quickly suggested another plan. Todd said, "I can take a small group of men into the city to handle all of the rioters personally with the sword."

Julius liked the idea of yet another way to punish the law-breaking rioters. He said, "Very well, that sounds like a great plan. We will put it in motion the day we arrive in Egypt."

Quintius agreed with the plan and had no objections. He advised, "I like it as well. This will be our plan for attack."

A short time later, Todd realized he was feeling tired and his thoughts had returned to Natilia and her safety. He stood up and announced, "Well, I think I'll be off to bed now. See you both in the morning."

Quintius turned to him and said, "Good night, Toddacis. Perhaps we can do some fishing in the morning."

Julius replied, "Good night as well, hero Toddacis."

Todd left the room and instead of going to his bed for the night, he went back to Julius' storage room to check on Natilia. When he entered the room, he whispered, "Natilia, where are you?"

Once Natilia heard his voice, she knew who it was and responded, "I am over here, Todd."

Todd quietly walked over to the crate she was hiding in and softly said, "That's a better hiding place than the one before." They smiled at each other.

Natilia replied, "Thank you, Todd. Why are you here again tonight?"

Todd answered, "Well, to tell you the truth, I came here to check on you and make sure you were safe. There was a soldier in the hall when I left earlier and I'm concerned he thinks someone is hiding in here."

Natilia understood immediately, "I know. I heard you talking to him after you left."

Todd decided to change the subject instead of dwelling on how worried he was for her and how odd it was to feel so protective of someone he'd just met. He said, "So that's why I'm back. And I want to ask you something. Why do you call me Todd and not Toddacis like everyone else?"

Natilia smiled and answered, "Well, I do not know. I guess I just feel that I should, for that is your name, right?"

Todd was surprised by her answer. He stated, "Oh well, yeah, that is my real name. But everyone in this time thinks it's strange and they all have insisted on calling me Toddacis."

Natilia thought it was sweet that he took an interest in why she called him by his true name. She told him, "Well, I, myself, find it a very strange name, but it is your name, is it not? So that is why I call you Todd."

Todd was very happy to hear that Natilia still wanted to call him by his name. He answered, "Well, I know it's weird to everyone here, but thank you for calling me by my real name."

Natilia was curious to know more about the background of his name and where he came from. She said, "You are welcome. Would you mind telling me about your name and where you are from? Did the gods bring you here to us?" She looked at Todd with much interest as she thought he may be a demigod.

Todd said to Natilia, "The truth is I don't know how I got here. I can tell you that I'm from the very far future, where the Roman Empire no longer lives and people no longer have to walk far to get to places. They just drive a car or fly in an airplane."

Natilia looked at Todd with great confusion. She was trying to understand what he'd just told her. She asked, "In the place where you come from people fly and move faster than a running horse?"

Todd laughed and answered, "Yes, in a way, but my point is that I'm not from this time period."

Natilia was still struggling to comprehend his meaning. After a few moments, she stated, "So, if you do not know how it is that you got to us and what you say about how people get around in your place, then this must mean the gods have brought you here to us as a hero of Rome!"

Now Todd was the one feeling confused. He thought, 'Could she be right?' He replied, "I guess that could be it. I just really don't have any idea how I came to be here. I sure would like to know how and why."

Natilia excitedly began to explain to Todd what she thought, "I think I may have figured it out. You do not know how it is you came to be here. You have a very strong sword that has cut through two whole people in one swing. Also you speak a little strangely and your clothes are quite peculiar. You must be of the gods!"

Todd thought to himself, 'I can explain most of those things.' But he replied to Natilia, "How can I be a hero of the gods if I can get injured with an arrow?" He undid his bandage and showed her where the arrow had gone into his right forearm.

Natilia studied his wound and answered, "No, Todd. I did not mean that you were a god, but a hero from the gods. You can still get hurt if you are a hero from the gods. Also, you are very skillful and brave, and kindhearted to so many people." She was staring deep into his eyes.

Todd felt his heart racing. Natilia finished her explanation, "This must be why you were brought here by the gods."

Todd looked down at his feet and let out a deep breath. He thought to himself again, 'I know the gods didn't bring me back to Roman times. Maybe it was from the wish I made before I went to sleep back in my room that first night.' He told Natilia, "You may be right. It does make sense and I did wish to come back in time to Rome. Maybe my God answered my wish."

Natilia replied, "See, you are a hero from the gods and will help Rome be very fruitful and prosperous for a long time."

Todd smiled at Natilia's statement. He was pleased and grateful that she was trying to help him figure out his problem. She also made him feel so happy and at ease. He looked into her eyes and said, "Natilia, you are very nice to me and you give me hope when I need it." Natilia smiled back at him as her heart filled with joy. Suddenly she hugged him and stated, "I do not know why, but when I hug you, I feel safer than I ever have before."

Todd's smile grew even bigger. He really liked making her feel safe. To him it just felt right. He said to her jokingly, "Well, maybe one day we can hug when I'm not in this cold armor and then you will feel even safer."

Natilia's smile faded as she thought of him leaving her for the night. His presence filled the little storage room. She knew without him she'd feel lonely and maybe even a little scared. She stated, "I wish you did not have to go to your chambers to go to bed."

Todd thought again of the soldier in the hall and hoped he wouldn't come back. He replied, "I know, me too. I'm sorry. But I will bring you a blanket, so you will not be cold tonight just in your robes."

Natilia was impressed by his thoughtfulness and delighted that he cared about her comfort and well-being. "Thank you, Todd. You are truly a very kind and generous man. This is unexpected as this is better than anyone has ever treated me."

Todd was shocked to hear such a thing. 'How could people be so uncaring for someone in trouble who needs help?' He replied, "Natilia, where I'm from, that's how you are supposed to treat everyone, with kindness and respect."

Natilia was surprised to hear that in his place people cared about the well-being of others. She responded, "I like that very much, Todd. Thank you."

Todd left the storage room and went to his room to get Natilia a blanket. When he returned to the storage room, she was still awake and waiting for his return. She was sitting on the ground and smiled up at him. He headed over to her and handed her the blanket saying, "Here you go. I hope this keeps you warm tonight. Now I better go get some sleep. It's been a long day. I'm beat."

Natilia knew Todd must be weary from the battle earlier in the day. She replied, "Thank you for the blanket, Todd. I know you must be tired, for you fought very bravely and saved many lives today."

Todd answered with a smile, "You're welcome. Now go find a good place to hide for tonight and I'll check on you in the morning."

As Todd headed towards the door to leave, Natilia said, "Good night, Todd. And thank you again."

Todd looked back and smiled at her. "Good night, Natilia. Sweet dreams." He exited the storage room, closing the door behind him, and went to his room.

When Todd got to his room, he untied his katana from his side and took off all his armor. He placed the katana and his shield right next to his bed in case of an emergency in the middle of the night. He continued to get ready for bed by taking off his shoes and putting his socks into them. He noticed that both his socks and shoes had a little blood on them from the battle earlier that day. Leaving his shorts and shirt on, he lay down on the bed and began to think of Natilia and his family. Shortly, he was fast asleep.

When Todd woke up the next morning, he found himself still on the ship with everything placed where he had put it the night before. He sat up and put on his socks and shoes. Then he stood up and grabbed his katana. He tied it around his waist on his left side like he normally did. He left his room and headed down to the storage room to check on Natilia.

As Todd opened the door, he saw Natilia's robes ripped and torn on the ground. He heard noises coming from behind some barrels and hurried over. He found Scipiio on top of Natilia holding her down as she struggled. He had his left hand over her mouth keeping her quiet so she couldn't scream. Scipiio was also attempting to remove her lower undergarments.

Todd rushed to Natilia's aid and threw Scipiio off of her. As Scipiio rolled to the ground, Todd drew out his katana.

Scipiio pulled out his gladius, a short sword, and lunged at Todd with it. As Scipiio came at Todd with his sword, Todd stepped back and to his right and slashed Scipiio in his back. Scipiio fell to the ground and was face down.

Todd rushed over to him and shoved his right foot down on his back so he couldn't get up. Todd then stabbed Scipiio in the back and through the heart. Scipiio lay choking on his own blood as life slowly seeped out of him. Then he was dead.

Todd released him and hurried over to Natilia who was huddled in a corner sobbing. She grabbed Todd and hugged him while continuing to sob. He held her and tried to soothe and comfort her.

Natilia began to calm, so Todd held her back to look into her face and asked, "Are you alright, Natilia?"

Natilia was still too scared and in shock to answer and just nodded. Todd continued to hold her but moved them together slowly to where he could reach her robes. They were too ripped up, so he grabbed the blanket he had given her the night before. Todd wrapped the blanket around Natalia's naked body and picked her up. He carried her and her torn robes out of the storage room and up to his room, where he set her down on his bed.

Natilia would not let go of him. Todd sat with her and tried to calm her saying, "You don't have to worry in here, Natilia. This is my room and no one comes in here but me. I'm so sorry. I won't ever let anything bad happen to you again."

Natilia looked up at him with tears streaming down her face but still said nothing. She buried her head in his chest and continued to cling to him. He hugged her back and she knew he truly meant what he said. Todd wanted nothing more than to keep her safe and make her happy.

Todd did not want to leave Natilia but knew he needed to go report the incident. Todd said, "I'm sorry. I have to go tell Julius what has happened. But don't worry. I will not tell him that you are here. Will you be ok?"

Natilia released him and nodded her head in acknowledgement. She wiped her tear-streaked face and laid down on the bed. Natilia curled up into a ball under the blanket.

Todd stroked her forehead and said, "I'll be right back." He got up and left the room, shutting the door behind him.

Todd walked down the hall and made his way up to the upper deck of the ship. As he came out of the ship's hull, he noticed the sun was high in the sky and it was almost midday. He scanned the deck and saw the soldiers rowing hard to make it to Egypt quickly. Towards the front of the ship, he saw Julius and Quintius standing at the rail looking out to sea. He wondered if they thought they might see Egypt soon.

Todd made his way over to them. Quintius perceived him first and called out, "Toddacis, you are up! Come let us fish and have another great meal today."

Todd was still trying to figure out how he was going to break the news. He answered, "I can't. At least, not right now, Quintius. Unfortunately, something terrible has happened this morning."

Julius had turned at this exchange and asked, "What terrible thing has happened this day, Toddacis?"

Quintius inquired as well, "Yes, please do tell us, Toddacis."

Todd took a deep breath and said, "After I woke up this morning, I went to Julius' storage room to find something to eat for breakfast. Instead I found Scipiio in there and he was stealing food. I told him to put it all back and leave. He came at me with his sword. So I protected myself and by doing so, I killed him with my sword."

Julius was shocked by Todd's statement. He asked, "By the gods! Is what you say true, Toddacis?"

Todd answered with conviction, "Yes sir, Julius, every word of it." Without further discussion, Julius and Quintius with Todd following, headed down to the storage room to confirm Todd's story.

They reached the storage room, opened the door and confirmed what Todd had told them. Julius turned to Todd and said, "Toddacis, I thank you, for you have killed a thief. This man tried to kill you, so it seems you had no choice. I thank you for letting us know what happened."

Quintius agreed with Julius and said, "Toddacis, this just proves to us more how much of a good man you really are."

Todd was relieved that they believed his story. He responded, "Thank you, Julius and Quintius. I just had to let you both know what happened. I am sorry for this unpleasant incident. I appreciate you both understanding I had no choice but to defend myself."

Julius was gratified by Todd's statement and proud of his actions. He stated, "You did well in letting us know of this occurrence, Toddacis. Now I will have some men dispose of this body."

Todd thanked them both again then advised, "I am going back to my room for a while. I think I need some peace and quiet to try to calm down some."

Quintius said, "You may go and rest, Toddacis, for this has been a vexing morning."

Todd left the storage room and made his way back to his room. When he entered his room, he found Natilia still naked on his bed asleep. He walked over to her and covered her up with the blanket. Then he went over to the other smaller bed in his room and went to sleep.

The next day, Todd gave Natilia the extra clothes he had in his room, since her robes were torn up. He never wore these clothes since he preferred wearing his t-shirt and shorts from his time. They were more comfortable to him.

For the remainder of the trip to Egypt, he made sure that Natilia was safe in his room. He would go down to his room every so often and keep her company. They had long talks learning more about one another. He also spent time going fishing with Julius and Quintius.

On the fourth day, they arrived in Egypt. Todd stood on the ship's deck with Julius, Quintius and Starpius. They could see fire spreading throughout the whole city. The rioting was out of control.

Julius quickly ordered, "Toddacis! I want you and Starpius to go into the city and do what you have planned. Now go! And make these fools pay for their treachery."

Todd understood immediately the urgency of the situation. He responded, "Yes sir, Julius!" Then he and Starpius prepared to disembark. As soon as the ship got close enough to the shoreline, they jumped off.

Before they jumped, Todd heard Julius giving orders, "Men, ready your bows and arrows and light them a flame! We are going to unleash hell on these rioting people and teach them a lesson!" The men cheered wildly at the announcement.

As Todd and Starpius made their way to the city, Todd said to Starpius, "So I met Natilia on the ship."

Starpius looked at Todd shocked. He asked, "But how?! I mean how did you find out about her being here with us on the galley?"

Todd smiled as he answered, "Well, I found her by accident. She made a slight noise as I walked by her hiding place – the storage room. I went to check it out and there she was."

Starpius replied, "I figured she would get found out sooner or later, but not by you, Toddacis."

Todd responded, "I promised her I wouldn't tell anyone about her being onboard. She told me about her cousin and how you have been helping her. I told her I would too." Todd smiled at him.

Starpius said, "Well, at least you helped her instead of taking advantage of her."

Todd's smile turned into a frown. He told Starpius about the awful incident. "Unfortunately, Scipiio also discovered her after he heard us talking. The next day, I found him trying to rape her. When I stopped him, he attacked me so I had to defend myself and Natilia. I killed him and would do it again to protect her."

Starpius was angry after hearing Todd's horrible story. He said, "Well good, he deserved to die then, for what he tried to do to my cousin. I would have killed him myself if I had known of this."

Todd was glad to hear Starpius thought he did the right thing. He told him, "I took care of him. He won't be a problem for anyone anymore."

After running the whole way, Todd and Starpius quickly reached the city gates. As they neared the gates, they both pulled out their swords and held their shields out in front of them. They ran through the open gates and into mayhem.

Todd saw people beating each other, some were robbing the people prone on the ground, others were stealing from the shops, some ran through the streets with torches, and there were also a few Roman guards trying to subdue the rioters and thieves. As they took in the crazy scene, Starpius asked, "So what is your plan, Toddacis?"

Suddenly a rioter came charging at Todd with a short sword in his hand and yelling angrily. Todd turned and quickly cut off the rioter's head. He said to Starpius, "I am going to try and save a lot of scrolls in the Great Library and stop as many rioters as I can on the way there."

Two more rioting civilians came running at Todd and Starpius. They both charged at the attacking rioters and ran their swords through them. As they both pulled their swords out of the dead rioters, Starpius said, "That sounds like an entertaining plan."

Todd replied loudly over the din of the riot, "Ok, then let's get a move on and go save some scrolls before the whole city is burnt to the ground!"

Starpius turned around and slashed another charging rioter across the chest while shouting, "Let us move!"

Todd and Starpius moved swiftly through the city, killing rioters and avoiding attacks as they made their way to the Great Library. Once they reached the library, Todd noticed all the flaming arrows in the sky headed towards the city – and them. He turned to Starpius and said, "We need to hurry!"

Without another word, they ran into the library. Todd told Starpius, "Find some bags or something to put the scrolls in. We need to save as many as we can carry!" They both started searching for something to transport the scrolls.

Starpius located three old supply bags and yelled out, "I have found only three bags, Toddacis!"

Todd was frustrated, not finding anything else and only having a few bags, when there were so many scrolls to save. But there was not time. They had to move quickly. Three bags would have to do. To be heard over all the commotion outside, he yelled to Starpius,"Put as many scrolls in the bags as you can. Be careful. Try not to damage them!"

Starpius answered reassuringly, "I will use caution, and do so with haste, Toddacis."

Todd was pleased and surprised to find the bags held more than he had thought possible. They now had a good portion of the Great Library's scrolls safe with them. Before heading towards the entrance, Todd placed two of the bag straps over his shoulder and across his body, so the bags were on his back. He then tied his shield to his back to protect the bags of scrolls.

Starpius also strapped his bag of scrolls to his back and tied his shield over it. As they came out of the library with the three bags full of scrolls, Todd saw many flaming arrows all over the ground and twice as many more buildings on fire than when they had come into the city. As he looked up, he saw yet another wave of flaming arrows coming down through the sky. As the arrows started to rain down, he yelled, "Let's move!!"

Todd and Starpius started to run quickly through the city back to the gates where they had entered. They stuck close to the buildings, trying to keep safe from the flaming arrows. They ran by many dead bodies of civilians and guards. The flaming arrows continued to rain down around them. The streets were ablaze with fire. People were running and screaming everywhere. Some caught fire right in front of them.

As Todd and Starpius made their way through the city, a few arrows hit Todd in the back. Luckily, he had put his shield on his back to protect the scrolls. He turned around and saw that one of the bags had caught fire from the flaming arrow. Todd stopped and yelled to Starpius, "Quick, help me put it out!"

Starpius hurriedly smothered the fire and checked the scrolls inside. It appeared nothing had been ruined.

With a sigh of relief, Todd turned to look back at the Great Library and saw that it too was now on fire. He quickly scanned the area and noticed many more flaming arrows littering the ground and more buildings catching fire. He again checked the sky towards the ships at sea and saw another wave of fire arrows coming at the city. He yelled out, "Starpius, we have to go. Now!"

Todd and Starpius started running again with their load of scrolls. They ran speedily, weaving in and out from left to right, trying to avoid getting hit from this new wave of flaming arrows.

Todd felt arrows hit his shield again. He also felt a sharp pain and burning sensation on his right calf muscle but kept moving as quickly as he could. He turned his head to look back at Starpius and noticed that he had been hit by an arrow in his right arm. But he was still keeping up with Todd, following right behind him. Todd thought to himself, 'Man, if I got hit like that, I doubt I would be able to keep moving so fast.'

Todd looked ahead and spotted the city gates where they had entered. They dashed through the gates and moved clear of the city. They stopped to catch their breath. As they looked back at the city, which was fully ablaze, another wave of flaming arrows rained down into the city.

Once Todd's breathing calmed, he said to Starpius, "Man, was that a close one. Starpius, I don't know how you did it, still running so fast with that arrow stuck in your arm."

Starpius laughed as if Todd had just told a joke. Todd didn't understand his reaction. He asked, "And what's so funny?"

Starpius thought it was Todd who was joking around. He responded amused, "You jest with me, Toddacis, for you think it was hard for me to run with an arrow in my arm. But you Toddacis, you have an arrow in your leg, there." He pointed to Todd's right leg.

Todd looked down at his leg and saw the arrow sticking out of his right calf. Suddenly he was hit by the pain from his injury. He said, "I was wondering what that sharp pain was that I felt in my leg. Now I see. Ugh! How come I always get hit with arrows, man?"

Starpius was surprised to understand that Todd wasn't joking and hadn't known he was hit by an arrow. He answered, "I do not know, Toddacis, but you are very strong to keep moving with that in your leg."

Todd removed his shield from his back and placed the two bags of scrolls on the ground. He noticed four arrows stuck in his shield. He said, "This is why we didn't leave our shields in the Great Library."   Starpius also removed his shield and bag and saw that he had been struck by six arrows. He replied, "Yes, I see, Toddacis. I am pleased we did that after all, for I thought it would have been too much to carry the bags of scrolls and our shields."

Todd had known it would be a difficult task to carry both but a much safer option. He said, "Yes, I knew it would be challenging, but we – the scrolls and us – needed the protection. That is why I said we must take them with us when we left the Great Library."

Starpius was curious as to why they saved the scrolls. He asked, "Toddacis, what are we going to do with these scrolls we saved from their certain doom."

Todd thought it was best to hide the scrolls to keep them protected. He didn't want anyone from this time or any future time to find and study them. He looked around for a place to keep them safe and saw a spot that would be a good hiding place.

Todd responded, "We will bury them over there near those large rocks."

Starpius thought this was a strange suggestion. He said, "Ok, if you think that is best."

Todd didn't have a better idea at the moment. He stated, "I do think it's best, for now anyway."

They both removed the arrows from their injured leg and arm and bandaged their wounds. They also took the arrows out of their shields.   Todd and Starpius picked up the bags and went over to the rocky area. They buried the three bags of scrolls underneath the large rocks.

After they had finished burying the scrolls, Todd and Starpius headed back to where they had been dropped off Julius' ship. As they saw the ship coming into view, Todd thought of Natilia hiding in his room and hoped she was still safe. As the ship neared, they could see Julius and Quintius at the front of the galley waving to them.

Quintius yelled to Todd, "Toddacis, did you complete what you set out to do?!" Todd hollered back so he could be heard, "Yes sir, we did. Unfortunately, with a little damage taken, but otherwise mission accomplished!"

Julius was eager to get underway. He shouted, "Well done! Now get aboard, for we make for Rome herself immediately." Both Todd and Starpius walked into the water, grabbed the ropes, and were pulled aboard.

Once they were on board, Todd heard Julius command that one whole legion of soldiers would be left behind at the burning city of Alexandria with instructions to try and regain order in Egypt. Julius' next command was for his galley ship to set sail for Rome. Todd slipped away and headed straight to his room to check on Natilia.

When Todd entered his room, he found Natilia sitting on the bed. She appeared to be anxiously waiting for him. She jumped up and ran to hug him. She said relieved, "Todd, I am so happy you are here. I was so worried for you, since I knew that you had gone into the city. They launched so many arrows of fire into the city. I feared the worst may have happened to you."

Todd confessed he had been thinking about her while he was gone. He said, "And I was worrying about you. Hoping you were okay and safe in my room."

Natilia smiled at his kind words. Then she looked down and noticed his right leg was bandaged and slightly bleeding. Her happiness turned to concern for Todd's injury. She replied, "Todd, you are hurt. Please come with me and sit down, so I may give aid to your leg at once."

Todd tried to tell her he would be fine, but Natilia kept insisting she needed to take care of it. He finally agreed and laid his shield and sword down near the door. He took off his shoes and all of his armor. He was left standing in his socks, tee shirt, and shorts. He sat down on the edge of the bed.

Natilia sat on a small stool, removed the makeshift field bandage and examined Todd's wound. She stated, "I will clean this with water and wrap it up in a cloth for you."

Todd knew quite a bit about modern day first aid. He advised her, "No, don't use just water, Natilia. Add salt to the water." He knew that salt water would clean his wound better. She looked at him oddly and asked, "Why salt water, Todd?"

Todd explained, "Because it will disinfect the wound. The salt will kill any germs or bacteria."

Natilia just stared at him wide-eyed and confused. Todd thought to himself, 'She obviously doesn't understand what I just said.' He added, "It will clean better. It's a good idea, I promise."

Natilia decided not to question it further. She replied, "I will go and make you some salt water, Todd."

Todd was pleased Natilia would follow his instructions and use salt water to clean his injury. He expressed his gratitude to her. He said with a smile, "Thank you very much, Natilia. I appreciate you taking care of me."

Natilia got up from the little stool and went over to the table. She mixed a bowl of salt water from the fresh water jug and the small bowl of salt on the table. Natilia came back over to Todd. She again sat down on the little stool and placed the bowl of salt water on the floor beside her. She looked up at Todd and said, "This may burn a little now that it is salt water, Todd. Please bear with me."

Natilia was reaching for the bowl and cloth when Todd, replied, "Yes, I know it will sting. Please give me your hand."

Natilia looked up into his eyes and without hesitating or questioning his request, she gave him her hand. It was soft and warm, and her touch was kind and tender. Todd felt much better just holding her hand and looking into her beautiful eyes.

Natilia stared deep into Todd's eyes and gently squeezed his hand to comfort him. He squeezed back. Natilia liked that Todd's hand felt smooth and soft. The kindness in his eyes and the tenderness and gentleness of his touch made her feel very safe and cared for.

Todd smiled and thanked her again for her comfort and her care. He said, "Thanks for giving me your hand, Natilia. I'm ready."

Natilia snapped out her daze and said, "Oh, yes. You are welcome, Todd. Now please try to hold still. I am just going to rinse your injury with the salt water."

Todd nodded and gritted his teeth as she poured the salt water onto the arrow wound in his leg. He continued to clench his teeth and hold his breath while at the same time flexing the rest of his body. Once all of the salt water had been poured out onto Todd's leg, he sighed in relief. Natilia patted the wound dry and stated, "There now. It is rinsed well. I will now wrap it up in clean cloth, so it will heal. We do not want it to get dirty. If it gets dirty, we would have to cut off the leg."

Todd was a little freaked out to hear her talk about his leg getting cut off. He replied, "Please wrap it good and tight!"

Natilia realized they were still holding hands. She smiled at Todd and said, "I am going to need you to let go of my hand. When I am done wrapping your wound, if you wish, we can hold hands again."

Todd was surprised to realize he was still holding her hand. He reluctantly let go. Todd responded, "Oh, I'm sorry. I didn't notice we were still holding hands."

Natilia tried to reassure him that it was okay with her. She said with a smile, "That is fine, I do not mind. I liked it."

Todd was happy to hear it but was also still worried about his leg. He replied, "I liked it too. But let's get my leg bandaged up first. Then maybe we could continue." Now they were both smiling.

Natilia said, "Yes, let me do this now so nothing bad will happen to your leg, Todd."

Todd agreed that they shouldn't delay any longer. He answered, "Please do what you need to do, Natilia."

Natilia proceeded to carefully and gently wrap Todd's injured leg, making sure it was tight so no dirt would get into the wound. With the bandage in place, Natilia was done ministering to Todd's injury. She let go of his leg and he lay down on his back in the bed.

Todd patted the bed next to him, signaling her to join him. Natilia lay down in the bed with him and laid her head on his chest. She reached for Todd's hand and squeezed it gently. She told him, "I hope your leg will heal properly, Todd."

Todd felt so happy being with Natilia. He could tell that she had feelings for him too. He wrapped his arm around her and said, "I know it will heal right because you did a good job, Natilia. Thank you." "You are welcome, Todd," she replied. They fell asleep in each other's arms.

For the eight-day sail back to Rome, Todd spent time fishing with Quintius and training with the sword with Julius. He would also hang out with Starpius and Bruteeni. Bruteeni, as usual, was always drinking. He spent his nights with Natilia in his room.

The day finally arrived when the docks of Rome were in sight. It was midday as they began to pull closer to the harbor. Todd was amazed by what he saw. 'Incredible. And this is only just the harbor,' he thought to himself.

Todd saw a large white lighthouse made of concrete and hundreds of other galley ships. Some of the ships were small, some average-sized, and then there were a few that were huge. They looked to be great war ships that protected Rome's harbor. Todd was overjoyed. He never thought his dreams would become a reality. He was in Ancient Rome!

As the galley ship docked, Todd noticed a large group of soldiers standing at attention and saluting. They probably numbered in the thousands. The soldiers continued their salute as they began exiting the ship. As Julius, Quintius and Todd walked down the ship's ramp, Starpius was hurrying Natilia back to her home in Rome to be sure she arrived there ahead of her father.

Once Julius, Quintius, and Todd had exited the ship and were back on land, they made their way over to the chariots that were made ready for them. Todd did not have his own chariot so he rode with Quintius in his. Julius rode in a chariot in front of them.

As they headed into the city of Rome and her grand gates, Quintius said to Todd, "Toddacis, you will now get to see my lovely daughter, who all of the Roman men wish they could be with. If you see her fit for you, then you may have her in marriage."

Todd tried to suppress his smile. Even though he had already started to develop feelings for Quintius' daughter Natilia, he said, "Only if she finds me to her liking and will love me. Then will I marry your daughter, Quintius." She was very beautiful and nice but he wanted to be sure she had feelings for him and wanted to marry him before he would agree to Quintius' plan.

Quintius laughed at Todd's statement. He said with a smile, "Toddacis, you are very noble, and I do believe she will find you to her liking."

Todd smiled at Quintius' kindhearted reply. He responded, "Well Quintius, I do hope so. I really do."

They had been heading up hill and had now reached the top. The whole city of Rome lay before them. Julius stopped his chariot, so they stopped as well. Julius called out to them, "Ah! There is my lady in all her glory! The beauty, Rome!"

Quintius leaned over to Todd and said, "It is a magnificent sight, is it not, Toddacis?"

As Todd looked down at Rome, he was amazed. He could see the great Coliseum, the Emperor's Palace, where the Roman Senate would be, and the great walls around the city. He also spotted the Hippodrome. All of Rome looked incredible and surprisingly modern. It also looked much cleaner and not as crowded as the pictures of Rome he'd seen in his time period.

Todd continued to stare in astonishment. "Wow it's bigger than I had imagined it to be."

Julius looked over and noticed Todd was thunderstruck. He said, "Come now. Are we just going to look at her all day or go into the great city herself?"

Todd felt like a little kid receiving a much desired present. He answered excitedly, "Yes! Please let's go now and see the glory of Rome!"

Quintius and Julius laughed at Todd's answer. Quintius announced joyfully, "Alright then, let us be off to Rome!"

They continued down the hill to Rome and as they arrived at the large gates of the city, they began to open. Once the gates were fully opened, Todd saw a long line of Roman royal guards in all black armor and shields standing on both the right and left sides of the roadway.

As the group rode their chariots through the line of soldiers, the people of Rome were behind the royal soldiers cheering for Julius as if he was some kind of super hero. They all loved him.

They continued to make their way through Rome and up to the palace. They arrived at the entrance to the senators' chambers. Julius jumped off his chariot and said, "Do not trouble yourselves with politics. I will handle these babbling old men alone. As for you two, Quintius, I do believe there is a matter you wish to attend to, if I am not mistaken."

Quintius understood what Julius was implying and answered with a grin, "Yes Julius, there is a matter. You are not mistaken, my good friend."

Julius was pleased to hear that Quintius was going to attend to matters right away. He said, "Then go do what you must, my friend. And once you are done, we will meet up for some gladiatorial games by this noon."

Quintius replied, "The games sound excellent. I look forward to it. See you soon, my friend. And, Julius, do go easy on the old fools in there."

Julius appreciated his friend's concern for diplomacy and said, "I will give it to them nicely, Quintius. Do not worry. Now go. Off with you two."

Quintius responded, "Very well, then." Quintius, with Todd in his chariot, set off for home.

As they rode away, Todd turned around and saw Julius walking up the steps to the Senate. Quintius eagerly said to Todd, "Now Toddacis, while Julius takes care of business with the Senate, I want you to meet someone very dear to me."

Todd knew exactly who he was talking about but asked, "Is it your daughter, Quintius?" He saw that Todd knew who he wanted him to meet and answered, "Yes Toddacis. Yes, it is. I hope you take her to your liking, for that would do me a great deal of honor."

Todd thought of Natilia and hoped she had feelings for him. He knew he had feelings for her. He said, "I hope so too, Quintius." He thought about her beautiful eyes, kind smile, and the touch of her tender hands. Todd truly hoped she did have feelings for him.

They arrived at Quintius' house. It was very large and well kept. The house was a typical Roman villa for the upper class of Rome during the glory times of the early Roman Empire.

As they were getting out of the chariot, Todd saw Starpius and Bruteeni riding up to meet them. He wondered why they would be coming to Quintius' home. Todd asked Quintius, "Why are Starpius and Bruteeni here?"

Quintius saw confusion on Todd's face. He enlightened him by answering, "They are my guards. And they guard my house as well." Before Todd could respond, he saw Natilia running down the steps of the house. She was dressed in beautiful robes of a stunning dark purple color. She ran straight to her father and hugged him tightly. She said to him, "Father, I am glad you are home, for I missed you so."

Quintius, hugging her back replied, "I, too, Natilia. It is so good to be home once again."

As Natilia and her father stood in their embrace, Todd and Natilia's eyes met. Her smile broadened as she gazed at Todd. He returned her smile.

Quintius recalled Todd was with him and introduced him to Natilia. He said, "Natilia, there is someone here I would like you to meet. His name is Toddacis." Quintius looked at Todd and waved him over so he could meet Natilia. Quintius introduced them to one another, "Toddacis, this is my lovely daughter, Natilia."

Todd looked into Natilia's eyes. As she returned his gaze, they both began smiling at one another. Todd kept up the ruse and said, "Hi, I'm Todd. It's nice to finally meet you, Natilia. I've heard a lot about you from your father. I feel like I already know you." And then he winked at her.

Todd put out his hand for Natilia to shake. She looked at his hand, then shook it and said, "Well, it's nice to meet you, Todd. You seem very charming."

Quintius was thrilled for them to finally meet and thought they would make a splendid couple. He said happily, "Let us go inside and have a fine meal to celebrate our safe return home to Rome granted to us from the gods."

As the group walked up the steps to go into the house, Starpius came to Todd's side and quietly said, "We just made it back in time." Bruteeni walked past them and stopped to stand beside the door to Quintius' house to guard the entranceway.

Todd was glad it had worked out well. He said, "Good man! I was a little worried it might be a problem."

Starpius felt a sense of accomplishment and said, "Well, there was no need to worry. I told you that I would be able to do this."

Todd appreciated Starpius' confidence. He said, "Yes, you were right, Starpius. No need to worry. I'm just glad it's done and everything is fine."

Todd was relieved Natilia had made it home in time without any problems. He headed into the house and could see the dining room straight in front of him, as well as a set of stairs leading to the next floor. Quintius and Natilia were already seated at the table. Todd took off all his armor and placed it up against the wall. He then headed over to the table and sat down for a wonderful meal to celebrate their arrival in Rome.

As they were eating the meal, there was a slight lull in the conversation. Quintius asked Natilia, "So what do you think of Toddacis, Natilia?"

Natilia looked across the table at Todd. Again they both stared into each other's eyes. After a few seconds she said, "I believe I love him father. I mean, will love him." She smiled and, this time, she winked at Todd. He was overjoyed by her words.

Quintius was a little surprised but very happy about Natilia's response. He asked Todd, "Well then, Toddacis. What do you say to that?"

Todd answered with a big grin as he looked at Natilia, "I would have to say that she is very beautiful. I believe I will love her too. And I hope to spend my whole life with her." They both could not stop smiling at each other. Quintius was smiling too.

Quintius said, "Toddacis, will you have my daughter in marriage?" Todd still looking into her eyes answered, "As long as she wants to be with me, then yes. I will, Quintius."

Quintius turned to Natilia with a raised eyebrow. Natilia excitedly replied, "Yes, father. I do very much wish to be with him."

Quintius was ecstatic. He stated, "Then it is settled. The both of you are to get married a week from this day!"

As the group was finishing their meal and continuing to celebrate the good news, Julius arrived at Quintius' house with his six bodyguards. Julius came into the house and approached the dinner table. He said jokingly, "What is this? No food for me? You could not save me any, Quintius? I am hurt."

Quintius was glad to see his friend and in such a good mood. He replied, "Ah! My friend, you know if I were to have known of your coming, I would have saved you a meal."

Julius laughed and said, "Yes, Quintius. That is why I did not let you know I was coming. Well now. I expect all went well with your plans while I handled the old fools?"

Quintius excitedly replied, "Oh yes, my friend. Natilia and Todd are to be married on this day next week. It will be a joyous occasion. But how did your meeting go with the Senate?"

Julius stated, "This is great news, Quintius. I will have to attend. Now you know very well how the Senate went. They were annoying, as they normally are."

Quintius responded, "Yes, I thought as much. So my friend, Julius, why is it you have come here on this special day?"

Julius answered, "Have you already forgotten, Quintius? We are to go to the games this day."

Quintius replied, "Oh yes! Well, let us get changed and ready to leave at once."

The party got up from the table to prepare to leave. Todd went back to the entrance area and grabbed his armor, shield, and sword. Natilia was waiting in front of the stairs to show him to his room. Todd followed Natilia up the stairs to the guest room, where he would be staying until the wedding. Quintius had also promised to have a nice house built for him and Natilia just outside of Rome.

Todd went into his room and stored his equipment in the corner. He turned around and Natilia ran into his arms hugging him tightly. As she slowly released him, their eyes met and they both kissed for the first time. It felt as though time had stopped. Usually whenever they were together time just seemed to fly by, but not this time!

Natilia was so happy to have Todd in her life. She told him, "I am very glad that my father found you, for you are the best man I could have ever asked for Todd."

Todd was also very happy to have met someone that really loved him. He said, "Same here. You care for me and are very kind to me, Natilia. There's not much more I could ask of you." She smiled at his thoughtful words and kissed him again. Natilia reluctantly left Todd to go prepare to leave for the games.

Todd sat on the bed and started to think about what the gladiator games would be like. He remembered from his history class how great the Roman games were. He thought they might be like going to watch a football game in his time.

Todd looked up as Quintius came into the room. He said, "Here Toddacis, I bring you a gift. You can wear this robe to the games."

Todd looked at the robe in Quintius' hands and saw it was a beautiful, bright, dark purple. Todd acknowledged his appreciation, "Thank you, Quintius. I will proudly wear this robe to the games."

Quintius left so Todd could get ready for the games. He put on the purple robe over his tee shirt and shorts. He picked up his katana and tied it around his waist.

Natilia came back to Todd's room to see if he was ready to depart. She noticed his katana and said, "Todd, I do not think you will need your sword at the games."

Todd knew she was probably right but answered, "You never know. And it's always good to have it in case of an emergency. Then you are prepared for anything."

Natilia agreed with his thinking. She replied, "Oh, I see. You have a good point."

Todd and Natilia headed back downstairs, where Julius was at the front entrance waiting for the group to depart. He saw them approaching and said, "Well now, you two make a great Roman couple."

Todd appreciated the approval of the great historical figure, Julius Caeser. He replied with a smile, "Thank you, sir."

Julius noticed Todd's sword and said, "Ah, I see you still carry your sword with you, Toddacis. That is very wise even in Rome."

Todd answered, "I am just being safe, Julius, sir."

Quintius had come down the stairs and heard this exchange. He said, "And this is why I like, Toddacis. He is very smart and I now know and see that he will protect and keep my Natilia safe."

Todd immediately responded, "I would never let any harm come to Natilia."

Julius was eager to proceed to the games. He said, "Well now, it would seem that we are all ready. Let us be off to the games so we do not miss the start."

The group all proceeded outside, down the steps, and got into their chariots. Their guards went with them as well. As usual, Todd had Starpius by his side.

When their party arrived at the Coliseum, Todd was amazed that it was larger than he had imagined in his dreams. The whole structure looked brand new with clean, freshly-made, cut stones.

They entered through one of the main archways and made their way to their seats, where the Senate and Emperor would be sitting. When they took their seats, the games had just started.

It was everything Todd had pictured it to be. There were teams of gladiators fighting against one another and there were times when they would have to fight lions and tigers as well. He knew most of the gladiators that were fighting in these games were criminals or prisoners of war from newly taken lands.

The games continued through the day and even went on into the night. At nightfall, they lit the columns in the middle of the ring, so the fighting could be seen and continue.

Julius and Quintius had been talking almost the entire time of the games. When one of the battles ended, Julius stood up from his seat. The crowd began to quiet for Julius' pronouncement.

Todd noticed that Quintius had a concerned look on his face in anticipation of what Julius was about to say to the people of Rome. As Todd was trying to figure out what might be going on, Julius yelled out, "My good people! My good people! Today I have with me a warrior that I met when I was out fighting and defeating the barbaric Carthaginians!"

The crowd cheered for his victory over Carthage. Julius continued, "That warrior is here with me today! He came to be known to my dear friend, Quintius, as he was headed to Carthage!"

The crowd's cheering persisted as Julius continued to tell of the quest to Carthage. He yelled even louder, so the people could hear what he had to say. "My dear friend believes that he is a warrior sent from the god Mars himself, for this warrior does not know how he came to be here!" After hearing Julius say this, the whole crowd of people fell silent.

Julius continued with his story, "My good people of Rome, I give you the warrior from the gods! They call him Todd. We call him Toddacis!"

Julius turned to Todd and told him, "Toddacis, take off your robe and come up beside me." Without saying a word, Todd took off the robe and set it in his seat. He was now in his tee shirt and shorts with his sword still on his side. He walked over to Julius and stood next to him.

Julius placed his right hand on Todd's left shoulder. He continued to yell to the crowd, "Look here. I give you the warrior from the gods themselves!"

The crowd went from a dead silence into a whisper. They had never seen clothing like his before. Now Julius made his big announcement. He called out, "Now my people! I will have him go up against our best gladiator! Martonius himself!"

The people were amazed to hear that they would get to see their great champion gladiator fight a warrior of the gods. The crowd went wild with cheering.

Julius said to Todd, "Go to the underside of the Coliseum and I will have one of my guards give you his full armor for this fight."

Todd was shocked and a little scared that he was going to be fighting in the middle of the Coliseum in front of all these people and with the champion gladiator, no less.

Todd replied, "Yes sir, Julius. I just need the same type of armor I was wearing for the attack on Carthage."

Julius was pleased that he seemed eager to do battle. He advised, "It will be done. Now go down there and make ready for the fight."

Todd walked away and quickly made his way down to the underside of the Coliseum. When he got down there, one of Julius' guards was there with all of his armor and equipment already off and on the floor for Todd to use. Todd grabbed the equipment and put it on, starting with the chain mail shirt over his shirt, followed by the steel shin guards on his legs.

As Todd put the shin guards on, he thought of putting on his soccer shin guards back in his time to go play in his soccer games. He continued getting ready by putting on the steel-plated body piece over the chain mail, followed by the leather bracers around his wrists.

Todd grabbed his sword and tied it on to his side again and took the helmet from the guard and put it on. The Roman helmet was made of steel and had red feathers on the top. He picked up the final piece to complete his armor, the large square Roman shield, which he was now used to holding and carrying.

Now fully equipped, Todd ran up to the gate and it began to open. The guard said to him, "Good luck to you, Toddacis."

Todd replied, "Thanks man, I'll need it."

Once the gates were fully opened, Todd ran out into the center of the Coliseum. The night sky was dim, but he could see well enough with the firelight on the columns that stood high above his head. At the other end of the arena, he saw the very large and muscular Martonius walking out of the other gate.

Martonius had on no armor, just a robe. His face was covered with a metal lion mask and he was carrying a large steel battle axe.

Todd heard Julius yell out once more, "Let the fight begin!" As soon as Julius gave this command, Martonius rushed at him and Todd quickly raised his shield to block the charging attack. Martonius hit Todd's shield with his large battle axe. The powerful axe blow knocked Todd backwards causing him to fall to the ground.

But as Todd fell to the ground, he used his katana to slash Martonius in the left leg. Todd rolled on the ground to avoid Martonius bringing the battle axe down on his head. As he rolled, he dropped his shield so he could move quicker.

Todd got up and ran at Martonius, while he was still catching his balance from being cut in the leg. Todd swung his katana at the lion mask Martonius had on his face. Now the mask had a big slash mark across it.

Martonius quickly reacted, hitting Todd with his battle axe directly on the center of his steel chest plate and denting it. The strike was so strong that it knocked Todd back on the ground again.

Since the violent blow had knocked the wind out of him, Todd was slow to get up. He looked up and saw Martonius standing over him and laughing. Catching Martonious by surprise, Todd quickly kicked him in the leg where he had cut him earlier in the fight. He had kicked Martonius' leg as hard as he would have kicked a soccer ball to clear it up the field.

After taking the kick in his wounded leg, Martonius fell to the ground in anguish. He had dropped his battle axe and was down on his knees.

Todd swiftly rose and had his katana aimed at Martonius' neck. Todd stopped himself from delivering the fatal blow to Martonius that would have cut off his head. As Martonius looked up, he saw Todd pulling the katana away from his neck.

Todd said to him, "I won but you will live. You do not deserve to die by my hand. You are a good fighter, Martonius. Now let me see if I can get you free."

After hearing Todd's words, Martonius took off the lion mask he was wearing. With tears streaming down his face, he said, "Thank you, Toddacis. Thank you. You are very kind."

Todd suddenly felt the weight of holding this man's life in his hands. He sighed and answered, "I try to be."

Todd looked up at Julius. Julius yelled to him, "Toddacis, why have you not finished Martonius off?!"

Todd did not want to take the life of someone who didn't really want him dead. He yelled back, "This man is a great fighter and I have defeated him. But he doesn't deserve to die by my hand."

Julius seized the moment to show that Todd was of the gods. He called out, "If you will not kill him, then it is by the words and choice of the gods, who have sent you for this man not to die today! Toddacis, your actions show us that you were indeed sent from the gods! And that you are kind and merciful to all Romans!"

Todd was relieved to hear that Julius did not want him to kill Martonius. He replied, "Thank you, Julius!"

Todd helped Martonius up to his feet and assisted him to leave the arena. As they were making their way out of the arena, the whole crowd started cheering for Todd and calling him the gods' warrior.

When they both made it over to the gate, Todd said to the guards, "I need you guys to take care of this man. Once he is healed, you free him, because he has earned his freedom today."

The guards were star-struck in believing Todd was of their gods. They responded, "Yes sir, Toddacis." They took Martonius from Todd and escorted him to receive aid.

When Todd gave the armor back to Julius' guard, he saw his purple robe had been brought down to him. He put his robe back on over top of his regular clothes. Todd then made his way back up to Julius, Quintius, Natilia, Starpius, and Bruteeni.

When Todd arrived, Julius said to him, "Toddacis, you have passed my test for you, and now I believe the words of my friend Quintius even more. You were sent by the gods for our help and to answer his prayers."

Quintius was relieved and amazed to see Todd was still in one piece. He said, "I do not know why I feared you might have died, even after taking that direct hit from the battle axe. But you arose from a hit that would have killed any normal man."

Starpius in awe over the whole battle said, "Toddacis, you did very well and I am greatly honored to be your guard."

Todd shared his thoughts. He told them, "Well, I didn't really want to fight, but I also didn't want to upset anyone. So I just said to hell with it, I'll go ahead and do it. And I did think it might be fun and exciting too." Todd also knew that it was a great honor for him to be asked to go fight in the arena.

Julius was even more impressed by Todd's comments. He said, "Toddacis you are extraordinary, for when you are thrown into danger you think of it as something fun to do. You truly are a warrior of the gods!"

Quintius was also certain that Todd was from the gods. He stated, "I am sincerely honored and blessed to be having a warrior of the gods marry my daughter."

Todd modestly replied, "Thank you, but I am no warrior of the gods."

Julius quickly corrected him by saying, "You may think so now, Toddacis. But you will find out soon enough what we know to be true. You are a god warrior." The games were over for the night so they said their goodbyes and headed to their homes.

Natilia had been very quiet since Todd's match in the arena. When they were back at Quintius' house, Natilia and Todd were finally alone in his room. She started crying and said to him, "Do not ever scare me like that again, Todd! I was afraid that I may have lost you out there tonight." She hugged him tightly and continued to cry quietly.

Todd felt bad for upsetting her. He lay down in the bed with her and said, "I'm sorry. I didn't mean to scare you. I won't do anything like that again. Just for you, Natilia. I promise."

Natilia stopped crying and they lay there quietly together. They talked for a long time until she reluctantly got up and went to her own room to bed.

Todd lay there thinking about the many amazing events of the day – the glory of Rome, his beautiful soon-to-be wife, the excitement of the Coliseum. He was shortly fast asleep and dreaming of life as a Roman.

Days went by and Todd remained in Roman times. He began to wonder if he would ever go back to his time period. Their wedding day came and Todd and Natilia were married, as Quintius had hoped and planned. Todd and Natilia spent a joyous day and blissful night together.

The following week, their house was finished being built just outside of Rome. They moved in and spent all their time together. They went to the races, the theater, and gladiator games. They even went to baths together. They also enjoyed visiting with Julius and Todd's new father-in-law, Quintius.

As the days passed, Todd often wondered if he'd ever make it back to his time period again. When they had lived there for about a month, he decided it was okay if it didn't happen. He had a new family in ancient Rome and was very happy.

One night when Todd was thinking about these things, he looked out his bedroom window at the stars and at a much bigger and brighter moon.

Natilia was already in bed. She asked Todd, "What is wrong, dear?"

Todd answered, "Oh nothing. I was just thinking about how I came to be here."

Natilia wondered why he was thinking of that again. She said, "I thought we already tried to figure this out, Todd, a long time ago."

Todd didn't want to worry or upset her. He replied, "Yes we did. It just came to mind." He walked over to the bed and got in with Natilia. He had on his same tee shirt and shorts from the day he had left his room back in time over a month ago. Todd had them washed regularly so they were clean. He also had similar copies of his modern clothes made for him to wear as well. Natilia gave him a kiss good night and rolled over to go to sleep.

Todd lay there thinking some more, he wasn't quite ready for sleep yet. He looked around the room and thought about his life in Rome. His sword was on a table right next to the bed and his armor and shield were also nearby.

Todd started to feel sleepy as his thoughts drifted back to why he was there. 'Why had he come back in time? Why to this point in time? Why not further back in time or a little more into the future from this point in time?' He just couldn't figure it out.

Todd finally fell asleep but was no longer thinking about why he was there. His thoughts had turned to why that night felt stranger than usual.

THE TIME THAT TRAVELED PART II FEUDAL JAPAN

The following day Todd woke up before Natilia. He sat up in their bed and gazed around the room. Everything looked the same as the night before. He got out of bed and went over to the window to determine the time of day.

As Todd looked out the window, all he could see was fog, an outline of trees and bamboo. The bamboo was right outside his window and was so close he could reach out and touch it. Todd thought to himself, 'Oh no! This can't be happening again.'

Todd turned around and hurried back over to the bed. He saw that Natilia was still there in the bed asleep. He stood stunned for a second thinking, 'So I'm not the only one this can happen to.'

Todd hastily rushed to get all his armor and equipment on. He started with his socks and basketball shoes. Next he put his chain mail shirt over top of his red tee shirt.

As he was hurriedly getting ready, Natilia woke up and saw Todd getting dressed in his armor. She rubbed her eyes and was not quite fully awake as she asked him, "Todd, why are you putting on all your armor?"

Todd answered Natilia as he strapped on his steel shin guards, "Because I traveled through time again. And this time you came with me." Todd put on his steel body plate and then his leather wrist bracers.

Natilia was shocked to hear what Todd said. She was trying to understand what was happening and said "No, this cannot be true. The gods would not take you and me away from Rome."

As Todd put on his Roman helmet, he replied, "Like I was trying to tell you, Natilia, I think there's more to it than just the gods." She looked at him stunned and with fear in her eyes.

Todd tied his sword to his waist on the left side, as usual. He then picked up his shield. He was fully armored and ready to go. Natilia was on the verge of panicking. She asked Todd, "What are we to do?"

He looked deep into her eyes and calmly answered, "Babe, we go find out where we are and what time period we're in."

Natilia took a deep breath and composed herself. She asked, "Ok, what should I do?"

Todd looked around the room while thinking. He spotted the gladius that Quintius had given him. He replied, "First, you need to change into my extra clothes instead of your robes. We may need to be able to run. Also, take my gladius over there. It will be yours to use whenever you may need it."

Natilia got out of bed and dressed in Todd's clothes. They were some of the ones he had made in Rome that were similar to the modern clothes he was wearing. She agreed this was a good idea, since they had no idea what lay ahead.

Once Natilia was dressed and ready, Todd opened the door to their room and stepped outside. As they exited their room and came outside, Todd guessed it was morning. He thought that would explain why there was so much fog around. He was also pretty sure it was still summer.

The sun was starting to come up and it was becoming brighter. He could tell it was already getting hotter outside and knew the fog would start lifting soon. They headed toward the nearby woods.

Todd and Natilia made their way through the woods and finally arrived at a clearing. As they came out of the woods and into the clearing, Todd saw the outline of a castle in the distance through the scattering fog. He knew right away what type of building it was. He could tell the roof was of an oriental design.

Todd was thinking perhaps they were in Feudal Japan, and knew for sure as he found himself and Natilia surrounded by samurai in green armor. He quickly drew out his sword and was ready to fight the four samurai that had him and Natilia encircled.

Todd whispered to Natilia whose back was against his, "Don't worry. I know they will not attack you, because you are a woman. Just put down the gladius and I will tell them to leave you alone."

Natilia had no idea what they were. She asked quietly, "Are they even men? They have faces of demons, not those of men."

Todd knew very well they were men. He answered, "They are just wearing masks. Now please, put down the gladius. I will not let them harm you." Natilia did as Todd asked and slowly laid her sword on the ground.

Todd spoke to the four samurai, looking at each of them as he said, "Leave this woman be. Your fight is with me, not her! Natilia, move away from me and go back in the woods. Please, just for now." No one moved or said a word as Natilia walked away from all of them and into the treeline of the woods.

Todd lifted his shield and said, "Now, let's start this." All four samurai warriors came charging at Todd at the same time. As they neared him, he ducked down and put his shield over top of his head. The four samurai came down on his shield at the same time with their katanas.

Todd had successfully blocked their attack. He spun around while he was still low to the ground and slashed all but one of the samurai's shins. As he thrust up with his shield, three of the samurai fell to the ground.

The one samurai he had missed stepped back as Todd jumped up with his shield. He looked at his fellow samurai that had been defeated, then ran at Todd again with his katana in the air.

Todd blocked the samurai's swing with his shield and then swiftly slashed the samurai across the chest. The samurai fell back from the blow, but it hadn't cut him. Todd had only taken off the front piece of the samurai's armor with his strike.

Todd charged into the samurai with his shield and he fell to the ground from the force of the hit. As the samurai slammed into the ground, he dropped his sword.

Todd stood over the samurai and held his katana to his neck. He asked the samurai, "Why did you attack me?"

The samurai responded, "You are the enemy. You wear red. You are with the Hojo kingdom."

Todd had no idea who the Hojo were. He avowed firmly, "I am not with the Hojo! I don't even know who they are! Who are you with?"

The samurai sighed and told him, "I was with the Takeda kingdom until you have now defeated me."

Todd was confused why the samurai said "was" with the Takeda kingdom. He asked, "But I have not killed you. Therefore, you are still with the Takeda kingdom."

The samurai simply answered, "No, I am not. Even if you will not kill me, I will kill myself, for I will not live with the dishonor of a defeat."

Todd tried to convince the samurai not to take his own life. He said, "I will not kill you. You deserve to live. And you should not kill yourself over one loss. There is no disgrace in losing. It is an opportunity to honor yourself by learning from your mistake in this battle. It is knowledge. That is all."

The samurai fell silent and thought for a minute. Then he responded, "You may be right but why spare me, since I attacked you?"

Todd answered, "Well, I know it was a mistake. You thought I was your enemy."

The samurai nodded in agreement and said, "Very well. You make a good point. But you must go kill my men, for they are dishonored by their defeat."

Todd did not want to disrespect the samurai's culture, but he was not going to kill the wounded men. He insisted, "Just because they were defeated in battle does not mean they should die. I believe it is honorable to learn from your losses. I will not kill them, but I would have your name."

The samurai was impressed by Todd's character and principles. He said "A name for my men's lives, this is very honorable. My name is Yoshoni. What is your name, warrior?"

Todd was relieved that the samurai had shared his name instead of continuing the talk of killing him and his men. Todd responded, "My name is Todd."

Yoshoni answered, "That is a strange name. I will call you Todaroshi. Is this fine?"

Todd thought to himself, 'Here we go again.' He said to the samurai, "Yes, it is fine, Yoshoni. Now, as I said, you and your men are free to go and can gain knowledge from this fight." Yoshoni nodded in agreement.

Todd put his katana away. Yoshoni sat up, grabbed his katana and put it back in his scabbard. Todd turned and called out to Natilia, "Ok, Natilia! It is safe to come out now!"

Natilia emerged from hiding behind a large tree and asked, "Have you finished them off already, Todd?"

Todd answered, "Yes, I have but Yoshoni here is going to help us out."

Todd headed towards Natilia to escort her from the woods. As Todd turned back towards Yoshoni with Natilia behind him, an arrow hit his shield dead in the center.

Yoshoni stood up and drew out his katana. He said, "So sorry, Todaroshi. We had you surrounded in case you may have been able to defeat us."

Todd glared at Yoshoni as he pulled the arrow out of his shield. He looked up at the castle walls and noticed the archers. The arrow had traveled a great distance to come all the way from the castle, and it had green featherings on it.

Todd knew he was outnumbered, so he decided it was best not to pull out his katana. He took hold of Natilia's hand and said to her, "Come, we have to go with them. They won this one, for now at least."

Natilia was frightened and worried what might happen to them. She whispered to Todd, "Do you think they mean to harm us?"

Todd was concerned but tried to reassure her, saying, "Don't worry, Natilia. You know I will always protect you. We will be fine."

Yoshoni did not want Todd to start up the fight again. He ordered, "Now come with me, Todaroshi! Or our archers will fire a wave of arrows on you."

Todd responded angrily, "Very well. We will come but let Natilia bring her sword."

Yoshoni nodded in agreement, picked up the gladius, and handed it to Natilia. With the archers covering them, Yoshoni felt no need to disarm them.

Natilia stowed her sword in its sheath. Yoshoni ordered his wounded men to return to the castle and receive attention for their injuries.

The samarai seemed confused and ready to protest. He repeated the order firmly and they departed.

Yoshoni turned back to Todd and Natilia and pointed them in the direction of the castle. They made their way across the clearing and Yoshoni followed with his katana in hand.

The captives arrived at the castle's gates where two samurai sentries stood guard. Yoshoni spoke to them and they opened the gates to let him and his detainees inside.

As they proceeded through the gates, Yoshoni said to Todd, "I am taking you in front of my Lord Takeda. He will decide what is to be done with you."

Todd was still angry with Yoshoni for turning on him after he had spared him and his men. He answered crossly, "Do whatever seems fair in your eyes, Yoshoni."

Yoshoni was surprised by Todd's reaction. He wondered why Todd wasn't asking to be spared being taken in front of his most feared Lord.

The group made their way to the castle entrance where four more samurai sentries stood guard. Again, Yoshoni spoke to them about taking them as captives to Lord Takeda.

The castle doors were opened to them. As they entered the castle and its great hall, Todd saw pillars of large wood beams. They were coated in green paint to show Lord Takeda's power. The wooden columns progressed all the way up to the foot of the throne where Lord Takeda sat. He seemed intent to hear what news Yoshoni brought.

The party traversed the hall to Lord Takeda's throne. Yoshoni told them to bow down like him when they reached Lord Takeda.

Yoshoni bowed down to the ground in front of the throne. He announced, "My Lord Takeda! I bring you the warrior that was roaming through your woods.

When we had him surrounded, we all attacked at once. Forgive me, my Lord, but he managed to defeat me and my men. This warrior, Todaroshi, should have killed me but has spared my life and those of my wounded men. And he would not allow us to take our own lives, saying we must learn from defeat. We have only captured him because of our archers on the castle walls. They made him see there was no option to run or fight."

While Yoshoni made this statement, Todd squeezed Natilia's hand and whispered to her, "Don't worry. I won't let them harm you. I'll get us out of this."

Natilia whispered back, "I trust in you, Todd."

Lord Takeda sat quietly for a few minutes, then ordered them all to stand up. He studied Todd and Natilia very closely. He finally said, "This is the warrior I have seen in my dreams."

Yoshoni was confused by this statement. He respectfully asked "I beg your pardon, my Lord, but what do you mean?"

Lord Takeda had been excited by Yoshoni's story and was thrilled to have Todd and Natilia in his presence. He responded, "I mean by this, he is what I dreamed of. A warrior, with his woman, who will help us finally destroy the Hojo and teach them a lesson with the sword!"

Todd was startled by Lord Takeda's declaration. He asked, "What are you saying, Lord Takeda?"

Takeda said with a slight smile, "I am telling you, I will not kill you, Todaroshi. Even though you were trespassing on my land and have wounded my men."

Todd now looked closely at Lord Takeda. He was dressed from shoulder to toe in a full suit of armor made of green jade. On his left side, at the top of the throne, was his green jade samurai helmet and mask.

Todd thought he had figured out what was about to be asked of him and perhaps why he had traveled through time again. He asked, "So you want me to go with your armies to fight and destroy this Hojo and all his lands too, right?"

Lord Takeda smirked at Todd's question. He responded, "No, I want you to go with my armies and take the village of Tokyo from Hojo. Then we will destroy his castle and kill him. I will take this journey with you."

Todd and Yoshoni were both shocked and exclaimed, "What?!" Todd was now beginning to feel a little less tense. He was relieved that they would not be harmed or need to fight their way out of this mess. He said, "If you think that's best, Lord Takeda."

Yoshoni was concerned for his lord's safety and stated, "My Lord, stay here where it is safe, so you will not come to any harm."

Takeda became angry that his plans were being questioned. He yelled, "Do not tell me what I should do, Yoshoni! I did not ask for your guidance!"

Todd hoped to diffuse the situation by asking Lord Takeda about his plans. He said, "When will we depart, Lord Takeda?"

Takeda was pleased to hear the warrior Todaroshi was eager to move forward with his plans for attacking Tokyo. He replied, "In the next morning, for now we rest. And I will have some proper armor made for you, Todaroshi. You must be a very skilled warrior to defeat some of my finest samurai."

Todd recalled his training sessions with Quintius and Julius and answered, "I was trained by some very good people, Lord Takeda." He looked at Natilia and winked. She smiled at him, knowing he was referring to her father and Julius. Thinking of them made her a little homesick.

Lord Takeda said, Todaroshi, you may call me Takeda." Todd replied, "Thank you, Takeda, sir."

Takeda was thrilled and anxious to advance his plans to retake Tokyo. He had much to think about - strategies, tactics, etc. He yelled out, "Servants! Take these two strangers and provide them with the honorable guest rooms."

A servant rushed forward and bowed low. She bid Todd and Natilia to follow her and led them down a hallway to their room for the night. The servant opened the guest room door and stated, "This is where my Lord wishes you to stay. I hope you will be comfortable." She bowed to them and quickly walked away.

Once the servant was gone, Todd said to Natilia, "Ok, we have to figure this out. How did this happen again?!"

Natilia thought for a moment and was unsure but shared her opinion with Todd. She replied, "I think perhaps it was the gods that willed this to happen to you, Todd."

Todd wondered why she would think it was the gods. He asked, "And why would they do that, Natilia?"

Natilia had started to believe that this might be some sort of trial. She answered, "The gods may wish for you to become a better warrior, so they could have sent you to this place to learn and train more."

Todd wished it was that simple, but he appreciated Natilia's optimistic view and was glad she was with him. He smiled at her and said, "I hope you're right, Natilia, I really do. One thing is for certain, I'm not alone this time. I'm happy you're still with me."

Todd walked over to her and wrapped his arms around her. As they stood together in each other's arms, she clung to him, thinking they could have been parted. She said, "I, too, am glad that I am here with you and not left behind."

Todd was still dead set on trying to find out why this had happened again. Now Natilia was involved also. He vowed to her, "I will figure this out. I promise you, I will discover why this has happened to us. And I won't let any harm come to you."

Natilia was touched by Todd's concern for her and his determination to understand their situation. She said, "I know you will, Todd, for I believe in you."

Natilia kissed Todd and they were still embracing when a different servant came into the room. The servant bowed and said, "Excuse me. My Lord wishes to see you, sir. Please come with me." Todd agreed to go with the servant to see Takeda.

Todd turned to Natilia and asked, "Hopefully I won't be long, Natilia. Will you be safe here without me?"

Natilia thought about the sword he had given her for protection and answered, "I believe I will be quite fine."

Todd smiled at her and headed towards the doorway where the servant waited. He was glad to see Natilia was confident but he still worried for her safety. He turned back to her and said, "If anything happens, you have my gladius. Use it if necessary."

Natilia nodded her head in confirmation. Todd exited the room.

The servant led Todd to Takeda. They went down a long hallway and came back into the throne room, which they only passed through. They continued down another hallway on the other side of the throne room. This area of the castle was new to Todd. A short ways down the hall, they stopped at an open doorway and inside stood Takeda. Todd took one quick look around the room and knew at once they had arrived at the castle's armory.

Takeda greeted Todd with a smile and said, "Come in, Todaroshi. It would seem that you are in luck this day." Todd wondered what this was all about. He asked "Why is that, Takeda?"

Takeda proudly answered, "For this reason. There is already a whole suit of armor made for you. It is a very fine armor of jade." Todd studied the magnificent suit of armor. It was a stunning shade of green, beautiful, shiny and obviously brand new. The suit of armor was extremely well put together as if by a master blacksmith. Todd was very impressed by the amazing craftsmanship. He was stunned that it was for him but eager to try it on. He told Takeda, "Thank you, Takeda. I will try it on right away."

Todd grabbed the green jade armored pants, which Takeda called grieves, and put them on over top of his steel shin guards and shorts. Then he took off his steel body plate and set it on the ground. Todd put on the long sleeved green jade body piece over top of his shirt and chain mail. He picked up the steel body plate, which he'd received from Julius, and put it on over top of the jade body piece.

Todd continued to get fully equipped by taking off his leather wrist bracers. He put on the green jade gauntlets and then put the leather bracers back on over top. Lastly, Todd took off his Roman helmet and put on the green samurai helmet instead. He did not put on the jade armor boots. He chose to wear his shoes from his time. Todd thought he'd be better able to move quickly, even with all this armor on. He also decided not to put on the mask. He did not want it to impair his vision in a battle. He also opted for his own Roman shield and katana. These items he refused to trade out.

Once Todd was fully armored, Takeda looked at him in amazement and said, "Well now, look at you. I would say you would be a feared warrior if I saw you on the field of battle."

Todd was a little embarrassed by Takeda's comment but did not want to be disrespectful. He also appreciated his gift of the magnificent jade armor. Todd responded, "Thank you again for the armor. I will do my best to be a feared warrior for you, Takeda."

Takeda continued to look at Todd, impressed by the armored soldier standing before him. He stated, "Now you look almost exactly like the great warrior from my dreams."

Todd was starting to think that his reason for coming to this time period was to assist Takeda. He stated, "Well, I don't know how I got here or why I'm here, but I will do what I can to help you."

Takeda was overjoyed by Todd's statement. He said, "Good! Now I will tell you what we are up against, great warrior, Todaroshi. In the morning, we make way for the village of Tokyo to take it back from Hojo. He took my village from me and has waged war upon me. But we cannot defeat him when we do battle with Hojo himself. You see, Todaroshi, Hojo possesses a very powerful sword that will cut through anything. I do not know how he came by this sword or if he made it himself. My spies tell me that when he uses this sword, it glows with a blue light and can cut down the tallest tree with one swing."

Todd was surprised by Takeda's description of the sword. It sounded like something out of a sci-fi movie. He also thought he knew what Takeda wanted him to do. Todd said, "So let me guess, you want me to kill Hojo and take his powerful sword?"

Takeda was impressed that Todd caught on quickly, but he hadn't yet told him a key feature of the sword. He explained further, "But I must also tell you the sword Hojo carries is magical. The blade of the katana will disappear when it is out of his hands."

Now Todd was shocked. The magical sword of Hojo was starting to sound a lot like a light saber from the Star Wars movies back in his time period. He thought it would be impossible for a light saber to be in the past, let alone in his own time. They were only movie magic. Then he thought to himself, 'Well, I've traveled back in time so anything's possible, but a light saber?!'

Todd's thoughts then returned to Natilia. He didn't want to leave her alone for too long and was now anxious to get back to her. He said to Takeda, "Ok, we'll see about this magical sword. I'd like to return to my room now. Please let me know when you're ready to leave in the morning, sir."

Takeda was pleased to see how eager Todd was to aid him in his struggles. He replied, "Very well. I will have a great meal sent to your room, Todaroshi. Thank you for the service you will be giving me in the days to come."

Todd appreciated Takeda's gifts, hospitality, and respect. He again thanked him and offered his support saying, "Thank you, Takeda. I look forward to our journey. Please call on me if I can be of service before then."

Takeda bowed to him and Todd bowed in return. Todd exited the armory and headed back to the guest room to Natilia.

When Todd came into the room, he found Natilia asleep on the bed. He wanted her to get some rest so he tried not to wake her. He quietly took off all his armor and shoes until he was just wearing his tee shirt, shorts, and socks. He got into the bed and nestled in close to her. He was fast asleep in a few minutes.

A couple hours later, one of Takeda's servants came into the room and woke them. The servant had brought their dinner. They both sat up and stretched. Todd got out of bed and walked over to the table as the servant set the tray down.

The meal consisted of bread, rice, fish, and what looked to Todd to be something like sushi. The servant, with his head slightly bowed so as not to make eye contact, asked if they wanted something to drink.

Todd answered, "No sake, please, just water for us."

The servant bowed and said, "Very well, sir. I will go and get you some water." The servant left the room. Natilia got out of bed and came over to the table.

The servant came back with four cups of water, two for Todd and two for Natilia. Todd took the cups from the servant and thanked him. The servant bowed and left the room.

After the servant had gone, Natilia pointed to the sushi on the tray and asked, "What food is this?"

Todd laughed at the face she was making as she looked at what was strange food to her. He explained, "That is sushi and it's very good for you. It is raw fish and rice, and some sea weed too, I think."

Natilia's face changed to slight disgust. She said, "Raw fish! I do not think that can be good for you, Todd."

Todd smiled at Natilia as he popped a piece of sushi in his mouth. After chewing and swallowing it, he advised her, "Not all raw fish is good for you, but these are okay to eat."

Natilia trusted Todd so she picked up a piece of the sushi and tried it. She thought it tasted okay, but would have preferred having it cooked. They finished their meal and enjoyed a quiet evening spent together. They went to sleep early after such a trying day.

When the morning came, Todd and Natilia were both awakened by the first sign of sunlight coming through the window in their room. Todd got out of bed and put on all his armor. He outfitted himself as he had the day before. Once fully equipped, he put on his shoes.

Natilia examined Todd now fully armored in jade and Roman steel. She smiled and said, "Todd, I have found one good thing about being here."

Todd smiled back at her and asked, "What is that, Natilia?"

Natilia went over to Todd with his samurai helmet and put it on his head. She answered him, "All your armor is your favorite color now." Todd laughed and gave her a kiss. He said, "You're right. That is a good thing."

Natilia then thought about his journey and the forthcoming battle. She was afraid of losing him and said, "Todd, I do not wish to see you fight, for I am afraid that you may come to harm."

Todd understood Natilia's concerns and tried to ease her anxiety. He responded, "Don't worry about me, Natilia? I'm doing this to keep you safe from harm. I'll be fine."

Natilia smiled and kissed Todd. She told him, "I know you would let no harm come to me and that is one of the many reasons I love you, Todd."

There was a knock on the door and a female servant entered the room. She bowed to them and said, "My Lord waits for you and is ready to make way towards Tokyo to take it back from the evil Hojo."

Todd was dressed and ready so he responded, "Very well. Let's go to your Lord." Todd grabbed his sword and tied it to his waist on his left side. He picked up his shield and nodded to Natilia. They all exited the room.

Todd and Natilia followed the servant out of the castle gates to where Takeda and Yoshoni were waiting on horseback. They had assembled in front of the gates men numbering in the thousands and were ready to head to war.

Takeda saw Todd and Natilia approaching. He called out, "Todaroshi, I see you are ready to go and do battle to kill the evil Hojo and his forces."

Todd knew Takeda would be anxious to leave as soon as possible. He answered, "I'm ready."

Yoshoni noticed that Natilia was still with Todd. He said, pointing at Natilia, "If you are ready, get on that horse and leave the woman behind."

Todd was not planning to leave Natilia behind. He answered angrily, "I only go if she comes with me." He knew she would be afraid to be left alone while he was gone to war.

Yoshoni felt dishonored by Todd's reply. He yelled "No, she is not! We cannot..."

Takeda had raised his hand up at Yoshoni and cut him off, saying, "If Todaroshi wishes for his woman to come with him, then so be it. Let her be his burden alone to bear."

Todd knew very well Natilia would not be any trouble. He replied to Takeda as he continued glaring at Yoshoni, "Trust me. She will not be any burden at all."

Todd grabbed ahold of the horse and tied his shield to the saddle on the left side. He helped Natilia up onto the horse. He then jumped up in front of her and took up the horses' reins.

Once situated on the horse, Todd looked at Takeda and asked sarcastically, "Well, are we going or not?"

Takeda, with a smirk on his face, yelled out, "Men! We make our way to the village Tokyo to take it back!"

All the men cheered at this announcement. After the cheering died down, Takeda further ordered, "Now, we move out!" All the soldiers started marching towards Tokyo with Takeda leading the way.

They marched until about midday but did not camp. They had reached the edge of a forest and took refuge in the shade. All the soldiers just sat for a few minutes to rest and eat a small portion of food.

Todd was wondering how long their trip would take, so he approached Yoshoni and asked, "Yoshoni, can you tell me how long our journey will be to Tokyo?"

Yoshoni stared at Todd, looking slightly annoyed. Todd thought he might still be mad about their earlier confrontation. Yoshoni finally answered, "It is a two-days journey, if the weather allows. But as it is mid-summer, we should not have any difficulty."

Todd was glad Yoshoni had answered him. He hoped their argument about Natilia was now in the past. Todd respectfully bowed to him and said, "Thank you, Yoshoni." He headed back over to Natilia and their horse.

Natilia wondered if Todd got an answer and asked, "Did Yoshoni tell you how long it will be?"

Todd answered, "He said it would only take two days. Let's get mounted. It looks like we'll be heading out shortly." The soldiers were packing up and preparing to leave, so Todd and Natilia got back on their horse and were ready to depart.

The rest period ended and the war party headed out through the forest. As they continued, the forest became dense woods full of bamboo. Everything seemed closer together. Even the air was thicker in this area with an overabundance of bamboo.

Natilia had never seen anything like bamboo. She asked, "Todd, what are these trees? They seem to be taking over the land."

Todd explained, "They are called bamboo. You may think they look weak, but bamboo is actually very strong and hard to cut down with an axe."

The soldiers continued their trek through the bamboo woods throughout the afternoon. When the sun was starting to set, they had reached an even denser part of the woods.

Takeda looked around and decided the area would be a good camp site. He yelled out, "Halt! We rest here tonight!"

The men stopped their march and started to set up camp. Later the soldiers had all the tents up and multiple fires going throughout the campsite. There were groups of men around each fire, relaxing and talking amongst themselves.

Todd and Natilia had set up and organized their tent. Todd had planned to stay the night in the tent with Natilia, but it had grown dark outside and he thought he saw shadows moving around in the woods. Todd started to have a bad gut feeling about the shadows. He said to Natilia, "Something's not right. Go in the tent and stay inside. No matter what happens or what you hear, do not come out. Understand?"

Natilia was frightened by Todd's request. She asked, "Why, Todd? What is going to happen?"

Todd was focused on the woods. He responded, "I'm not sure. I think there's movement in the woods."

Natilia put on a brave face and said, "Ok, I will stay in the tent while you go survey the area. Please be careful, Todd."

Todd smiled at Natilia and tried to reassure her, saying, "Don't worry. I'll be fine. It's probably nothing but keep your gladius nearby just in case."

Natilia went in the tent and sat on the edge of the cot. She hoped Todd wouldn't be long.

Todd slowly and quietly crept over towards Takeda's tent, where he'd seen the shadows moving around. He kept his shield held up and his right hand on the hilt of his sword ready to be drawn.

As Todd neared Takeda's tent, he thought he could make out a dark figure, as it disappeared around the back of the tent. He hurried over to see if he could locate the figure. Todd knew someone was definitely creeping about. He hadn't imagined it.

When Todd reached the back of the tent, he was shocked to see there was one long, straight-line cut into the fabric about five feet in length. He thought to himself, 'Assassins!'

Todd stealthily peeked in through the cut and saw two figures in black facing away from him. He soundlessly went through the hole in the tent.

Now that Todd was inside, he could see the two figures were ninjas. They both had their swords in hand, ready to attack Takeda as he lay asleep on the bed. Todd ran at the two ninjas and tackled them both to the ground.

As the ninjas fell, one of them dropped his sword. Todd grabbed the sword and stabbed one of the ninjas through the chest. He released the sword, leaving it in the assassin's chest, as the other ninja slashed at him.

The uninjured ninja had recovered quickly and was on the attack. He had slashed again and cut Todd on his right shoulder.

Todd rolled away and hastily pulled out his own sword. He swung at the ninja and cut off both of his legs. As the ninja fell to the ground, Todd stabbed him in the heart to finish him off.

Takeda had woken up in time to see Todd kill the second ninja. Takeda's shock quickly turned to anger. He knew he could have been keen killed in his sleep. He jumped up and yelled out to the soldiers, "Assassins!"

The men reacted immediately. Some relaxing around the fires didn't have their weapons and had to run into their tents for their swords.

Once Takeda raised the alarm, a large group of ninjas came out of the darkness. They were all dressed in black to blend in with the darkness of the night. The two groups of combatants began fighting.

As the samurai warriors were out in the camp fighting, Takeda grabbed his sword to join his men in battle. Before he could exit the tent, four more ninjas pushed in through the hole cut in the back.

Todd immediately reacted and rushed over to Takeda. He stood with his back to Takeda's back and raised his shield and sword. Todd said to Takeda, "I get two and you get two, sound fair?"

Takeda was amused by Todd's comment. He also appreciated his assistance. He responded with a slight smile, "Yes, sounds fair to me."

As soon as they had agreed on this plan, all four ninjas attacked. Todd turned his sword sideways and raised it up to block the two swords of the ninjas. As there blows fell, he pushed them both away from him. They stumbled backwards. Todd swiftly and forcefully swung his sword and cut them both in half with just the one swing.

Now that Todd had defeated the two ninjas, he turned towards Takeda and saw him cutting off the head of one of the ninjas. The final ninja was badly injured and began to shake and tremble with fear.

Trying to save himself, the ninja made a sudden dash for the hole in the back of the tent. Takeda saw that his quarry was trying to escape, so he violently threw his sword at him. The sword caught the ninja in the back. It stabbed all the way through him and ended up sticking out of his chest.

Todd and Takeda heard loud yelling and cheering coming from outside. They exited the tent and saw that all the ninjas had been slain by the samurai. The men were cheering about their victory.

Takeda turned toTodd and said, "Thank you, Todaroshi. I am in your debt."

Todd reminded Takeda that he was just honoring his commitment. He answered, "No thanks are needed and you're not in my debt, Takeda. I'm just doing as I promised you."

Takeda was still very grateful for Todd's efforts. He said, "Yes, but I will still repay you for saving my life. Once we are done with our journey to destroy the Hojo, I will give you the reward you have so much earned."

Todd replied, "Thank you, Takeda. Now, please excuse me. I will see you in the morning." Todd was anxious to return to Natilia to be sure she was alright.

Takeda said, "Yes, Todaroshi. I will see you at first light. Also, may I say, you are an honorable man."

Todd responded, "Thank you, Takeda. You are a great warrior and leader for your people." He didn't want Takeda to know he was worrying about Natilia, so he added, "Now I'm off to bed to get some sleep. Good night."

Todd gave Takeda a quick bow and headed back to his tent. He came into the tent and found Natilia sitting on the bed with the gladius sword in hand. She was ready and waiting to lunge at any enemy that might enter.

When Natilia saw it was Todd, she dropped the sword and ran over to him. She embraced him and noticed that his right shoulder was cut. She asked him, "Are you hurt, Todd? You are cut in the shoulder."

Todd had forgotten about the cut. He looked at his right shoulder where his armor had been slashed by the ninja. He noticed there was no bleeding. He answered Natilia, "I don't think so. There is no blood coming out."

Natilia still wanted to be sure Todd was alright. She said, "Please let me take a look at it." She helped him remove his body plate. She looked closely at the jade armor where it had been cut. Then they took off the jade armor piece as well. There was no cut on the chain mail. It appeared that the ninja's sword had been stopped by the chain mail. Todd's skin had not been touched.

Natilia was surprised that there was not even a scratch on Todd. She said, "Todd, you are very lucky. The sleeve of the chain mail protected you. Otherwise you could have been cut to the bone."

Todd recalled who gave him the chain mail and smiled. He replied, "Well then, we better thank Quintius for this one. I might have lost my arm tonight if he had not given me this fine Roman chain mail shirt."

Natilia smiled at Todd and continued helping him out of his armor. She thought about her father and how much she missed him. She said, "My father did the best he could to look after you, for you were the only son he ever had." Natilia started to feel incredibly homesick thinking about her father. Her eyes started to well up with tears.

Todd felt bad for upsetting Natilia. He took her in his arms and said, "Don't worry, Natilia. I'm here for you and we will find a way to get back to your father and Rome." Todd said this even though he was still hoping to get back to his own time and home to his own family. He wanted to cheer her up.

Natilia appreciated Todd's kindness. She wiped her eyes and said, "I know you are here for me, Todd, and that we will find a way back home soon."

Todd decided they needed to focus on the here and now, which meant getting some rest for the long journey ahead. Tomorrow he could think more about how they might get back to their own times. He said, "Come on, Natilia. Let's go to bed. We have a lot to do tomorrow and now with little sleep."

Natilia wiped away the last of her tears and replied, "Yes, you are right, Todd. We do need to get our rest for tomorrow." They got into the bed and fell asleep in each other's arms a short time later.

When morning came, Takeda came into Todd's tent to wake him. Seeing that he and Natilia were both still asleep in bed, he said, "Wake up, Todaroshi, for the sun is up and we are all getting ready to make leave to head to Tokyo and take my village back."

Todd opened his eyes and replied, "We'll be ready shortly, Takeda. He and Natilia got up and quickly dressed.

Todd put on all of his armor with Natilia's help. Once fully armored, they hurriedly packed up their tent and put it into one of the carts that were being moved with the army.

Todd and Natilia headed over to the horse after stowing the tent supplies. Todd assisted Natilia onto the horse. After she was mounted, he tied his shield onto the horse's left side and saddled up in front of Natilia.

Takeda was impressed to see how quickly they both had made ready to depart. Now that everyone seemed to be prepared to head out, he shouted, "We march to Tokyo to take back what is rightfully ours!" The whole army cheered at this announcement.

Takeda steered his horse over to Todd and said, "I have figured out what I will do for you as your reward for saving my life."

Todd wasn't surprised Takeda hadn't let it go. He asked, "And what would that be, Takeda?"

Takeda was glad to see Todd was interested in his reward. He answered, "I will train you to be even better with your katana, Todaroshi."

Todd was surprised and very happy. It would be an incredible opportunity to receive training from Takeda. He said, "Thank you, Takeda. I would be honored and very much look forward to training with you."

Takeda was glad to see Todd was eager to train with him. He replied, "Have no fear, Todaroshi. We will have our chance to train once we take back Tokyo."

Todd reassured him by saying, "I have no doubt we will take back Tokyo. Then with the village in our control, we can train all day if we like." Takeda laughed at Todd's enthusiasm.

All day long the soldiers continued their march to the village Tokyo. They finally arrived at the edge of the thick bamboo woods and came out into a clearing. The white stone walls and red wooden gates of Tokyo could be seen in the distance.

Takeda halted the war party and gave orders. He said not too loudly, "Alright, men. Go with haste and cut down a good many bamboo trees. Tie them together to make a large battering ram. Be sure there are at least six handles so many men can carry it."

A group of soldiers headed off to make the ram as Takeda ordered. He dismounted his horse and gave more orders. He said, "I need archers to form a line and prepare to fire on the village Tokyo on my command."

The archers quickly moved into place forming a line. They had their arrows loaded and bows ready to fire on command.

Todd sitting astride his horse watched the men making the ram. The task was completed speedily. Before long, the ram was assembled and ready to be carried into battle.

Todd had also been surveying the village. He shared his thoughts with Takeda saying, "Takeda, sir, seeing how small the village is and that there's not many Hojo samurai posted to protect it, I would only fire two waves of arrows on the city."

Takeda was impressed to hear Todd's view of the battlefield. He said, "Very good, Todaroshi. This is what I plan to do. But are you forgetting one important thing?"

Todd wasn't sure what he had missed. He asked, "What is that, sir?"

Takeda smiled and answered, "Keep your archers' firing on select targets after they fire the two waves."

Todd thought about it for a second and realized why this would be a very good strategy. He replied, "Oh, I see. That way your samurai have cover when they go up to the gates to break them down with the ram."

Takeda was delighted that Todd had caught on to his tactics so quickly. He answered, "Exactly, Todaroshi! And then we will not lose too many of our good men."

Yoshoni approached Takeda and gave a quick bow. He advised, "We have everything ready now, my Lord."

Takeda was excited to see everything moving forward as he had planned. He responded, "Good work, Yoshoni. Now we attack! Archers, fire two waves of arrows into the village, then focus on just the Hojo samurai on the village walls!"

Todd wondered if the arrows would be able to reach the village. From the edge of the woods, they were still a great distance away. However, the bows of the samurai archers were very large, extending from knee to head.

The archers fired the first wave of arrows into the village. It appeared they hit in the dead center of the village and a lot of screaming could be heard. The archers proceeded with their orders and fired the second wave. As soon as they fired, several of them were hit by incoming arrows. The Hojo archers, aiming from the village walls, were returning fire. The Takeda archers now focused on the Hojo archers defending the village.

Takeda yelled out more orders, "Men, go ram open the village gates and take Tokyo back from the Hojo scum!"

The samurai moved forward with the battering ram and were protected by the archers who continued firing upon the Hojo defenders. The Hojo archers were being overwhelmed and their numbers were dropping quickly. Soon there were so few archers on the wall that they knew they had to retreat.

The Hojo samurai archers left the wall and went behind the red gates. They would have to defend the village with the other soldiers if the Takeda samurai could break through the gates.

Todd saw that the archers had retreated from the walls and decided to take advantage of the situation. He got off his horse, untied his shield and took his sword out of its holder. Todd said to Natilia, "Wait here. You'll be safe. I'm going to help them out up at the gate."

Natilia was concerned for Todd. She replied, "Please be safe, Todd. I was scared for you last night. Please do not make me fear losing you here."

Todd smiled and responded confidently, "Come on, Natilia. It's me. What could possibly happen?" Todd gave her a quick wink, then turned and ran off towards the Takeda samurai at the gates to help them break through.

As Todd was running to the gates, he noticed to his left there was a ladder leaning up against the village wall. He quickly ran over to it and stood it up against the wall. It was tall enough to get him to the top. Todd decided he couldn't pass up this opportunity. He tied his shield onto his back so it would be easier to climb the ladder.

Todd quickly reached the top. He made sure there were no Hojo samurai waiting on the embrasure from where the archers had been firing. It was clear, so he proceeded over the wall and removed his shield from his back. He moved forward with his shield in front of him and headed for the door at the end of the embrasure. He knew it would lead down to the gates.

Once Todd reached the door, he decided to take a quick look over the edge to see into the village. He was hoping to see how many Hojo samurai were waiting down near the gate. Todd was surprised to see that there were only about ten samurai behind the gate. He scanned further into the village. Todd's eyes widened in shock as he spotted a large group of Hojo samurai. They were near the center of the village and were lying in wait. Todd realized it was a secret counterattack. The Hojo would strike the Takeda samurai once they entered the village.

The ten samurai at the gate was just a ruse. The Takeda samurai would think that they had easily taken the village. But in fact, there were about 1,000 Hojo samurai in the village center ready to attack. Takeda had only sent 100 men to attack the village gates. Todd knew Takeda had thousands more samurai soldiers and hundreds of samurai archers waiting on the edge of the bamboo woods. He had to warn the attacking Takeda samurai and get some back up from the supporting troops.

Todd hurriedly opened the door and descended the stairs from the wall. He stealthily looked out to see if the ten Hojo samurai were still stationed behind the gate waiting to face the Takeda samurai on the other side. It appeared no one had noticed him yet, so he decided he better act fast.

Todd sprinted as fast as he could with his shield raised up through the middle of the ten Hojo samurai. He knocked five of them down with his shield and slashed two others with his sword. Three of the fallen Hojo samurai got back up, so there were eight men angry and ready to fight.

Three of the Hojo samurai charged Todd. As they came at him, he raised up his shield blocking two of them. The third samurai he kicked back. Todd pushed away the two blocked samurai with his shield. As the third one was trying to catch his balance, Todd swung his katana and violently cut off his head.

After seeing the decapitated samurai fall, the other two Hojo samurai came at Todd again. He charged back at them and blocked the samurai on his left with his shield. He slashed at the Hojo samurai on his right and cut him along his chest. The samurai fell to the ground.

The other Hojo samurai continued his attack and struck Todd's shield with his sword. He continued to strike Todd's shield but his blows seemed to be lessening.

Todd could tell the Hojo samurai's arm was wearing out. He reacted quickly by turning his shield out as if opening a door and quickly moved towards the samurai, slashing him down the middle of his face and upper body.

As Todd defeated the last of the three Hojo samurai, he heard a loud bang and cracking noise. He turned around to see that the Takeda samurai had just broken through the gates. They had dropped the ram and stood shocked. They were surprised to see the five Hojo samurai standing there ready to fight Todd, not them.

Taking advantage of this slight pause in action caused by the gates being opened, Todd charged at one of the Hojo with his shield. He knocked him down and as soon as the samurai hit the ground, Todd swiftly stabbed him through with his sword.

Now two other Hojo samurai charged at Todd. As they neared him, Todd blocked their sword swings with his own sword. He then used his shield to disarm them. By slightly tilting his shield, he used the edge to hit the bottom of both of their swords' hilts. The blow knocked their swords out of their hands and up into the air. Todd then rapidly slit them both across the waistline and they were dispatched.

Todd turned to the last two remaining Hojo samurai. They seemed to now be afraid of him. He charged at them and blocked a swing from one of the Hojo's swords. He counter attacked and slashed the Hojo across his chest. The Hojo collapsed from the strike.

The last Hojo turned and started to run away as fast as he could. Todd dropped his shield so he could run faster and chased him down. He rapidly caught up to him and stabbed the samurai in the back and through the chest in one vicious blow. Todd pulled his sword out and let the samurai fall face forward to the ground. He shook the blood off his sword, retrieved his shield, and headed back to take his place with the Takeda samurai.

As Todd was almost to the gates and the Takeda samurai, suddenly three arrows struck Todd in the back and he fell to the ground. He pulled his shield up to protect him. He also used it as an aid to pick himself up.

Todd was back on his feet and hurrying to the Takeda samurai. They seemed awestruck. He guessed they were surprised to see him get up after such hits.

Todd knew he had to warn them about the large number of hidden samurai. He yelled out, "Signal for more men. We need back up now!"

The Takeda samurai were stunned and impressed by Todd's actions. They didn't hesitate to listen to his instructions. They immediately signaled for reinforcements.

Seeing the signal, Takeda sent 1,000 samurai forward to help in taking back the village Tokyo. The additional samurai included some of the archers.

Todd was pleased to see the archers and hastily gave orders. He said, "Archers, I want you up on the wall and to fire on the Hojo samurai waiting near the center of the village." Todd turned to the rest of the samurai and said, "Everyone else, head to the middle of the city. We will surprise their 'surprise attack.'"

Todd went with the archers up on the walls. He watched as the Hojo samurai were struck down by the Takeda arrows. The Takeda samurai were nearing the now smaller group of Hojo samurai. Todd knew the archers needed to stop shooting. He ordered, "Cease fire, men! We don't want to hit any of our own." The archers halted the attack and watched with Todd as the battle raged on down in the middle of the village.

The battle ended when there were only Takeda samurai standing. Todd signaled to Takeda that the fighting had concluded. Now that it was safe to enter, Takeda, Yoshoni, and Natilia came to the village with the rest of the army.

As they entered the village, Takeda noticed that there were ten dead Hojo samurai at the gate and not one single dead Takeda samurai. Takeda was surprised by this and asked, "Who is responsible for the deaths of these ten Hojo samurai?"

Todd had come down from the wall and was waiting at the gate for them. He answered Takeda, "Me, sir. Why do you ask?"

Takeda looked Todd up and down. This warrior from another place continued to impress him. He replied, "Never in my life have I seen a single man take down ten fully armored samurai. And it looks like you weren't even touched by any of them."

A Takeda samurai soldier spoke up about another amazing feat he'd witnessed, "My Lord, he also took three Hojo arrows in the back that knocked him down. He got up as if he had not even taken these vicious strikes. He is a great warrior."

Todd was a little embarrassed by this but did turn around to show Takeda his back. Takeda could see the three arrows still stuck there. Todd explained, "Yes, as you can see, I haven't had a chance to take them out yet."

Takeda was now even more impressed. He was so stunned and amazed that Todd had done all of this by himself and he seemed to be indestructible. He asked, "Todaroshi, were you sent by the gods to come and help me defeat Hojo and his samurai?"

Todd was shocked by Takeda's question. He asked, "What?! Did you pray to the gods?"

Takeda advised, "I prayed for a great warrior to come and aid me in taking back the village Tokyo. And to help me defeat and kill vile Hojo and his samurai, so I could rule this land in peace. Were you sent by the gods to assist me, Todaroshi?" Takeda already felt like his prayers had been answered, but he was anxious to hear what this great warrior had to say.

Todd was unsure how to respond, since he didn't know himself how he had come to be there. He simply told the truth. "Well, to be honest, I don't really know how I got here."

Takeda was thrilled to hear this response. He excitedly replied, "Splendid! You must have been sent by the gods to aid me in defeating Hojo to stop his reign of evil over this land."

Todd thought it was strange. Again his presence couldn't be explained, so people believed that the gods must have willed it to answer their prayers. He still wasn't sure what to think, but maybe it was true that the gods or God had sent him to these time periods to help these people. He said, "Well, I guess that could be the reason, but I'm not really sure."

Takeda insisted, "I am sure this is the reason, Todaroshi." He expressed his gratitude to Todd, congratulated the samurai soldiers on the day's victory, and then rode away towards the center of the village, where most of the action had taken place.

Once Takeda had departed, Natilia rode over to Todd and dismounted. She was very happy to see him still in one piece. She was also anxious to share her thoughts about his conversation with Takeda. She said, "Todd, I believe Lord Takeda may be right."

Todd was surprised by her statement and asked, "What do you mean, Natilia? How is he right?"

Natilia was very confident in her answer. She replied, "First my father prayed to the gods for a son and received one through you. Then Lord Takeda prayed to the gods for a great warrior and we came here. You are a very skilled combatant and the best fighter my people have ever seen in their lifetimes. I believe the gods answered my father's prayers and now Lord Takeda's prayers. Don't you see, Todd? You are a warrior sent from the gods."

Todd thought she made good points but wasn't convinced. He asked, "Ok, that may all be true, but how do you explain why you are here, Natilia?"

Natilia reasoned that it must be the gods' desire. She answered, "I am only here for the gods must have willed it. I think they knew I would try my best to support you and help you understand it to be their doing."

Todd smiled at her honest and thoughtful reply. Natilia smiled back at him but then abruptly stopped and said, "I asked you to be careful, Todd. I can't believe what's happened to you!"

Todd was startled by her sudden change of demeanor. He responded, "What?! What happened to me?"

Natilia couldn't believe he'd forgotten so quickly. She answered loudly, "You have three arrows stuck in your back!"

Todd reached his right hand around to his back and felt the arrows. He was embarrassed as he responded, "Oh, yeah. I forgot about them for a minute. Sorry." Todd then gave her a sheepish grin.

Natilia laughed at him and said with a smile, "Todd, what am I to do with you? For you seem to always be fighting evil, putting your life in danger, and risking death. But I know you are trying to help people and I guess that is just what happens, when you marry a warrior of the gods."

Todd didn't really think he was 'of the gods.' He said, "Or maybe it's just me. And this is what happens to me in these places."

Natilia turned him around, so she could get a good look at the three arrows stuck in his back. She told Todd, "These are pretty deep. I am going to have to break the arrows so I can pull off your body plate."

Todd replied, "Natilia, do whatever you need to do." Natilia told him, "Todd, this may hurt when I break the arrows."

Todd braced himself and said, "Go ahead. I'm ready." Natilia took a deep breath and quickly broke off the three arrows.

Todd didn't move and appeared not to have felt anything. Natilia was surprised by this and asked, "Todd, are you alright? Did you feel that?"

Todd was a little confused by her question. He answered, "I felt you pull on my armor, that's all."

Natilia stared at the broken arrows she was still holding. She said, "I just broke the three arrows, Todd. I'm surprised you didn't' feel it." She showed him the broken ends of the arrows, which had red feathers on them to match the Hojo samurai's all red armor.

Natilia removed Todd's body plate. She said in amazement, "Remarkable! If you had not been wearing the samurai armor, then the arrows would have went deep into you."

Todd replied, "Yes, that's why I always put on all of my armor."

Natilia took off Todd's jade upper body armor and said, "I see now why you weren't hurt, Todd." She held up the jade armor to show him the back. It had the other halves of the three arrows stuck deeply into the jade plate pieces.

Todd said, "Wow! That was a close one."

Natilia removed the broken arrow heads and said, "From now on, you need to be more careful. Please, for me."

Todd felt bad to have distressed her. He said, "Yes dear, I will. And I'm very sorry to have upset you."

Natilia could tell he felt bad for worrying her. She smiled and said, "It is okay, Todd. I am not upset with you, for I know you will not perish easily. You are a warrior from the gods and you have more strength, wisdom, and resolve than a mortal man."

Todd knew that he had indeed become strong from lifting weights, knowledgeable from studying and reading, and had a very determined personality, but he was definitely mortal. He didn't want to argue the point or trouble her again. He replied with a smile, "I'm glad you're not upset with me."

Natilia smiled back at Todd as she threw the three broken arrows to the ground. She said, "I guess we should go find Lord Takeda and see what's next?"

Todd nodded in agreement and said, "Yes. He headed toward the center of the village. Let's go."

Before they departed, Natilia securely tied to the horse Todd's jade armor, body plate and his shield.

Todd was now only dressed in his tee shirt, which was underneath his chain mail shirt, and his shorts, which were underneath the jade leg plates. He also still had on the jade gauntlets with his leather bracers over top. Todd put away his katana in its holder on the left side of his waist and carried his samurai helmet.

Todd and Natilia walked in the direction of the village's center, where the big battle had taken place. As they were looking around this town center, they spotted an inn and Natilia decided to rest there with the horse.

Todd continued his search for Takeda and noticed the temple of Tokyo. He decided to take a quick look inside. He entered the temple and found Takeda sitting inside talking with his advisors. Todd was glad to have found him so easily. He approached the group and made a small bow. Todd asked, "Takeda, sir, what is our next plan of action?"

Takeda replied, "We will stay here for the night. Then we will move out to the open field, which we call the sea of grass. Once through the sea of grass, we will travel through the woods that lead us to the Hojo castle. And it would seem we may have to travel in the rain, for it looks as though the clouds are gathering."

Todd wondered how long the journey might be. He asked, "How much time does our trip through the sea of grass and the woods to the Hojo castle take, sir?"

Takeda thought for a few moments then responded, "I would say only four days, so long as the Hojo do not attack us on our travels."

Todd was pretty sure the Hojo would retaliate, since the Takeda had attacked and taken Tokyo from them. He said, "I believe they will. I'm sure they want revenge for our victory today."

Takeda was eager to fight them head on. He replied excitedly, "Then we will have a fierce battle with them and it will do us a great honor."

Todd figured he was no longer needed for the day and was keen to return to Natilia. He said, "Yes, sir. Well, if you need me for any reason, I will be at the inn here in the village."

Takeda understood Todd wanted to go rest with his woman. He gave a slight bow and Todd bowed in return. Todd turned, exited the temple, and headed back towards the inn.

As Todd neared the inn, Yoshoni spotted him and came running over. Yoshoni called out, "Todaroshi! Might I speak with you?"

Todd halted in front of Yoshoni who continued, "You are a truly great warrior, Todaroshi. I would be honored if you would let me teach you more of the ways of the sword, for I could show you how to swing it more easily than you have been doing so in your battles."

Todd was startled to hear such a proposal from Yoshoni. He answered, "I would like that very much. Thank you for your generous offer."

Yoshoni was overjoyed to hear Todd's acceptance. He bowed and said, "I will not let you down. This will be hard training, so be prepared for it when we depart on our travel to the Hojo castle."

Todd thought to himself that the sword training probably wouldn't be too hard. He answered, "I will be ready, Yoshoni. Thank you again." Yoshoni nodded, then turned, and walked away.

Todd proceeded to the inn. He entered to find a lot of the Takeda samurai sitting around talking and drinking sake and water. As he moved into the room, they noticed him and fell silent.

Todd looked around the room as they all stared at him. He quietly said under his breath, "Okay..." and continued on in search of Natilia.

Todd found Natilia in one of the rooms. As he entered the room, he noticed she had brought in his shield, Roman body plate, and jade body plate. They were stowed in a corner.

Natilia smiled at Todd as he entered the room. She asked, "Did you find Lord Takeda?"

Todd smiled back at Natilia and answered, "Yes, I did. We are going to move out in the morning. The journey to the Hojo castle should take about four days, if we don't run into any of the Hojo samurai on the way."

Natilia was glad to hear the trip would not be lengthy. She said, "Good. At least we now know the journey will not be a long one."

Todd started removing the rest of his armor. Natilia came over to him to help get it all stored away.

Todd advised, "I have a feeling we will encounter some of the Hojo forces on our way to the castle."

Natilia turned back to Todd after stowing his last gauntlet. She clasped his hand and reminded him, "Todd, if we do, you just remember to be careful, for you promised me."

Todd smiled at her and gently pulled her to his chest. He gave her a soft kiss. She wrapped her arms around his neck and hugged him tightly.

Todd whispered in her ear, "Thank you for your care and concern. I'm so lucky to have found your love."

Natilia looked into Todd's eyes and shared, "You know I do love you so very much, Todd. And that is why I worry for you every time you must do battle."

Todd was very happy to have Natilia by his side. He kissed her again, then stated, "Let's not worry about tomorrow. Right now we need to get some sleep. I'm sure we'll be leaving this place early in the morning."

Natilia released Todd, agreeing that they should gather what rest they could. She said, "Yes, let's get to bed and not lose another moment's rest."

Natilia laid down in the bed. Todd stretched his tired muscles and also got in the bed. They fell asleep in each other's arms.

Todd and Natilia both woke the next morning to Yoshoni banging on their door. Todd jumped out of bed and went to open the door.

When Todd opened the door, Yoshoni saw that they were not out of bed or dressed. He said, "You must hurry. My Lord is waiting so we can start our journey."

Todd was stressed out realizing everyone was ready to leave. He said, "I'm sorry. We'll be right out."

Yoshoni looked a little panicked, like he might be in trouble for Todd's delay. He replied, "Be quick!"

Todd closed the door and turned around to see Natilia already preparing his armor and equipment. He hurried over to her and quickly dressed. Now that Todd had all of his equipment on, he tied his sword to his waist on his left side as he always did and picked up his shield.

Todd headed for the door with Natilia right behind him. When he opened the door, he saw Yoshoni was standing there waiting.

Yoshoni was surprised to see Todd come out so quickly. He said impressed, "That was fast! Let's go! My Lord wants to be at the Hojo castle in four days time and he will not be pleased if anything delays his travels."

Todd didn't want to be the cause of any holdup and risk Takeda's fury. He said, "I understand."

As Todd exited the inn, he saw Takeda sitting on his horse waiting. Takeda noticed Todd, Natilia, and Yoshoini and called out, "Well now. That was faster than I had expected."

Todd was relieved to see that Takeda was not upset having to wait for them. He gave a quick bow and replied, "I was anxious to begin our journey with the thought of many battles ahead."

Takeda smiled at Todd's reply, then yelled out to the soldiers, "Men, we make way to the sea of grass and from there to the Hojo castle!"

The Takeda samurai cheered in response to Takeda's command. Todd helped Natilia onto the horse, then mounted in front of her.

As the cheering died out, the soldiers began their march and headed out of the village. Todd and Natilia rode out with the war party.

As the samurai were leaving the village, Todd noticed that Takeda was leaving about 2,000 samurai behind to maintain control of the village. This meant that only about 4,000 samurai were marching to the Hojo castle. Todd was concerned about this decision. He hoped Takeda was making the right move. They exited the village on the opposite side from where they had entered and traveled into the bamboo woods on the other border.

The samurai traveled all morning through the bamboo woods. As they continued their trek, the bamboo was starting to lessen and the woods grew thicker with other trees. When it was nearing midday, there was no more bamboo in sight. They entered a small clearing between the trees and Takeda called out, "We rest now for a short time!"

Todd dismounted the horse and helped Natilia off. They were just sitting down, when Yoshoni came over to them and said, "It may be time for everyone else to rest but not for you, Todaroshi. Now is the time when we will train you with your sword and help you to bring more damage with it."

Todd was surprised by his statement and thought maybe he was joking. He asked, "But when will I eat, Yoshoni?"

Yoshoni laughed at Todd's reply and said, "Eat? Todaroshi, you will not get your midday meal today, for you will instead be training during this time of rest. Now! Come with me away from the other samurai, so you will not be distracted."

Todd thought about it for a minute and decided he wanted to see what Yoshoni had in mind. He answered, "Fine, but this better be good."

Yoshoni gave him a big grin and stated, "It will be very good, Todaroshi. Do not worry yourself."

Todd let out a sigh and got up. He gave Natilia a quick kiss and followed Yoshoni deep into the woods.

After a little over an hour, Takeda yelled "We leave now! Everyone pack up and let us make way to the sea of grass!"

As everyone was packing up to depart, Todd and Yoshoni came out of the woods. Todd looked very tired and worn out. He approached Natilia and helped her up onto the horse.

Natilia was curious to know about Todd's training with Yoshoni. She asked, "Todd, please tell me about your time in the woods. You appear exhausted."

Todd replied, "He made me do a lot of running and wielding my sword until I was dead tired. Then he told me to put away my sword. He tossed me a wooden sword and said, "Now you fight me."

I told him I was too tired and he said that was the point. When we fought, my reflexes were a lot slower, because I was so beat. He just kept coming at me with what felt like full force, but he said he was using only half of his strength and skills to combat me."

Natilia thought she understood Yoshoni's plan. She said "Oh, I see what he is training you to be able to do, Todd."

Todd wearily mounted the horse with Natilia and asked, "And what would that be besides beating me so much?"

Natilia turned to Todd and smiled. She explained Yoshoni's strategy, "He had you wield your sword the correct way until your arms got really tired. Then he dueled with you, so that you would continue swinging the sword the proper way in battle even when you are fatigued. That is what you were doing in the woods."

Todd thought for a minute, then it was as if a light bulb had come on over top of his head. He said, "Oh, I get it! I was already in the mindset of swinging my sword the proper way, so even though I was tired this is what my reaction would become when I was being attacked."

Natilia was pleased to see Todd understood and agreed with her. She said, "Yes. And it sounds like his training will enhance your strength and endurance as well."

Todd was so thankful to have his beautiful, intelligent wife with him. He replied, "Natilia, I hope you know how very smart you are." Natilia gave him a kiss and thanked him for his kind words.

The Takeda army of samurai soldiers continued on their journey. They traveled the rest of the day until the sun started to set.

Takeda ordered, "We rest here until morning! Our journey will lead us to the sea of grass by midday tomorrow!"

The samurai halted and began to set up their tents. Todd jumped off his horse and helped Natilia down. He had decided that a thorough inspection of the campsite was needed before he could rest. Todd asked Natilia, "Are you okay with the tent? I'm going to survey the camp to make sure there is no danger, like ninjas, so we can sleep in peace tonight."

Natilia thought this was a wise suggestion and agreed saying, "Yes, this sounds like a good idea. I will set up the tent and make our bed ready for the night." Todd gave her a hug and a kiss and headed off to walk around the perimeter of the camp.

As Todd patrolled the camp, a full moon rose in the sky. It was a cloudy night, so the moonlight was intermittent. He thought he saw movement in the woods. He quietly crept toward it.

As the moon came out from behind a cloud, Todd saw a white tiger. The tiger saw him and let out a low growl. The tiger stared him down and continued to growl.

Todd slowly backed away and the tiger stopped growling. Not wanting to make any sudden movement, Todd gradually raised his shield up to protect himself. The tiger approached him leisurely. Todd had his hand on the hilt of his sword as the tiger neared. The tiger simply brushed its head against the shield as if it were a house cat needing a scratch.

When the tiger brushed the shield, Todd let go of his sword hilt and tentatively touched the white tiger's head. The tiger began to make a purring noise just like a cat would if it was being petted.

Todd cautiously scratched the tiger's head for a minute or so, then continued to slowly back away. The tiger just stared at him with its yellow eyes.

Todd somehow knew the tiger wouldn't pursue or trouble him at all. The tiger turned away and walked back into the woods.

After the odd experience with the white tiger, Todd continued his survey of the camp. He found no indication that enemies were lurking. Since Todd was comfortable that the camp was safe, he returned to his tent and Natilia.

Todd entered the tent and found that Natilia was in bed but waiting for him to return. She was relieved to have Todd safely back with her and curious to know about his patrol. She asked, "How was your survey of the camp and surroundings, Todd?"

Todd was still amazed by the strange incident with the tiger. He answered, "It was fine but there was one odd thing. I ran into a white tiger."

Natilia's face suddenly filled with fear and confusion. She asked, "It did not try to kill you?"

Todd was confused himself. He replied, "No, it was very strange. When we spotted each other, I thought it would try to kill me. But the tiger actually came over to me, rubbed against my shield, and let me scratch its head. I don't know why it would do that?!"

Natilia was astonished by Todd's story, but she knew why he was unharmed. She smiled and said, "I believe it did not attack you, because you are a warrior of the gods."

Todd didn't know what to think. He was just grateful the white tiger had let him be and walked away.

Todd took off all his armor and got into bed with Natilia. He continued to think about her reasoning of the situation. He stated, "I'm still not really sure but perhaps you're right. Maybe I am protected by the gods."

Natilia was confident that Todd was 'of the gods.' She kissed him good night and said, "I am sure you will find out soon, Todd."

Todd kissed her and replied, "I really hope so, Natilia. Good night." They held onto each other as they fell asleep in their small bed.

Todd had a strange dream that night. He dreamt he was riding the white tiger into battle. And every battle he fought, he won. He knew he was winning, because the tiger took him to the fight. The white tiger also seemed to be moving him through time.

Todd was startled awake from his dream by Yoshoni yelling outside his tent, "Wake up, Todaroshi! We leave now! Get dressed and be ready to move out shortly!"

Todd and Natilia both got out of bed. Todd hurriedly put on all of his armor and readied his equipment. Natilia packed everything up as Todd got dressed. Once they were packed and ready to go, Todd helped Natilia onto the horse.

Takeda came over as Todd jumped up behind Natilia and asked, "Did you get any rest last night, Todaroshi?"

Todd was not quite sure what Takeda meant by this question. He answered, "Yes, sir. I did."

Takeda presumed that Todd had protected the camp overnight. He said, "Am I right that you are the one who made sure the camp was safe last night from the three Hojo ninjas that came near."

Todd was surprised by Takeda's statement. He said, "No, it was not me! I did not see any ninjas when I patrolled the camp, but I did see a white tiger."

Takeda was shocked and intrigued. He asked, "Tell me about this white tiger. Did it see you? What did it do?"

Todd explained, "Well, I saw it when the moon came out from behind the clouds. It spotted me and growled. So I moved backward slowly and raised my shield. The tiger came up to me but it did not attack. It let me scratch its head, then went on its way."

Takeda exclaimed happily, "The gods are truly with us! And more so with you, Todaroshi, for that white tiger must have killed the three ninjas in the night and did so to protect you from their harm."

Todd looked over at Natilia and saw that she agreed with Takeda's assessment. She smiled at him and he could tell she was thinking, 'I told you so.'

Todd was stunned and concerned. He asked Takeda, "Do we know if the tiger is okay?" Takeda reassured him, "We did not find any tiger, just the dead ninjas with slash marks across their chests."

Todd was relieved to learn the white tiger had not been harmed by the Hojo ninjas. He was also still skeptical about believing he was being protected by the gods. He said, "Well, I'm glad to hear that the tiger protected all of us from the Hojo ninjas, not just me."

Takeda replied, "Yes, Todaroshi. And you do not have to believe or understand what all these signs mean. You continue to do things your own way."

Todd could tell Takeda thought he had sent the tiger to kill the ninjas. He knew better. He had run into the tiger by sheer luck. Todd also knew better than to try to argue the point. He simply said "Yes, sir. Thank you."

Takeda laughed and stated, "No thanks are needed for me. But they are for you, Todaroshi, for you are the warrior from the gods, who sent the white tiger to guard our camp last night. And the white tiger protected us well."

Todd just smiled at Takeda. He was at a loss for words. When Todd didn't respond, Takeda yelled out to the soldiers, "We move out now men! And we do not stop until we get to the sea of grass!"

Once Takeda gave these orders, the whole army started their march through the woods. When they arrived at the edge of the woods near the sea of grass, it was a little bit past midday. The sky had also turned very cloudy.

Todd sensed the shift in the air and told Natilia, "It's going to rain shortly, Natilia. I can feel it in the air and smell it too."

Natilia looked up at the sky and replied, "Yes, it does look as if the rain is coming soon."

Takeda was very pleased they were making good time. He advised the soldiers, "Now warriors, we rest and eat our midday meal. Then we will move out across the sea of grass."

Todd and Natilia found a spot to rest and started to prepare their meal. Todd was just about to take his first bite when he saw Yoshoni approaching. Yoshoni saw the look on Todd's face and stated, "Do not worry, Todaroshi. You eat your meal. We will not train this day, for the weather will only get in the way of our forms."

Todd was hungry and thankful to hear this good news. He let out a sigh of relief and asked, "Is that all you wanted to tell me, Yoshoni?"

Yoshoni laughed and answered, "Yes, I only came to say enjoy your meal and rest for today."

Todd was grateful for this break from training and happy to be able to enjoy some rest at this stop in their journey. He gave Yoshoni a slight bow and said, "Thank you, Yoshoni." Yoshoni bowed and walked away.

As Todd sat eating his meal, he looked out at the sea of grass. He could not see the wood line that would be on the other side. Instead all he could see was small hills out in the grass fields.

Natilia thought they were advancing well in their travels. She said, "I believe by the end of the day we may be half way in our journey."

Todd continued studying the sea of grass and was growing uneasy about its openness. He replied, "I hope so. But I'm concerned about the sea of grass. It's a very open field with no cover. We could easily be attacked if the Hojo see us out there."

Natilia looked out at the sea of grass and asked, "Yes, but if they see us out in the grass, then we will be able to see them as well, right?"

Todd knew they would be able to see the Hojo if they tried to strike, but he felt they should stay in the woods and go around. He simply answered, "Yes, that's true. But why risk exposure. Unfortunately, I'm not the one giving orders and deciding our route."

Natilia knew what Todd meant. She could see it in his eyes as he looked out at the grassy fields. She said, "No, but I wish you were, for you would pick the longer, safer route to the Hojo castle."

Todd moved over to be beside Natilia and stated, "Yes, I would. But I doubt I have a say in it right now." He continued to eat his meal of rice and bread and drank his water.

Natilia put her arm around Todd's shoulder and said, "Do not worry, dear. For I know if we do run into any trouble, you will defeat the enemy and keep us safe from harm. You will be sure we make it to the Hojo castle."

Todd smiled at her confidence in him. He said, "I will do my best, Natilia. I promise." Todd gave Natilia a soft kiss.

Todd and Natilia had finished eating and were packing up when Takeda came over. He asked Todd, "Are you rested and ready to move out, Todaroshi?"

Todd stood up and answered, "Yes, sir, whenever you are ready."

Takeda was pleased to receive a positive reply. He said, "Good! Then we make leave now."

Takeda turned and walked away. He advised his samurai army to get packed up and ready to leave.

Todd and Natilia had already mounted the horse. They rode over to the clearing on the edge of the sea of grass and waited there for Takeda and his samurai soldiers.

Takeda made his way to Todd's side and stated, "We should be to the other side of the sea of grass before nightfall comes upon us."

Todd turned from looking out into the hilly fields and looked at him. He replied, "I hope so. I really don't think we should stay out in the open for too long, especially now that we're getting close to the Hojo castle."

Takeda understood Todd's concern about being exposed out in the open. He was still dead set on proceeding as quickly as possible. He said, "Very wise, Todaroshi, very wise. But we need to make it to the Hojo castle swiftly to catch them unawares.

So we must go this way, for they will never expect us to go across the sea of grass with such a large number."

Todd now grew concerned that the Hojo samurai might think of doing the same thing. If so, they would be in for a big battle. Todd responded, "True, they might think we have gone the long way. Regardless, we need to get across quickly so no Hojo see us."

Takeda was happy to see that Todd agreed they need to move fast. He said "Yes, we will make haste to get across the sea of grass."

Takeda ordered the men to start forward at a rapid pace. They all headed toward the first hill which was a good distance away. As they neared the hill, Todd got off his horse and said, "Please wait here, Takeda. Let me make sure the way ahead is clear."

Takeda nodded in conformation and said, "Very well. Go and see if it is clear on the other side of the hill." Todd nodded and sprinted up the hill.

As Todd headed up the hill, he noticed the sky was getting darker. It wasn't that the day was getting late, but the darkness came from storm clouds starting to move in overhead. Once he reached the top of the hill, he slowly peeked over it to see what was on the other side. As Todd looked over the hilltop, he saw a Hojo army of samurai marching towards him. There looked to be about 8,000 Hojo total. They were making their way down another hill further in the distance.

As soon as Todd saw the army, he ran back down the hill and over to Takeda. "An army of Hojo is coming this way. I'd guess it to be about 8,000 in size."

Takeda was shocked to hear this report. He said "We must turn back now and go to the village Tokyo and protect it. There we can match their numbers."

Todd didn't want the distance they'd traveled already to be wasted. He quickly thought of a way to engage the Hojo now. He replied, "No! Takeda, sir. We can defeat them here and now."

Takeda was surprised by Todd's statement. He wondered how this could be accomplished. He asked, "How, Todaroshi? How do you plan to do this against 8,000 Hojo samurai?"

When Todd had spotted the Hojo samurai, he noticed they looked very tired and worn out. He answered Takeda, "Easily, just think about it. First of all, they looked weary like they had been marching all day. Next, they are marching into a slight valley between this hill and the next. If we send our archers up to the top of the hill and fire several waves of arrows on them, we may be able to drop at least half of their samurai. And that's just with the archers. After the archers have done their damage, our samurai warriors can charge down the hill and engage them. We may be able to crush them here and now instead of retreating."

Takeda was silent for a few moments considering Todd's daring plan. He decided it just might work and to put the plan in action. Takeda immediately ordered, "I want all archers to the top of the hill now! And all of the samurai warriors right behind them ready to attack but hidden on this side of the hill! Do this now!"

All of the samurai obeyed Takeda's commands and swiftly started moving into their positions. Todd smiled at Takeda then ran over to Natilia.

Todd untied his shield from the horse and told Natilia what was happening. "There is a very large Hojo army of at least 8,000 men headed this way and we are going to attack them now. If we should fail, you must ride as fast as you can to the village Tokyo and warn them of these Hojo reinforcements."

Natilia looked down at Todd from the horse and tried to put on a brave face. She said, "I have faith in you, Todd, and I know you will do well. But please try to come back to me with no injuries or arrows sticking out of you."

Todd grabbed Natilia's hand and said, "Don't worry, Natilia. I will stay safe and come back in one piece. I promise."

Todd kissed Natilia's hand, told her he loved her, and darted away. As tears streamed down Natilia's face, she watched Todd run up the hill to be with Takeda and all the samurai soldiers.

Todd rushed up to Takeda, anxious to put his plan in motion. Takeda asked, "Are you ready, Todaroshi?"

Todd answered, "Yes! Let's do this now, while they are still unaware of us and tired."

Takeda nodded and called out, "Archers, fire! Take down as many as you can!" The archers stood up and all fired the first wave of arrows at the exact same time. The arrows rained down and many of the Hojo samurai in the front lines started to drop. The archers quickly prepared for a second wave.

The Hojo army reacted to the first wave of arrows and had started running towards the hill, where the Takeda archers were positioned. As the Hojo headed towards the archers, they fired the second wave. This time they took down even more Hojo samurai.

The charging Hojo samurai were getting closer to the hill, but they seemed to be slowing down and getting winded. The Takeda archers took advantage of this and quickly fired another wave of arrows. The closer the Hojo came, the more of them dropped as the Takeda archers found their mark.

The Hojo samurai had taken great losses, but they continued to press forward. They reached the bottom of the hill where the Takeda archers stood and started to run up it. The archers fired a fourth wave of arrows at the attacking Hojo and large numbers continued to fall.

Takeda ordered his samurai soldiers to attack. The archers quickly stood aside to make way for the samurai who would now engage the enemy. As the Takeda samurai came over the top of the hill, the Hojo samurai had made it about halfway up the hillside.

Takeda ordered the archers to fire one more wave of arrows at the Hojo to aid the Takeda samurai charging them. They took out another large number of the Hojo.

Swords already drawn, the Hojo samurai were about to collide with the Takeda. The Takeda samurai had also drawn their swords as they were coming down on top of the Hojo. Takeda stood at the top of the hill with the archers and watched the battle commence.

Suddenly the storm clouds let loose. The rain started to pour and the sky was full of lighting and thunder.

Todd and Yoshoni were at the front line of the Takeda army. As they charged the enemy, Todd put his shield in front of him and Yoshoni had his sword out in front of him.

The Hojo samurai reached the Takeda samurai and the clash began. The warring samurai fought a battle in the sea of grass. Fortunately, the grass was only about knee high, so Todd and the samurai were able to move well in the combat.

As Todd reached the Hojo samurai, he knocked down two of them from the impact of his shield. He kicked another Hojo back that had started to swing at him. Todd swung his sword in a 180-degree arc in front of him and sliced in half three of the Hojo. He then knocked another Hojo down and stabbed him thorough. Todd immediately pulled his sword out of the dead soldier and blocked two more charging Hojo with his shield. He quickly evaded a sword strike coming at his head.

The fight raged on. After watching for a time, Takeda decided to join the conflict and destroy his enemy. He spurred his horse and raced down the hill. When Takeda charged into the Hojo, he cut down four soldiers. The horse also trampled two Hojo underneath it as they rode through the battle.

The fighting persisted but the Hojo continued to fall. At one point, Todd almost got his head cut off. A Hojo was charging Todd from behind with his sword ready to strike. Fortunately, Yoshoni spotted the attacking Hojo and ran him through with his sword, saving Todd.

The fighting had gone on for several hours and the battle was starting to die down. Todd and Yoshoni found themselves in the middle of all the enemy Hojo. They stood back to back and tried to catch their breath. They were both soaked from the rain.

Todd asked, "Which half do you want?"

Yoshoni laughed and answered, "There is plenty for the both of us."

Todd replied, "Ok, I like the sound of that."

The Hojo that had surrounded them attacked. As they charged, Todd used his shield to block each swing. The Hojo recoiled from the block and Todd counter-attacked. He sliced them across the chest or slashed them in the arm, leg, or even the head.

Yoshoni was deadly with his sword. He skillfully blocked the Hojo with his sword and swiftly reversed his swing, so that he could strike them. He viciously slashed them along the chest or the head.

Yoshoni and Todd were still fighting back to back. Todd noticed a Hojo running straight at Yoshoni from his right side. Yoshoni was busy with other Hojo and didn't see him coming. Todd quickly moved his shield to protect Yoshoni and block the charging Hojo. Todd struck the Hojo as he fell back from the block and killed him.

While Todd had his back turned shielding Yoshoni, a Hojo came at him and cut Todd in the back left calf muscle. The blow caused Todd to fall to the ground. He rapidly rolled to his back and pulled his shield up over top of him. Todd's shield blocked the Hojo from stabbing him in the chest.

Yoshoni was stabbing another samurai through, when he noticed Todd on the ground. He turned to help Todd as the Hojo continued his assault.

Todd moved his shield aside and stabbed the Hojo in his neck. At the same time, Yoshoni slashed the Hojo's back. Their strikes dropped the Hojo.

As the samurai fell, Todd and Yoshoni could see there were a lot less Hojo nearby. But as they looked around, they saw that they were still in the middle of only red armored Hojo samurai.

Seeing only the enemy in sight, Yoshoni was concerned this could be their end. He said, "Todaroshi, it was a great honor to fight by your side."

Yoshoni helped Todd up. Todd tried putting weight on his injured leg. It wasn't too bad, but he shifted most of his weight to his other leg. He answered, "It's not over yet, Yoshoni. I can still fight. And I promised Natilia I would come back in one piece. Let's give them hell!" Todd stood boldly and ready to meet the enemy.

Yoshoni appreciated Todd's confidence. He replied, "Yes, let us battle on, so we do not die here in the sea of grass today." Yoshoni also stood ready to fight.

Todd nodded in agreement and said, "I like the sound of that much better than giving up and waiting for them to end us."

Just then Takeda, still on horseback, and a large group of his samurai warriors advanced and engaged the Hojo surrounding Todd and Yoshoni. After the last of the Hojo samurai fell, Takeda rode over to Todd and Yoshoni.

Takeda said to them, "I saw you from afar combating the Hojo scum. You appeared to be in a field of red, so I thought you could use some support. But I must tell you that you have both fought with great honor and courage today, taking down many of our enemy. I am grateful for your service."

Yoshoni was thrilled to receive this great praise from his Lord. He said "Thank you, Lord Takeda. We did this for you to ensure that a victory came to us this day."

The rain continued to pour down on them. Todd looked around the battlefield and saw they were successful. He shared, "Yes, we are victorious. I knew we had the strength to confront them even though we were outnumbered. And we triumphed today despite the rain."

Takeda was grateful for the enemy's defeat, but he also did not want to fall behind on his schedule to reach the Hojo castle. He replied, "Even with these obstacles, we had a great victory this day. Now we must bind up the injured and prepare to move on, so we can try to reach the edge of the sea of grass before nightfall."

Todd agreed with Takeda's plan, but knew he needed to tend to his injury before they departed. He said, "Sounds good to me. And I doubt we'll be seeing any Hojo for a while. But I might need a bandage myself before we move out. I believe my leg is wounded."

Takeda now realized Todd was hurt. He was anxious to depart but knew that they must take time for the injured. He said, "Yes, Todaroshi. Go to your woman and have her care for your wound. We will put up a few tents for the injured, so they can be out of the rain while being bound. Once you and the others are tended, we move out to the Hojo castle."

Todd was relieved that he would have a few minutes rest and a chance to take care of his leg. He said, "Very well, Takeda, sir. Thank you."

Takeda smiled down at him and said, "You are very welcome, Todaroshi." Takeda turned his horse and rode off to check the battlefield for any more Hojo.

The tents were quickly put up for the injured. Todd slowly walked over to Natilia on his injured leg. She had rode down the hill and was waiting near the bottom for him.

When Natilia saw Todd approaching, she noticed he seemed to be limping. She quickly rode over to him and said, "What has happened? Are you alright?"

Todd was happy to see her still on the horse. She seemed fine and untouched by the battle that had just been fought. He replied, "Natilia, I'm fine. It's just a cut on my leg. I'm glad to see you stayed well away from the conflict."

Natilia was only concerned about Todd's injury. She said, "Of course. But let us hurry and put up a tent, so you can get out of this rain and I can take a look at your leg."

Todd responded, "No need. Takeda has already ordered tents for the wounded, but we must go quickly. He wants to head out of the sea of grass as soon as the injured are tended."

Natilia realized they only had a short amount of time. She said, "Alright, Todd. Let's hurry so I can take care of your leg."

Todd and Natilia made their way to one of the tents that had been put up and went inside. After they entered the tent, Todd took off only his greaves and shin guards and put them aside.

Now that Todd's lower armor was off, Natilia examined the cut on his left calf muscle. She was relieved to see it was not as deep as she'd feared. She said,

"Fortunately, this wound is not too severe, Todd. You won't need any stitches, just a bandage to hold the skin together. It should heal very well."

Todd was surprised to hear this report. He had thought it was a deep cut needing stiches. He asked, "Really? It's not that bad after all?"

Natilia smiled and answered, "No, it is not, Todd. You were very lucky."

Todd was thankful to learn the injury wasn't too serious, but he felt bad for scaring Natilia again. He said, "Well, I'm still sorry, Natilia."

"And why is that, Todd?" Natilia asked. She didn't realize he was referring to his earlier promise.

Todd was a little shocked she had forgotten his pledge. He answered, "Because I didn't keep my promise to you. I got hurt when I had assured you I would stay safe from harm."

Natilia finished bandaging his leg and gave him a kiss. "Todd, you did the best you could to keep that promise to me. I am just glad you are alive and well."

Todd held Natilia's hand, looked deep into her eyes, and shared, "I love you, Natilia. Thank you for understanding how hard I tried to do my best to keep that promise to you today."

Natilia squeezed his hand and smiled. She replied, "I love you too, dear. Now please try to stand up and see how that feels."

Todd stood up and felt a slight pain from the injury. He tried putting all his weight on the wounded leg. It felt much better than it had before. He took a few steps and was now better able to walk instead of limping around like he was earlier.

Todd turned to thank Natilia, but before he could say anything Yoshoni burst into the tent. He said, "I am sorry, Todaroshi, but we must take leave now. Takeda does not wish to be any further delayed this day."

Todd didn't want to be the cause of any delay and upset Takeda. He responded, "Ok, Yoshoni. I'm ready now."

Yoshoni exited the tent and went back out into the rain. Todd quickly put his greaves back on over top of his shin guards and his shorts. He tied his sword onto the left side of his waist and walked out of the tent with Natilia into the pouring rain.

Todd's shield was already tied to the horse, so he only had to help Natilia up. Once she was up on the horse, Natilia offered Todd assistance since he was injured, but he was able to mount the horse unaided.

Takeda called out to the samurai, "Warriors, pack up these tents and let us move out! We will proceed through the green sea section and hope to reach the edge of the woods on the other side of the sea of grass this day!"

Once the tents were packed and put away, the samurai advanced. As they went through the sea of grass, they came to a more hilly part of the grassy plains.

As they proceeded through this area of the plains, Todd realized why they called it the green sea. It was like being out in the ocean, going up and down over waves of water while being unable to see the horizon. It was the same for the green sea, except they would walk up and down many hills instead of sailing up and down them. And as they went over many of these hills, Todd was unable to see the edge of the woods.

After the samurai journeyed further, they arrived in more of the flatter areas of the plains. They had reached the other side of the green sea and were back in the sea of grass.

The rain was finally beginning to let up. The sky was still cloudy and overcast. As they continued on through this side of the sea of grass, they could now see the edge of the woods a far distance ahead.

Once Takeda spotted the woodline, he ordered, "We will stop for the night once we are in the woods! Continue forward!" Takeda knew his samurai were tired and wanted to rest, so he shared this to motivate them to finish the day's journey.

Yoshoni came up next to Todd on his horse and said, "Ah, the fresh air after a nice summer's rain. Would you not say so, Todaroshi?"

Todd took in a deep breath to capture the smell of the fresh rain water on the ground and answered, "Yes, Yoshoni. I would have to agree. It is nice."

The samurai continued forward and were nearer to the edge of the woods. The sky was getting very dark as night set in and the rain clouds still lingered on.

Even with the approaching darkness, Takeda wanted to press forward. They needed to reach the woods before they could rest for the night. He knew it would be safer, so they continued on until they had made it into the woods.

Once inside the woodline, Takeda called out, "Alright, my samurai warriors, we rest here! Now we are shielded from the enemy!"

The whole army stopped. They were very winded and weary from travel as they set up camp.

Todd and Natilia put up their tent. Once they had it set up, Natilia headed into the tent. When she realized Todd hadn't followed her in, she came back out and found him still standing there looking around. She asked, "Todd, are you going to come into the tent and rest now?"

Todd replied, "Not just yet. I'm going to do a walk-thru of the camp to make sure there are no enemies around."

Natilia knew he couldn't rest until he was sure the camp was safe. She said, "Alright. I will be waiting for you, Todd. Please hurry back to me." Todd gave her a hug and a kiss before she went back into the tent.

Todd headed into the woods to circle the camp. As he was walking around the campsite, he saw movement on his left. While staying focused on the area of movement, Todd slowly raised his shield up and grasped his hand around his sword's hilt. When the figure moved closer, he was glad to see it was only Yoshoni approaching him.

As Yoshoni neared Todd, he observed Todd was prepared for an attack. Yoshoni stated, "I notice you always take a defensive stance before you fight any one. And you do not attack except in battle. You only defend yourself or others if needed."

Todd lowered his guard and explained. "Well, I prefer not to fight someone or something unless I have to, Yoshoni. I'm glad that it was just you and not a ninja."

Yoshoni was impressed by Todd's way of thinking. He replied, "I am no ninja and would not be one in a hundred years, for they fight with no honor. Sneaking up on you in the dark or catching you while you are asleep. It shows their fear of not being able to face us head on, for they know they are far too weak."

Todd understood what Yoshoni meant but thought there may be more to it. He said "Well, that may be true, but we don't know for sure. They may be afraid to fight us in the daylight and appreciate their advantage in the darkness."

Yoshoni wondered about continuing Todd's training. He asked "So how is your leg feeling, Todaroshi? Is it well?"

Todd answered truthfully, "It's a little sore but feels much better than it did before. Natilia takes good care of me."

Yoshoni was glad to hear that it wasn't serious and they could continue to train. He said, "Very well. I can give you your final lesson of the samurai forms the next day then."

Todd was a little shocked that Yoshoni was going to train him while he was hurt. He decided not to stress about it just yet and wondered how the samurai were doing after the battle. Todd replied "Sure, I guess. And how are the men managing after today's events, Yoshoni?"

Yoshoni thought about the remaining troops and the wounded soldiers. He answered, "I believe they are all faring well. We still have about 2,000 samurai. The few injured are bound and healing."

After hearing the number of men they had left, Todd worried that it might not be enough. He asked, "Do you think we have a large enough force to take the Hojo castle or should we send a message for reinforcements?"

Yoshoni knew Takeda's plans and concerns. He advised, "No, samurai reinforcements would take too long. Takeda does not want any further delays. And he wants to finish our undertaking quickly, so the men can return to our Takeda castle and the village Tokyo to keep them both secure.

Todd thought about Takeda's concerns and agreed. He replied, "Well, I guess we'll just have to do this the old-fashioned way. Right, Yoshoni?"

Yoshoni liked Todd's response. He said smiling, "Yes, the good old ways. There is much pride in these. We will fight with few men and against great evil. This will be a thing of great honor."

Todd asked about their remaining journey, "Yes, it will. So we should reach the Hojo castle after tomorrow, right?"

Yoshoni thought about it for a moment and answered, "Yes, we will arrive at the Hojo castle on the fourth day of our journey, the day after next."

While Todd and Yoshoni were talking, they had circled the camp. They saw no signs of the enemy anywhere nearby.

Todd was ready to head back to his tent and Natilia. He asked, "Yoshoni, I will see you in the morning at first light?"

Yoshoni agreed that all was safe and they should get their rest. He replied, "Yes, Todaroshi, you will. And be ready to train well the next day, for we are going to work very hard, but you will enhance your sword skills by the end of training."

Todd gave Yoshoni a slight bow and said, "Thank you, Yoshoni. I will do my best. Good night."

Yoshoni said good night as well. "Very well, Todaroshi. Good night. If you are not up before me, then I will wake you." Yoshoni bowed to Todd and walked away towards the samurai sitting around the campfires.

Todd headed back to his tent and entered it. Natilia was waiting up for him to return. She was glad he was back and asked, "Are we safe for the night, Todd?"

"Yes, we are secure for now, at least," Todd replied. He put his shield and sword down next to the bed and started taking off all his armor.

Natilia put Todd's gladius down by her side and laid back on the bed. She asked, "Todd, will you teach me how to fight?"

Todd was surprised by her question. He smiled and asked, "What? You want to learn how to fight? Why?"

Natilia answered very seriously, "For many reasons, Todd. I want to be able to protect myself when you are not around. And, once you teach me, maybe I can come with you or be by your side when you fight. And also I could then protect you if any harm may come to you."

Todd was pleased by her response. He said, "Of course, Natilia. I will teach you how to fight. I should have thought of it myself. I'm glad you asked."

Natilia sat looking shocked. Todd suddenly realized why she was so serious in explaining her reasons. A woman fighting and being a warrior would be a rare thing in Natilia's time or this time in feudal Japan.

Natilia asked, "You are not going to ask me for more reasons or even laugh at me?"

Todd got into bed and gathered her in his arms. He answered, "You told me your reasons. Why would I laugh at you, Natilia?"

Natilia replied, "Most men would have, for I am only a woman." Todd laughed at her response and explained, "Now you thinking like that makes me laugh, but I would never laugh at you for wanting to learn how to defend yourself. It does not matter if you are a man or a woman. I believe anyone should be able to protect theirself."

Natilia squeezed Todd tightly and excitedly said, "Thank you, Todd! Thank you, so very much! I love you!"

Todd hugged her back and said, "You don't need to thank me, Natilia. I wouldn't have ever told you no anyway."

Natilia was overjoyed. Todd was going to train her with the sword. She said, "But I must thank you, for I am grateful and love you so."

Todd kissed her cheek and realized she was crying. He knew they were tears of joy and not sadness. He was elated to know that he had made her so happy. They said good night and fell asleep in each other's arms.

As usual, Todd and Natilia woke up the next morning to Yoshoni coming into their tent. He announced, "Wake up, Todaroshi! We are now getting ready to leave for the Hojo castle!"

Todd jumped out of bed and started to put on all of his armor. He said to Natilia, "We will begin your training right away. When we are not busy, we will make time for it."

Natilia smiled at Todd and promised him, "I will do my best, Todd. I won't let you down." She got up and put on the clothes that had been made for Todd back in Rome. The shirt and shorts were similar to the one's he wore from his time period. He had given them to her, so she could move around more freely. She was now very comfortable wearing them.

Todd wanted to give her confidence for the upcoming training. He said "I'm sure you will do your best, Natilia. But don't worry about letting me down. Training is difficult and some things may not come very easily. Just remember no one is perfect. Even I have made mistakes when training or fighting. Why do you think you have to bandage me sometimes?"

Natilia asked Todd, "Why? Is it not because you were hurt?" Todd replied, "Yes, it is because I was injured. But I only became injured because I made an error in battle or training."

Natilia looked surprised by Todd's reply. She asked, "So that is how you get hurt sometimes?"

Todd replied honestly saying, "Yes, it's because I made a miscalculation. But you must also learn from your mistakes. Now for your first item of training, I want you to tie your gladius on your waist on your left side. You need to get used to always carrying a sword on you like I do with mine."

Natilia was thrilled to begin her training. She immediately tied the Roman short sword to her waist and asked, "Is this right?"

Todd inspected her work and decided it needed to be tighter. He tightened up the knot and said, "You did very well. Just be sure it's tight and secure, because you never want to lose your sword."

Todd turned away from her, put on his helmet, and picked up his shield. Natilia saw that he was fully dressed and ready to go. She stated, "I will make sure that I do not lose it, Todd."

Todd smiled and said, "Excellent. Now let's see how you do with this as a starter for today. I was taught that you should first know how to carry a sword before you learn to use it."

Natilia thought about Todd's instruction. She said, "I will do my best and carry this sword all day. I will not untie it until we rest tonight."

Todd was pleased that Natilia was a very earnest student. He smiled and said, "Very good. Let's go." They exited the tent. Todd went over to their horse and tied his shield on its side.

Natilia oversaw the samurai taking down their tent. Once it was packed up, she walked over to their horse where Todd was waiting.

Todd advised her, "I will not help you up onto the horse. You must have the strength yourself to get up."

Natilia struggled a little bit but made it up on the horse. Todd was impressed by how well she did. He said, "Very good. I knew you would be able to do it by yourself. It will become easier after a few more times. This is another important way to be able to protect yourself."

Natilia was pleased that Todd was helping her be more independent and safe. She smiled at him and said, "I understand, Todd."

Todd jumped up onto the horse and wrapped his arms around Natilia's waist. She asked startled, "Todd, what are you doing? Are you not going to be the one controlling the horse?"

Todd replied, "No, that is your job now that you are going to be a warrior. You need to learn to be able to take the lead in any situation that may call for it. Taking charge of this horse is another important first step."

Natilia turned to Todd and saw him grinning at her. She smiled back and said, "Very well, I can lead the horse. I will learn this lesson." She gave him a kiss and turned back around to begin directing the horse over to Takeda.

As Todd and Natilia approached, Takeda noticed Natilia had the horse's reins instead of Todd. He asked, "Todaroshi, is all well with you, for your woman is controlling the horse?"

Todd was not surprised by Takeda's question. He answered nonchalantly, "Yes, I'm fine. My leg is feeling better today. Natilia is directing the horse because she wants to."

Takeda laughed at Todd's answer for Natilia controlling the horse. He said, "Todaroshi, you are very funny! You make me laugh so!"

Todd felt Natilia tense and knew she was probably angry and embarrassed by Takeda's reaction. He whispered in her ear, "With humiliation comes honor." She relaxed a little.

Todd thought he better be sure Natilia's anger was subsiding, so he started to rub her stomach. He knew she loved it and it would calm her.

Todd didn't want to be disrespectful to Takeda. He simply stated, "Well, that is how I treat my wife. You may find it funny. Are we ready to move out?"

Takeda became solemn and answered, "Yes, we need to proceed now before the sun rises any more in the sky."

Todd was glad Takeda was again focused on their plans for the day. He said "Yes, we should be off before it gets any later."

Takeda yelled out to his troops, "Men, we make for the Hojo castle to destroy their evil ways!" The samurai cheered at Takeda's orders and for the great battle with the Hojo that was to come.

They began their march to the Hojo castle through the woods. As the day progressed and they traveled on, the rain clouds had all dispersed. The sun was shining and the day grew hotter. Fortunately, they had plenty of shade as they passed under all the trees in the woods.

As the samurai journeyed closer to the Hojo castle, the woods started to get a lot thicker. Todd began to have an eerie feeling about this part of the woods. Yoshoni rode up beside him and said, "We are now getting near to the Hojo castle and have entered what some call the Woods of Old."

Todd noticed the trees were getting larger and a lot taller. They were also closer together than they had been previously. The air felt strange and Todd was growing concerned. He asked, "Is this a bad place, Yoshoni?"

Yoshoni shared the story of the Woods of Old. He answered, "No, this is a sacred place. They say the oldest tree in here is at the very center of these old woods. And if you can climb all the way to the top of it, you can have one of its fruits. This tree bears the fruit of healing and it can cure any wound or ailment you may have."

Todd was curious to see this so called oldest tree. He asked, "Will we pass it or camp near it on our way to the Hojo castle?"

Yoshoni was eager to see the tree as well. He advised Todd, "No, I am afraid not, for my Lord does not want to go into such a thick part of the woods. He feels it would also just waste time. But when we stop for our midday meal, you and I will go to the Tree of Healing and it will be a part of your training today, the last part."

Todd was excited to have the opportunity to check out this fabled tree. He responded, "Great! I wanted to go and see this Tree of Healing as soon as you mentioned it."

Yoshoni was pleased by Todd's enthusiasm. He smiled and said, "Do not worry yourself, Todaroshi, for we will go to see the tree and you will undergo a great training."

Todd wondered what Yoshoni meant by this and was about to ask, but Yoshoni had moved away and was headed over to Takeda.

As the samurai continued to march through the thicker woods, it was becoming very hot. Takeda decided they should stop for the midday meal. This thicker part of the woods would conceal his army better as they rested.

As Todd and Natilia sat down together, she said, "Good luck with your training today, Todd. Please tell me about it when you come back, dear."

Todd was excited for his training today and reminded Natilia of hers. He replied, "I will, Natilia. And you keep to your training as well, ok?"

Natilia was very eager to please him and show that she was capable of becoming a warrior. She assured him, "Yes, I will, Todd. I most certainly will."

Yoshoni came over to where they were sitting and asked, "Are you ready, Todaroshi?" Todd was anxious to go see the extraordinary tree he'd heard about. He answered, "Yes, let's go." He got up and they headed into the deeper part of the woods.

As Todd and Yoshoni traveled further into the woods, the trees were even taller and thicker. It was so closed in and humid that it became more difficult to breathe.

Todd and Yoshoni continued on and struggled to make their way through the now extremely thick trees. They finally came to a clearing and were relieved to find the air much easier to breathe.

Todd took in a big, fresh breath of air. He looked around and noticed there was only one extremely tall and massive tree in the center of the Woods of Old. This incredible tree, which stood all by itself, must be the Tree of Healing.

Yoshoni saw the amazement on Todd's face at the sight of the tree. He said, "This is the Tree of Healing, if you have not already guessed. It has been told in legend that only one person has ever gotten a fruit from this tree. And that person did not climb the tree. The fruit fell from the tree, which is very rare, for no fruit had ever fallen before or since from the Tree of Healing. It would seem the Tree of Healing has only ever given one fruit to one person."

Todd scanned the tree all the way to the top. He had to bend his head far back to see the highest branches. He noticed the tree's fruits were blue and there were many of them bunched up at the top.

Todd wondered why the tree didn't drop its fruit. He asked, "So the tree never loses its fruit, not even with the change of seasons?"

Yoshoni smiled and answered, "No, it does not, for the trees in this wood are so close together that they trap the warm air in amongst them. The Tree of Healing stays green all year round."

Todd was in a state of awe. He replied, "And that also explains why it's so tall. It never stops growing throughout the year."

Yoshoni was pleased to see Todd understood the tree's mystique. He said proudly, "Exactly. And now here is the last part of your training. You, Todaroshi, must climb to the top of the Tree of Healing and claim a single fruit for yourself in order to gain the true strength of a warrior and be as strong as a god."

Todd loved a challenge. And he recalled how he used to always climb trees for fun when he was younger. He replied confidently, "This shouldn't be too hard." He looked around the lower area of the tree for a starting branch. He found no low limbs to begin with. In fact, he realized there were no branches around the whole tree except for those at the very top.

Yoshoni reminded Todd of the tree's nature and purpose. He stated, "Remember, Todaroshi, this is the Tree of Healing. If you get high up and fall, you will not die when you hit the ground, for the grass is very soft as well as the ground below it. It will catch you. Also, in order to obtain the fruit from the top of the Tree of Healing, you must have, as they say, a leap of faith."

After hearing Yoshoni's statement, Todd felt the ground. It was not soft but hard as a rock. He thought Yoshoni might be embellishing the legend a little bit. Todd replied politely, "Ok, I understand."

Todd tried to start climbing up the tree and found it to be very difficult. He decided he needed to remove all of his armor and equipment. He stripped down to just his shirt, shorts and shoes.

Todd then tried to climb up the tree again. It was much easier going than before. He was finding small gaps and crevices in the tree into which he could put his hands and feet to help him move up. He hadn't notice them before. He thought that was a little odd but continued to climb higher.

Todd was only about half way up the tree and was already very tired. He pressed upward and continued to get closer to the top where the fruits were located. Todd suddenly thought to himself, 'Man, this is just like climbing the rock wall at an amusement park when I was a kid. Not like climbing a tree.'

Yoshoni was watching in amazement and was thrilled to see Todd had gotten so high very quickly. Todd finally made his way to where he was right under the top of the tree with all the branches.

Todd reached up and grabbed hold of a branch. His arms were very tired and worn out, so he struggled to pull himself up. He planted his shoes firmly against the tree and walked a few steps up. He nearly fell as he finally pulled himself up over the branch.

Todd sat and rested on the branch for a few moments catching his breath. Then he carefully stood up and keeping his balance, reached for the next branch and pulled himself up. He continued to go up a few more branches. Todd was passing many of the blue fruits of healing. He had decided he wanted to reach the top.

Todd, determined to make it to the very top of the tree, pressed on. When he finally reached the topmost part of the tree, Todd found a single large golden fruit sitting there by itself. He studied it for a minute. It appeared to be made of pure gold. Todd felt it and it was soft to the touch. Not hard like real gold would be. He picked the golden fruit from the tree top and started to make his way back down.

When Todd arrived at the lowest tree branch he had first reached on his way up, he realized the gaps and crevices he had used to climb up the tree earlier were no longer there. Todd was shocked by this and thought they couldn't just disappear. He continued to look for a way to climb back down. He found none. He couldn't believe it.

As Todd stood there on the branch with the fruit in his hand, he recalled what Yoshoni had said about a leap of faith when he had gotten the fruit and that the grass was softer than it seemed.

Todd sat down on the branch and looked down. He felt hungry and tired. His injured leg was starting to throb. He looked at it and noticed he was starting to bleed through the bandage. He let out an exhausted sigh and took a bite of the golden fruit.

As soon as Todd swallowed the delicious bite of fruit, he felt full of energy and as if he'd just woken from a long, good rest. He also noticed his cut leg wasn't hurting anymore.

As Todd sat on the branch, he looked down and saw Yoshoni at the base of the tree waving his hand. At least that's what Todd thought sitting high up in the tree. He recalled again what Yoshoni had told him about the Tree of Healing.

Todd said aloud to himself, 'Just as you have faith in your gods, have a leap of faith and jump into their arms. When you have the faith to jump into your gods' arms, you will be safe and earn the same bravery of the greatest warriors.'

Todd found courage in this and jumped off the tree's branch. As he was falling fast towards the ground, he thought it probably was not very smart to jump from the tallest tree in the woods and plummet to the earth.

Now certain he was about to die, Todd closed his eyes. When he hit the ground, it turned to soft mud and took him in all the way past his knees and nearly to his waist.

Todd realized he had stopped falling and opened his eyes. He found Yoshoni standing in front of him grinning ear to ear. Todd looked down and realized he was stuck in really soft mud.

Yoshoni burst out, "Do you see now, Todaroshi! This tree is from the gods and the ground too, for it was hard before you jumped off the tree branch. I am very proud of you, Todaroshi, for you have past the last test of the training I had for you. Now you have the courage of a true samurai and you now know of the Bushido Code, life in every breath. Because of your leap of faith you have experienced the Bushido Code."

Todd was still dazed. He thought to himself, 'Why did I jump? How am I still alive?' He couldn't explain any of it. He pulled himself out of the mud hole and noticed that none of the mud was sticking to him or his clothes.

The whole experience was astounding. Todd was still in shock and trying to understand what had happened. He went over to where he had placed his armor and equipment and picked everything up. His mind and heart were still racing as he walked back over to Yoshoni. He finally found his tongue and replied to what Yoshoni first said to him, "I understand now and I will take this lesson to heart, Yoshoni."

Yoshoni was very happy that Todd had passed his training but was also in a hurry to get back to Takeda and the troops. He said, "Very well. For now we must return to Takeda. Keep that fruit with you, Todaroshi. You may need it and as it is from the Tree of Healing, it will never spoil."

Todd was surprised to hear the fruit would not go bad. He was also anxious to return to Natilia and the others. He responded, "Alright, I will keep it in mind. Let's go."

Todd and Yoshoni headed back through the very thick trees to Takeda's camp. As they arrived at the camp, they could see the samurai were packing up everything to head out. It was about an hour or so past midday.

Takeda spotted Todd and Yoshoni coming back to the camp. He approached them and said, "You have been a long while Yoshoni and Todaroshi. I hope you did everything that needed to be done, for I cannot spare any more time at this rest. Now go and prepare, for we depart shortly."

Todd headed over to Natilia and was glad to see she had everything already packed up and ready to go. Natilia saw Todd was carrying all of his armor and equipment. She asked, "Todd, why are you not in your armor?"

Todd was so glad to see Natilia and thankful to be alive. He hugged her tightly and answered, "I didn't have time to put it back on. Yoshoni wanted to be sure we were back in time to leave with everyone else."

Natilia wondered why he'd taken his armor off, but was happy to take advantage of the opportunity. She said, "Since your armor is off, please let me check your leg and apply a new wrapping before you put everything back on."

Todd remembered his injured leg and again realized it no longer hurt. He replied, "Ok, but it feels a lot better now, Natilia. There is no pain."

Natilia was relieved to hear this, but still wanted to replace the soiled bandage and check the wound. She said, "I am glad you are not having discomfort, Todd. Let us see how it is healing."

Natilia took off the wrapping over his wound. As she removed the last cloth piece and examined his leg, she saw the wound was completely healed. All that remained was a faint scar on his calf muscle. She was shocked but happy to see that he was fully recovered.

"Todd! Your leg is completely healed with only a scar. How can this be!? What did you do to your leg to make it heal so fast?"

Todd was stunned by Natilia's statement. He looked at his calf and confirmed that his injury was now only a small scar. He thought about what had happened when he took a bite of the fruit. He responded, "I guess it must be that fruit I ate from the Tree of Healing. That's when my leg started to feel so much better."

Natilia was confused. She asked, "Tree of Healing? I don't understand, but I am very happy your leg is better. Now I do not have to worry for you or be concerned about it healing well."

Todd thought showing her the golden fruit would help explain what had happened. He presented it and said, "It was this fruit from the Tree of Healing that mended my leg and restored my strength."

Natilia's eyes grew wide as she stared at the fruit. She was baffled by what she saw and asked, "This fruit is golden. It healed your leg? This must be from the gods."

Todd was not able to explain it. He agreed saying, "Well, it would seem so. I better get dressed so we're ready to depart."

Todd put on all of his armor. When he was finished, he tied his sword to his waist on the left side as usual. Then he put his shield on the horse and tied it on.

Natilia mounted the horse and Todd got on behind her. He put his arms around her waist.

Natilia and Todd had just mounted, when Yoshoni rode up to them and asked, "Are you ready, Todaroshi?" As Todd looked over Natilia's shoulder he answered, "Yes, we're ready, Yoshoni."

Yoshoni smiled and replied, "Good! We make leave now to the Hojo castle, for Takeda told me to come and move you two along."

Natilia was proud they were ready in a timely manner and was now becoming much bolder. She stated, "We are ready, sir."

Todd smiled at Natilia for having spoken up. He was glad to see her getting braver.

Todd confirmed what she had said, stating, "Yes, we're right behind you." Yoshoni turned his horse and rode back to Takeda.

Natilia, in control of the horse, followed Yoshoni over to Takeda. Once they reached Takeda, he called out, "Good! It is time. My loyal samurai, we make leave to the scum Hojo's castle to burn it down!"

The whole army of 2,000 samurai let out a very loud cheer. Then they all started the march towards the Hojo castle.

After traveling awhile through the thicker part of the Woods of Old, the group was pleased to reach a less dense area. They traveled on for nearly the whole day and finally made it out of the Woods of Old.

Once they'd exited the Woods of Old, Yoshoni rode up to Todd and Natilia to let them know what lay ahead. "Todaroshi, now that we have cleared the Woods of Old, we have only to travel through these woods to make our way to the Hojo castle of evil and destroy it. Now this part of the woods may be thinner than the Woods of Old, but it goes on for a long ways and it is now nearing night fall. Have no worry though, for at midday on the next day we should reach the treacherous Hojo and their vile castle."

Todd was happy to hear their journey to the Hojo castle was almost at an end. He replied, "Great! I'm glad to know we don't have much longer in these woods. I was starting to wonder if they would ever end."

Yoshoni laughed at Todd's reply. "Oh! They end and right where we need them to." Yoshoni rode back over to Takeda and was still smiling, amused on his way.

The samurai continued to march until it was completely dark. They were only about halfway through the long stretch of woods to the Hojo castle.

Takeda stopped and yelled, "Halt! We rest here for the night and in the morning we besiege the Hojo scum!" All the samurai came to a sudden standstill when he gave this order and started to set up camp for the night.

Once they stopped, Todd jumped down from the horse and Natilia followed right behind him. They quickly put up their tent for the night.

When they finished with the tent, Todd said to Natilia, "Since you're now in training, tonight I want you to come with me as I patrol the camp. And I want you to wear this." He took off his steel body plate that was over his jade armor and helped Natilia put it on.

Todd wanted her to get a feel for what it was like to wear armor and to know how to put it on whenever she got her own one day.

Now that Natilia had on the body plate, Todd looked at her and asked "Do you still have the helmet from your father? The one he had given me that I wore when we arrived here."

Natilia knew she still had it with her. She replied, "Yes, I did not let it get left behind at Takeda's castle."

Todd was glad to hear she had brought it with them. He said, "Good! I want you to put on the helmet as well. You need to get used to wearing armor and a good strong helmet too." Todd showed Natilia how to put on the helmet.

Natilia was ecstatic that Todd was training her. She smiled and said, "Well, how do I look? How did I do for my first time?"

Todd smiled at her with great pride and answered, "You look like a strong warrior. And you did great putting on the armor. I think you probably already knew how to do it, since you're always helping me with mine."

Natilia hugged Todd and the steel body plate clanked against his jade armor. They laughed at this, but Natilia turned serious and stated, "Todd, you are very special and mean the world to me. I will never let you go. I will be only yours and no one else's wife. I will always love you." She embraced him again even tighter.

Todd held her back and looked into her beautiful eyes. He said, "I love you with all my heart, Natilia. And believe your every word. I will never let anything happen to you." He gave her a long kiss while she held onto him. They released each other and Todd said, "Now let's go and circle the camp to make sure there are no enemies nearby tonight."

Todd and Natilia set out and surveyed the camp. As they made their way around, Todd would periodically stop and show Natilia some forms of how to use the sword.

As Todd and Natilia continued their trip about the campsite, Yoshoni spotted them and came over. He said, "Todaroshi, you are patrolling the camp once more and this time with company, I see. So tell me, have you seen any danger so far this night?"

Todd had not noticed anything suspicious. He answered, "No, Yoshoni. But I will warn you if there is any trouble."

Yoshoni was impressed that Todd wanted to ensure their protection. He said "Very well. I will leave you to your duty, Todaroshi. And will see you in the morning."

Todd knew it would most likely be Yoshoni waking them up in the morning. He said, "Yes, we will see you in the morning. Good night, Yoshoni." Yoshoni walked back into the campsite.

Natilia asked, "Where were we, Todd?"

Todd looked at her and smiled. He knew she was enjoying both the training and the patrol. He replied, "Right, where were we? Ah! I remember. I was teaching you how to use the sword properly."

Natilia was very eager to learn how to protect herself. She said, "Yes that's it. Please carry on."

Todd continued to show her more sword forms and taught her how to use the sword correctly as they finished their tour of the camp.

They arrived back at their tent and Todd held the tent open for Natilia. She entered and he went in after her. Natilia took off the body plate and gave it back to Todd. He placed it on the ground near the bed.

Natilia removed her helmet and gladius and put them next to Todd's body plate. Todd took off all of his armor and equipment and placed them beside the bed as well.

Natilia got into bed and waited for Todd to enter the bed with her. When he got into bed, she laid down facing him and wrapped her arms around him. They kissed good night and fell asleep in each other's arms.

In the morning, Yoshoni came into their tent to wake them. He said, "You must hurry now, for Takeda is most eager to reach Hojo as soon as possible this day. My Lord does not want any delays today."

Todd and Natilia both sat up immediately. Todd rubbed his eyes and said, "Alright, we'll be ready shortly."

Yoshoni knew they would be quick. He said, "Very well," and exited the tent so they could get dressed.

Natilia and Todd both quickly got out of bed and put on their armor and equipment. They would be reaching the Hojo castle today, so Todd would need his body plate. Natilia just had on her helmet and gladius for armor.

After they were both geared up, Natilia and Todd quickly dismantled the tent and packed it up. They hurried over to their horse and Todd tied his shield to it while Natilia got mounted.

Once Natilia was on the horse, Todd got on in front of her. Today he would be directing the horse, since they were headed to battle and would be fighting the Hojo at the castle.

With a worried look on her face, Natilia said softly, "Todd, please come back safely to me by the end of this day."

Todd gave her a kiss on the cheek and said, "Don't worry, Natilia. I promise to come back safely to you."

Natilia let out a soft sigh and Todd guided the horse towards Takeda. Natilia was apprehensive. She feared losing Todd. She hoped he would return to her unharmed. She took a deep breath and knew she must be brave.

As they approached Takeda, he looked at them and said, "Todaroshi, are you prepared for this glorious victory we will have today?"

Todd replied with great confidence saying, "Yes! And the sooner we get there, the sooner we will take the Hojo down."

Takeda was enthused to see Todd ready to do battle. He replied, "I like the sound of this, Todaroshi." Takeda called out to the troops, "We march to the Hojo castle to bring them to their end!"

All the Takeda samurai shouted out their support louder than Todd had ever heard before. Now that they were very close to the Hojo homelands, they sounded very eager for the battle and anxious to engage the enemy.

The samurai started their final march towards the Hojo castle. As they marched through the woods, the sun rose in the sky and misty fog rolled in.

By midday, they knew they were getting very close to the Hojo castle and the fog finally started to lift. They were also getting near the edge of the woods.

Takeda ordered the archers to the front of the army and slowed the march forward to make sure they would not step out of the cover of the fog in the woods.

As they proceeded forward slowly, the archers reached the treeline and could see the Hojo castle. The archers immediately stopped marching as Takeda had instructed. Takeda, Todd, and Yoshoni moved forward to see the Hojo castle for themselves.

Todd noticed the Hojo castle looked very similar to Takeda's castle, except it was a little bigger and red, not green like Takeda's.

Takeda gave his commands saying, "I want all the archers to stand at the treeline and fire five waves of arrows in the direction of the Hojo castle on my order. As for you, Todaroshi, before we fire the first wave of arrows, I want you to charge the Hojo's opened gates, just you alone, for they will not close the gates for a one-man army. Once you have charged directly out of the woods, we will start firing the waves of arrows to cover you. Todaroshi, I know you can handle ten or more samurai on your own and that is why you were chosen to do this task."

Todd was a little concerned that he might not live through Takeda's plan but answered boldly, "Ok, I can do this. No problem." He was thankful for the golden fruit he had in the right pocket of his shorts which were under his greaves.

Takeda still firmly believed Todd was sent from the gods. He said, "Good, I knew you would do this task for me, Todaroshi. And I know you will succeed. You are an honorable and brave warrior, and of the gods."

Natilia was fearful about Takeda's plan and what Todd must do. She got down from the horse and said softly, "Be safe, Todd." She was still trying to be brave but felt miserable. She looked away sadly.

Todd could see she was about to cry. He replied, "Don't worry about me, Natilia. You just go take cover behind a tree and stay safe. I'll be back soon."

Natilia nodded but wouldn't look at him. She knew she would cry if she did. She turned, walked away, and slipped behind a tree.

Yoshoni had great confidence in Todd but still shared, "Good luck, Todaroshi. I will see you inside the castle or with the gods."

Todd was starting to have a bad feeling about this plan of action. He replied, "Thank you, Yoshoni. I'll need all the luck I can get to complete this task."

Takeda was keen to take the castle. He asked, "All my archers are in position and ready to fire, Todaroshi. Are you ready?"

Todd knew there was no turning back now. He replied, "I'm ready whenever you are, Takeda, sir."

Takeda ordered, "Go, Todaroshi, and show the Hojo the power of the gods."

On Takeda's command, Todd rode his horse as fast as he could up the hill towards the castle. His shield was in his left hand as he used it to also control the horse. In his right hand his sword was held high up in the air.

As Todd charged out of the edge of the woods, he yelled "AHHHHH!!!!" to grab the Hojo's attention. When Takeda heard Todd's bellowing, he ordered the archers to fire the waves.

As Todd sped ahead on his horse, he spotted the arrows flying over his head. He was glad to see that the arrows were taking out a good number of Hojo archers and samurai. They had been focused on him and were caught unaware.

The Hojo archers began to return fire on the Takeda archers. A few of the Takeda archers were hit, but most of the Hojo arrows hit the trees. A few Hojo arrows flew towards Todd as well. Luckily he was riding so fast that all the arrows missed him, flying right over his head.

As Todd rode his horse up the hill to the wide-open Hojo gate, the Hojo samurai standing guard started to close it. The second wave of Takeda arrows flew over Todd's head. They found their mark and hit more archers, as well as a few of the samurai trying to close the gate.

The Hojo archers continued to fire back at the attacking Takeda archers. The Hojo could not see the Takeda in the treeline and were only able to hit a few again. More Hojo arrows came at Todd. This time two of the arrows hit his shield and another hit him in his left shoulder. He ignored the pain and kept riding forward.

Todd was getting very close to the Hojo gates, when he saw the third wave of Takeda arrows go over his head. Again they took down more Hojo archers and samurai. There were now only a small number of Hojo archers remaining and they were getting desperate. Most of them decided to focus their fire at Todd, hoping to kill the one enemy they could see. A few others continued to fire into the woods. They were firing blind and hit no Takeda archers this time.

The Hojos firing on Todd had better luck. Three of their arrows had struck his shield hard and were followed by four more arrows hitting him brutally in his chest. Another two arrows had struck his horse. The horse reared up and fell to the ground on its right side.

As the horse fell, Todd jumped off so he wouldn't get pinned. He landed hard and dropped his sword from the impact. He'd held tight to his shield, knowing he'd need protection from the Hojo arrows.

Todd kept his shield held in front of him and slowly picked himself up. He saw the fourth wave of arrows flying towards the Hojo castle. Again Hojo archers and samurai fell.

As Todd moved slowly towards his sword with his shield in front of him, three more arrows hit his shield from the few Hojo still targeting him. The remaining Hojo archers also fired into the woods once more.

Todd reached his sword and bent down to pick it up. As he did, he spit up blood onto the ground. He was shocked by this and now feared for his life. He didn't want to die in this field. Todd took a deep breath trying to calm his nerves. He took off and ran as fast as he could with all the arrows still stuck in him towards the gate of the castle.

The Hojo samurai had stopped trying to close the gate, when they saw Todd and his horse get shot down by the barrage of arrows. There were now only five Hojo samurai standing at the gates to stop him. When he neared the gate, the five Hojo samurai charged at him. The fifth wave of Takeda arrows came down right in front of Todd and took out three of the Hojo samurai. Unfortunately, one of the Takeda arrows also hit him in the left shoulder blade. Even though he was struck by another arrow, he still charged at the two Hojo samurai coming at him.

When Todd and the samurai ran into each other, Todd used his shield to block both of them. The two Hojo samurai recoiled from hitting Todd's shield and stumbled backwards. Todd's left arm was weak from the arrows that were stuck in his shoulder, so the force of the two Hojo samurai hitting his shield knocked it out of his hand.

One of the Hojo samurai rebounded quickly and came at Todd swinging his sword. Todd swiftly blocked the Hojo samurai's sword with his own. As they connected, Todd shoved the samurai back fast and slashed at the other samurai's throat as he was preparing to attack. He fell to the ground clutching his wound.

The last samurai advanced again as Todd was dispatching the other Hojo samurai. Todd's back was slightly turned, so the samurai took advantage and surprised him with a swift slash to his back. Todd reacted immediately and elbowed the Hojo samurai hard in the stomach. He then spun around quickly and cut him from the top of his head all the way down the middle to the ground, cutting him in two.

Todd turned around towards the woods and raised his sword up to signal Takeda to charge the gates. After having signaled Takeda, Todd moved forward and postioned himself at the gate to make sure it stayed open. As he stood at the gate, he looked back down the hill and saw all of the 2,000 Takeda samurai charging up the hill towards the Hojo castle as fast as they could.

Todd heard a loud cracking noise behind him. He turned around and saw the inner castle gates being opened. As they swung open, Todd could see what looked to be about 3,000 Hojo samurai charging at him. He thought to himself, 'And I was worried about keeping the gates open!' Todd backed up slightly to be out of the main roadway through the gates but still held his sword and position.

Before the army of 3,000 Hojo samurai could reach Todd and try to kill him, the Takeda samurai ran by him and collided with the Hojo samurai. Once the forces collided, Todd dropped to his knees and used his sword to hold himself up. He didn't want to fall on the arrows and push them in even deeper.

Yoshoni saw Todd on the ground as he ran up to the gates with the army of Takeda samurai. He was surprised to see him like this and asked, "Todaroshi! What are you doing on your knees!?"

Todd was still trying to keep himself up. He was starting to shake and continued to spit blood from his mouth. He said, "I'm......trying not to fall over."

Yoshoni now worried Todd's injuries may be fatal. He thought of the fruit from the Tree of Healing and stated, "Well, pull out these arrows and eat the fruit!"

Todd had forgotten about the golden fruit. He recalled that it was in the right pocket of his shorts. He hoped it was not crushed from when he fell off of his horse earlier. Todd struggled to pick himself up, even though he really wanted to collapse to the ground. He finally stood up and slowly pulled the arrows out of his chest. Yoshoni stood by to protect him as the battle raged on nearby.

As Todd pulled the arrows out of his chest, he threw them on the ground. Blood was coming out of the arrow holes of his armor, running down the body plate, and dripping onto the ground. Todd pulled out the arrows in his shoulder and threw them on the ground as well. He reached into the pocket of his shorts that were underneath his greaves and pulled out the golden fruit from the Tree of Healing.

Todd was surprised and pleased to see it was still in one piece. He took a bite out of it and immediately noticed that the blood stopped pouring out of his chest. He began to feel very strong again. He took a couple deep breaths and was gratified that he was no longer fearful for his life. He was also no longer tired. He felt full of energy and ready to rejoin the fight.

Todd went to find his shield. He located it and removed all the arrows stuck in it. He was about to head for the battle, when he remembered his wounded horse.

Todd found the horse still lying on the ground. It was alive and suffering with the two arrows still stuck in it. He knelt by the horse's side and placed his shield and sword on the ground. Todd removed the arrows from the horse and cut off a piece of the golden fruit of healing. He gave the fruit to the horse.

Suddenly the horse got up and seemed completely recovered. Todd turned the horse towards the treeline, and with a pat on its backside, sent it back to the edge of the woods where Natilia was waiting.

Once the horse had run off, Todd sprinted back to the battle and found Yoshoni in the middle of fighting samurai. Todd fought his way through the Hojo samurai, striking them down as he went, and came up beside Yoshoni to fight alongside him.

The Hojo samurai continued to fall as the combat raged on. The Takeda samurai persisted in moving forward to the Hojo castle gate as they slaughtered and killed all of the Hojo samurai. Now there were only about 500 Takeda samurai left with Todd and Yoshoni.

Takeda, seeing his samurai overpowering and defeating the enemy, had advanced to the Hojo castle gate. He advised his army of samurai, "You have all brought great honor to yourselves and your families. Now only I, Yoshoni, and Todaroshi are to go forth into this treacherous castle to destroy the evil Hojo." The samurai let out a loud cheer for their victory.

As the samurai looked to their fallen soldiers, Takeda and Yoshoni with Todd went into the castle to fight Hojo. As they entered the castle they found it was very similar to Takeda's on the inside. The main difference was that it was red instead of green. Yoshoni, Todd and Takeda advanced slowly, ready for an enemy attack. There was none.

As they neared the throne, the group could see Hojo sitting there staring at them. He was flanked by two samurai holding a sword in each of their hands and dressed in all black jade armor with red demon masks on their faces.

Hojo had quietly watched them enter his castle and slowly move forward to his throne. He said, "I am surprised you made it so far, old Takeda."

Takeda seethed with anger at seeing his enemy. He couldn't wait to kill Hojo. Takeda replied, "The gods willed it to be." He moved his sword slowly in front of him as if ready to attack.

Hojo looked at each of them scornfully and laughed. He said, "The gods willing you to beat me! That is very amusing. Old man, Takeda, you must be losing your mind or perhaps you already have!"

The insult met its mark and Takeda responded angrily yelling, "We will see about that, you fool! For I have with me a warrior from the gods! Todaroshi! Come forward now!"

Todd quickly stepped up beside Takeda. He had his shield raised and was ready with his sword in hand. Todd thought to himself, 'I hope this will be the final battle. I only have about one more bite left of the golden fruit of healing.'

Hojo looked Todd up and down studying him. With a malicious stare he said, "If he is a warrior of the gods, then he should be able to kill me. But you forget, Takeda, I possess "the sword" from the gods!"

Hojo grabbed an object from his left side and switched it on. The object looked like a silver flashlight, but what came out of its end with a snapping and hissing noise was a bright blue laser that extended out about two to three feet.

Todd was shocked by the sight of it. He thought it was impossible that Hojo could be holding this object. It was a light saber. A movie creation, not something that had been invented even in his time. Todd cast his shield aside. He knew it would be of no use against this weapon.

Takeda was stunned that Todd dropped his shield. He looked at him in disbelief. Hojo let out a wicked laugh and stated, "Look, Takeda, even your warrior from the gods will not fight me, for he knows this is the true sword of the gods!"

Todd answered angrily that he was not throwing down his arms. "No! You are very wrong, Hojo. I got rid of my shield, so I can move quicker and kill you faster." Takeda smiled after hearing Todd's answer.

Hojo was enraged and yelled with a face of hate and disgust, "You are the one who will die fast, warrior from the gods! I will enjoy cutting you to pieces! Guards! Destroy them!"

The two black armored samurai ran at Todd and Yoshoni. As the Hojo guard swung at Todd, he blocked the samurai's sword with his own and kicked him away. As the samurai was falling back, Todd lunged forward and stabbed at him. At the same time, the Hojo guard swung his other sword and knocked Todd's sword out of his hand.

Todd backed away and spotted his discarded shield. The Hojo guard tried to take advantage of Todd being disarmed and charged at him a second time. Todd quickly bent down and picked up his shield. He was able to block both of the guard's sword strikes with his shield.

Todd swiftly shoved his shield hard up against the Hojo guard and used all his strength to push him backwards. He overpowered the guard and rammed him up against the wall with great force. The guard slammed into the wall so hard that he dropped his swords.

Todd continued to crush his shield into the guard's body, keeping him pinned to the wall. He could hear the Hojo guard's labored breathing. Todd swiftly moved his shield away and with considerable power punched the Hojo guard in his face mask.

Upon being hit, the guard collapsed to the ground. The Hojo guard tried to pick himself up, but Todd gave him a hasty kick to the head and he passed out from this final blow.

Todd kicked away both of the guard's swords that were on the ground near him. As he turned around, he saw Yoshoni cut off the other Hojo guard's head dropping him dead to the floor.

Todd hurried back over to Takeda's side. Takeda had stood still waiting for Hojo to make a move and strike first. As Yoshoni came over to flank Takeda's other side, Todd noticed Yoshoni's right shoulder was bleeding badly from his fight with the Hojo guard.

Takeda was pleased and confident about how the battle was proceeding. He boasted, "It would seem your samurai need more training, Hojo! Now you see you may have the sword of the gods, but I have the warrior of the gods with me."

Todd set his shield down again and stood ready with just his sword. Hojo was furious at Takeda's remarks. He yelled indignantly, "We shall see who is the greatest of the gods!"

Filled with pure rage, Hojo furiously ran at Takeda. As Hojo neared, he swung the light saber at Takeda.

Todd knew Takeda couldn't defend himself against the light saber, so he pushed him out of the way. Todd also rolled out of the way as he moved Takeda. All Hojo managed to do was cut Takeda's sword in half.

Yoshoni reacted to the attack and swung his sword at Hojo. As his sword came down, Hojo quickly spun around and sliced Yoshoni's sword in half. Hojo then immediately pulled back the light saber and thrust it into Yoshoni's stomach. He stabbed Yoshoni through with ease. Hojo laughed and said, "Oh, too easy, Takeda!"

As Todd got up, he saw Yoshoni fall to the floor as Hojo pulled the light saber out of him. Hojo turned towards Todd and Takeda. Todd knew he had to disarm Hojo to defeat him. He sprinted full force at Hojo and tackled him to the ground.

Hojo tried to stab Todd with the light saber as they both lay on the ground. But Todd again quickly rolled out of the way and got to his feet.

As Todd stood up, he kicked Hojo in his left side as hard as he could. The force of the blow caused Hojo to howl in pain, drop the light saber, and roll aside. Todd took advantage and hurriedly grabbed the light saber where it lay on the ground. He stabbed Hojo in the chest with his own weapon, the light saber.

Todd located the button to turn off the light saber and put it on his right hip. He ran over to Yoshoni, who was mortally wounded and lay dying. Todd knew the only thing that would save him was the fruit of healing. He said, "Yoshoni, you must eat this and you will be better."

Todd took his last piece of the fruit of healing from his pocket and gave it to Yoshoni. Yoshoni swallowed the fruit. Instantly his whole body was healed. He no longer felt as though he were dying.

Yoshoni sat up and looked at Todd with relief and surprise. He said, "Thank you so very much, Todaroshi. You have saved my life more then once now. There is no way that I can ever repay you."

Todd reassured Yoshoni that he was not indebted to him. He said, "You have already repaid me enough, Yoshoni. There is nothing you owe me."

Yoshoni stood up and bowed to him saying, "You are most honorable, Todaroshi. I will never forget the great deed you have done for me this day." Todd bowed and simply replied, "Thank you, Yoshoni."

Todd went over to Takeda who stood in disbelief. He said, "Takeda, sir. I have the sword of the gods. I think we should find a box here in the castle so that we can transport it securely."

Takeda was amazed by the sword of the gods and that Todd was able to use it to kill Hojo. He answered, "Yes....yes. I will find something for us." He ran quickly through the castle searching for a suitable box for the sword of the gods - a light saber.

As Todd waited for Takeda to return with a box, he studied the light saber and wondered how something like this could have ever been made in this time period. He examined it closely and noticed writing. Printed on the bottom of the light saber was, "MADE IN THE UGA." He thought to himself, 'What is UGA? What does this mean?'

Takeda returned with a box and held it out to Todd. He said, "Here, Todaroshi, warrior of the gods. I have found this box. Is it suitable?"

Todd looked at the box and saw that it was a bright blue color with some cherry blossom flowers painted on the lid. Todd continued to play along with the light saber being a sword from the gods and said, "Very good. This will do for the gods' sword."

However, Todd knew it wasn't really a weapon from the gods. It was a light saber that had been made somewhere - UGA?! And that somewhere was a place he had to find, and hopefully figure all of this mess out.

Takeda asked Todd as he handed the box to him, "What will become of the sword, Todaroshi?" Todd thought of an appropriate answer to his question and replied, "I will take it and bring it back to the gods."

Takeda said, "Yes, very well. I thought as much."

Todd was thankful that Takeda agreed to this and didn't think to try to keep the light saber for himself.

Takeda continued, "We must destroy all remnants of Hojo and his castle. First we must gather our spoils of victory, especially the stores of silver and gold. Then we will burn this place down to the ground."

Todd was relieved that Takeda only seemed concerned with destroying anything that was of the Hojo. He replied, "Very well, Takeda, sir." Todd placed the light saber in the box and gathered up his sword and shield. He then proceeded to exit the castle.

As Todd came out of the castle gates, all the remaining Takeda samurai entered the Hojo castle and began their raid. Todd continued on and made his way down the hill leading away from the castle. As he reached the bottom of the hill, Todd looked back at the Hojo castle and saw smoke starting to come out from it.

Todd reached the edge of the woods and started looking for Natilia. He found her waiting with the horse he had healed with the fruit.

When Natilia saw Todd, she rushed over to him and hugged and kissed him. She looked at him with teary eyes and said, "I was so worried for you. When the horse came back without you, I feared the worst. And it was disturbing that the horse came right to me and didn't just run off."

Todd tried to soothe Natilia. He replied, "I'm fine Natilia. I promised you I wouldn't let any harm come to me. I did my best to stay safe for you."

Natilia was proud and honored to hear he'd kept his promise to her. She gave him another kiss and said, pleased, "Thank you, Todd. I love you so much."

Todd was glad to see Natilia had calmed down. He replied, "I love you too, dear. Now you don't have to worry anymore. I'm here and safe."

Natilia smiled at Todd and released him. She asked, "What happens now?"

Todd answered her with a smile saying, "We wait for Takeda and his samurai. Then we'll all head back to Tokyo and on our way I will continue training you how to fight."

Natilia's face lit up with excitement and she asked gleefully, "Really, Todd?!"

Todd enjoyed making her happy and seeing her beautiful smile. He replied, "Yes, really, Natilia."

They heard Takeda's samurai approaching and turned to see Takeda riding towards them.

Takeda stopped his horse in front of them and he said, "We are done here. Thank you, Todaroshi, for what you have done for us this day. Now mount your horse and we make for Tokyo to tell of our great triumph."

Todd nodded in acknowledgement and asked Natilia to get on the horse first. He tied his shield to the horse and then jumped up behind Natilia. As a part of her training, he continued to let her lead the horse as they rode with the marching samurai army.

It was late afternoon when the army reached the Woods of Old. Todd asked Takeda if they could stop there and rest for the night. Takeda agreed to this, since they were all tired from the battle and had won a great victory that day.

After Todd and Natilia had their tent set up, they headed into the Woods of Old. Todd took with him the box that had the light saber stored inside. He found his way back to the Tree of Healing and buried the box near its base.

After Todd buried the box, he thought of getting another fruit. He looked around the tree for a way back up, but could find nothing. The way he had gone up the tree before, the footholds, was gone. Not being able to find a way up, Todd and Natilia headed back to the camp.

On their way back to the army campsite, Todd stopped them in front of a tall tree. He watched as Natilia climbed up and back down the tall tree as he'd instructed. He told her it would help her gain strength and bravery.

After they arrived back at the camp, Todd engaged Natilia in a short training session with the sword. As the day grew dark, they headed into their tent to get some rest.

The next day, they carried on with their march to Tokyo. As they traveled, Todd continued to train Natilia. She was an excellent student and was becoming skillful with the sword.

After a few days, Todd increased the difficulty of her instruction. He was very proud of her dedication and talent. As her training continued, Todd appreciated her exceptional ability with the sword and knew she was becoming an excellent warrior.

The army had traveled for several days and were now only one day away from Tokyo. They had made camp for the night and were getting ready for bed. Natilia asked, "Todd, do you think we will ever get back to Rome?"

Todd considered that most important question. He answered, "Well, to tell you the truth, Natilia, I really don't know."

Natilia looked very sad and said, "Oh, I see." She turned away from him and got into bed.

Todd layed down beside her and rubbed her belly to help make her feel better. He said, "Please don't worry, Natilia. Takeda has promised to give us a nice home here. He's very grateful for all we've done for him."

Natilia replied, "Yes, I know. I am sure it will be nice."

Todd wanted to reassure her that everything would be alright. He said, "Yes, I'm sure it will and we'll find out soon enough. I love you, Natilia. And at least we are in this together. Now let's get some sleep so we are rested for tomorrow."

Natilia felt comforted as Todd held her. She believed and trusted in him. She responded, "And I love you as well, Todd. Good night, dear." She gave him a kiss and fell asleep in a short time.

It took a little while for Todd to fall asleep. He recalled Natilia's question about returning to Rome and started to feel strange. It was the same odd sensation he'd felt on the two other nights, when he'd traveled through time. Todd tried not to worry about it and held tight to Natilia. He focused on the quiet rhythm of her breathing and shortly drifted off to sleep.

THE TIME THAT TRAVELED PART III ANCIENT GREECE

As Todd woke up the next morning, he was surprised to realize he was not waking up to Yoshoni bursting in as usual. He also noticed it was much hotter than it had ever been since he arrived in Japan. Todd felt like he had overslept.

Natilia was still asleep in the bed beside him. He figured Takeda would be anxious to depart, so he got out of bed and exited the tent.

As soon as Todd stepped outside, he noticed they were not in the bamboo woods anymore. Instead all he saw was an open field with a little grass. There was really more dirt than grass. Todd thought to himself, 'Why and how could this have happened a third time?!'

Not knowing when or where he was, Todd hurried back inside the tent and put on all his armor. After dressing in his armor, he proceeded to put on his shoes and the gauntlets over top of the leather bracers. This completed his armor, consisting of Roman and Japanese equipment. Todd picked up his sword and tied it to his waist on the left side as usual.

Todd moved over to the bed and gently woke Natilia. As he softly nudged her shoulder, she slowly opened her eyes. She sat up with a start and asked, "Why are you dressed? Has something bad happened? Were we attacked last night?"

Todd wished it was only an attack. He answered, "No, it's worse. We went through time again. And I have no idea where we are now." He put on his samurai helmet and picked up his shield. He was ready to head out.

Natilia was shocked to hear this news. She stared in disbelief, wondering why this would happen again. She asked, "What?! You don't know where we are! Todd, why do the gods keep moving you around to different places and peoples?"

Todd had the same question and others – who, how, why, etc. But he had no answers and simply said, "I do not know, Natilia. But we need to find out and try to put an end to it, because I'm getting pretty tired of all this. Please hurry and get your armor on. And pack up all the food you can carry. Then we will head out. I think it's already midday."

Natilia quickly put on her helmet and tied her sword to her waist on her left side. She then packed all the food. Natilia was trying to understand why they might keep moving to different places and to different time periods. She said, "I think the gods love you, Todd. And perhaps that is why they always choose you to do their undertakings for them now."

Todd was pleased to see that Natilia was trying to look on the bright side. He responded, "Well, I'm not sure about that, but we're going to get to the bottom of this once and for all."

Now that they were both dressed and the food was packed, Todd and Natilia headed out of the tent. Todd decided to leave the tent behind, because he knew it would be too much to carry in this heat. He stuck with his ritual for moving forward in a new time location. They just walked straight ahead and didn't turn left or right as they traveled away from the tent.

Todd and Natilia proceeded forward for awhile. The sun was getting lower in the sky, so they guessed it was approaching late afternoon. As they traveled on, a city came into sight. It looked similar to a Roman city, but it wasn't.

Natilia recognized their location and happily announced, "This is the Greek city of Athens, Todd! We may be back to our time and can now return to Rome!"

Todd continued to study the city but wasn't sure he agreed with Natilia. He said, "I don't know, Natilia. Something is not quite right."

They continued to walk towards the city of Athens. They were anxious to get a closer look and find out more about their situation. As they reached the city entrance and proceeded to go inside, they both thought everything looked normal. It appeared to be a typical Roman city state.

Todd wondered if anything would truly be "normal" anymore. He asked Natilia, "So, what do you think? Are we back or not?"

Natilia replied, "I am not sure." They continued further into the city and studied their surroundings.

People stared at them as they moved on. Natilia stopped and slowly turned around in a circle, examining the buildings and people. She stated, "I cannot tell, Todd. The city does look very much like Athens and so it must be Athens. But there are no Roman guards keeping watch. And there is no arena for the gladiator games."

Todd and Natilia kept walking through the city nearing its center. Todd thought he'd figured out where and when they were. He said, "I think I have an idea of what time period we are in."

Natilia stopped and looked at him with uncertainty. She asked, "When we are?! Are you saying this is not Roman times?"

Todd looked at Natilia and nodded. He answered, "Yes, I believe we may be in Ancient Greece before the time of the Roman Republic."

Natilia was shocked to hear Todd's idea. She exclaimed, "No! This cannot be! Are we just going to keep moving further and further back in time until we come to when the gods made the world?!"

Todd stepped forward and hugged Natilia, hoping to calm her down. He tried to soothe her saying, "I'm sorry, Natilia. I don't know. But I won't let anything happen to you. I promise to keep you safe, ok?"

Natilia felt comforted by Todd's protection and concern. She replied softly, "I know you will, Todd. I am just so very worried." Todd knew exactly how she felt. They had to again proceed cautiously and do their best to stay alive and well. Todd said, "I understand, Natilia."

Todd and Natilia decided not to talk publicly for the time being. They needed to just observe and try to figure out more about where they were and what might be going on. They proceeded a short way and found themselves in the center of the city. In the city's center plaza, there was an old man speaking to a large crowd of people.

Todd was curious to hear what the old man was saying. He grabbed Natilia by the hand and walked over to the crowd. They worked their way into the group of people to get closer to the old man. Once they were near enough to hear him well, they stopped to listen to his speech.

The old man was yelling to grab the crowd's attention, "My good people! My good people! If I may, I will tell you of the great Achilles, who fights with the King Agamemnon and how they are planning for war with the Trojans. And I will tell you of the reason for this war. They go to take down the mighty walls of Troy for the most beautiful woman in all of Greece. This will restore the honor of Agamemnon's brother and all of Greece and return Helen to his side. King Agamemnon is gathering a force, the largest that anyone has ever seen before in the whole of Greece, and will be sailing for Troy in three days' time."

Todd now knew what time he was in for certain...Ancient Greece. But he still wasn't sure why he was there. The old man continued to preach his message to the people, "The King needs all great warriors at his side for this glorious battle that will take place. It would be a grand honor to have your names remembered for all eternity and to become immortal like the gods themselves.

Beware to all of those who journey with the Greek warriors, for the Trojans are loved by the gods and more so by the god Apollo. The gods have built for them the high walls around their city, and what is more, Apollo has given the Trojans some of his fire. It is a bow from Apollo himself that shoots blue flames at Trojan enemies. It will burn right through you and any with the greatest armor. So, my good people, go on this great journey to become immortal, be remembered for an eternity like the gods, and have your names never be forgotten by anyone."

The old man finished delivering his message and went silent. The crowd started to break up and people headed off on their separate ways. Some of the people from the crowd gave the old man gifts of food, drink, gold, and silver, thanking him for sharing his time and thoughts on the impending war.

Todd figured this old guy probably knew a lot about what was happening in this time period. He said to Natilia, "Let's go talk to this old man. Maybe he'll know what we should do."

Natilia agreed with Todd after hearing the old man's speech. She replied, "Yes, that sounds like a good idea, Todd." They both moved through the dispersing crowd toward the old man.

They approached the old man and as they neared him Todd said, "Hello! Sir, how are you?"

The old man answered Todd with another question saying, "I am good, if the asking of how I am is for good meaning?"

Todd understood what he meant and replied, "It is for good meaning, sir. I have a question and maybe you can give me the answer to it."

The old man still had not looked at Todd and Natilia. He was busy securing his possessions. He said, "First, tell me of your name, stranger."

Todd realized he had forgotten to introduce himself. He replied, "Oh, I'm sorry. My name is Todd and this is my wife, Natilia."

The old man tilted his head slightly then looked up at them from where he was sitting on the ground. He stared at them for a moment then said, "That is an odd name. I am to guess that your name is Toddacis in our words. And your wife, if I may say, is quite lovely. She has the beauty of a goddess."

Natilia was flattered by the old man's comment and blushed. She asked, "Thank you sir. Would you be so kind as to give us your name?"

The old man smiled at them and seemed very pleased to be asked. He responded, "My name is Homer and I am the storyteller for the gods. As for you, Toddacis, you are a warrior for the gods, I would say by the looks of you. What is it you seek of me, god warrior, Toddacis?"

Todd wondered why everyone kept saying he's 'from the gods' or 'their warrior.' But what could he expect considering how he was dressed and that he'd just traveled through time again.

Todd was also thrilled and excited to meet Homer in real life. He knew he had to just stick to the matter at hand and asked, "Well, I need you to tell me how to get to Sparta, so we can join this war or at least how to find the King of whom you spoke."

Homer looked at Todd with a raised brow. He didn't appear surprised by this request. He responded, "Very well, Toddacis. You will need to head up north along the road to Sparta. When you rest on this journey, which is a two days' travel, you will come across a man to help you. He is the son of a god. This man will travel with you to Sparta and to war.

But you must not tell anyone of his name, for the gods wish his name to only be known to you and your beautiful wife. This man will assist you and stay at your side during all of your travels until you return to the gods."

Todd was glad to have some direction and was anxious to begin. He said, "Thank you, Homer. We will remember all you have told us. We are grateful for your guidance."

Homer held up his hand as if to stop him and said, "Wait, Toddacis! Before you go, I must warn you that this will be a very dangerous journey. Once you get to Troy, it will not be easy for you to get the weapon of Apollo."

Todd was surprised by Homer's comment. He didn't understand why Homer would think he was going to try and take this 'weapon of Apollo.' He responded, "I'm not planning on taking anything from Troy."

Homer realized he had revealed too much. He said, "I am sorry, Toddacis. I mistook your reasons. Or perhaps you do not yet know your own reasons for being here."

Todd was stunned. How could Homer know or understand what was going on. Todd was reluctant to respond. He didn't want to show his uncertainty so he simply replied, "Again, thank you for the directions, Homer. Good bye."

Todd took Natilia by the arm and they turned to walk away, but Homer stopped them once more. He said, "Wait, Toddacis! Before you leave I have some very good armor to help you on the journey you are about to undertake this day."

Todd and Natilia turned back to Homer and saw sitting in front of him was a gold suit of armor. There was a golden body plate and a pair of golden shin guards. They were similar to Todd's Roman body plate and the shin guards he wore underneath his greaves. There was also a golden Greek helmet, a golden square shield, and a golden short sword.

Todd was surprised to see an entire set of armor made of gold. He asked, "This is extraordinary armor, Homer. Why are you giving us this incredible gift?"

Homer smiled and looked at Natilia who was lightly armed. He answered, "Your lady needs better armor than just a helmet. She should have magnificent armor to accompany her beauty."

Natilia was surprised to hear that the beautiful golden armor was for her. She went over to it and touched its smooth shiny surface. Natilia turned to Homer and said, "Thank you very much, Homer. The gods will surely reward you for this great gift and the kind deed you have done." She began to gather up the golden armor.

Homer was pleased to have her thanks and blessings. He replied, "You are welcome, Natilia. You are very fortunate to have had a warrior from the gods choose you as a wife. You deserve no less than this stunning golden armor, for you are a very beautiful woman."

Natilia smiled at Homer's generous words. She brought some of the golden armor over to Todd so he could help her carry it. She again acknowledged Homer's kindness saying, "Thank you once more, Homer." She collected the rest of the golden armor and returned to Todd's side.

Todd was glad that Natilia finally had some proper armor, so that she would be protected. He said, "Homer, thank you for everything. You are a good and honorable man."

Homer was now anxious for them to depart. He hurried them along saying, "Go now! You must not be late to the gathering of armies at Sparta or you will not be able to get the bow of Apollo."

Todd agreed they needed to be on their way immediately. He replied, "Very well. Good bye, Homer. Thank you again."

Todd and Natilia both carried the golden armor as they made their way out of the city. They exited the south side of Athens. Once they were out of the city, Todd helped Natilia put on her new armor. He assisted her with the golden shin guards first, followed by the golden body plate, which she wore over top of her shirt. Todd took off Natilia's Roman helmet and put on the golden Greek helmet in its place.

Natilia strapped the golden shield to her left arm. It was very heavy and difficult for her to hold up. She would have to get used to its weight. She kept her gladius tied to her waist on her left side. Natilia gave the golden short sword to Todd, which he tied to his back to carry.

Todd surveyed Natilia in all her armor. The golden armor was impressive. She sparkled in the afternoon sun. He was also thankful to see her better protected. He said smiling, "You look like a golden warrior."

Natilia laughed and before she could say anything Todd stated, "We better keep moving. So we follow this road all the way to Sparta, right?"

Natilia recalled what Homer had told them. She answered, "Right, we follow this road. Then we should be to Sparta in two days' time."

Todd was glad to see that they both remembered correctly and were heading in the right direction. He said, "Alright, that sounds like good timing. Let's get going."

Natilia was very happy. She had beautiful new armor, and knew that Todd was proud of her and pleased to have her on this journey with him. But she simply replied, "Yes, let us be on our way, dear."

Todd and Natilia began to travel along the road Homer had directed for them to take all the way from midday until nightfall. Once nightfall came, they stopped on the side of the road to find a place to rest. A man stepped out from behind some bushes and asked, "Excuse me, do you need a place to sleep for the night? I have an extra tent set up here, for Homer told me to be expecting two travelers that would need my help along their journey. And that one of the travelers was a warrior of the gods. He said that this warrior has come to take back the bow of Apollo from the Trojans and return it to the gods."

Todd was surprised to hear this stranger's story. He wondered how Homer could have foretold that he was coming or believe that he was a warrior of the gods. Todd thought it was all very odd, but knew that they needed a place to sleep for the night. He replied, "Yes, we are the two travelers. And you are the man Homer told us would help us on our journey. He said that you are the son of a god."

Todd studied the man and noticed he was very big and muscular. He had no shirt on, only a garment covering him from his waist to his knees. The man also had a short iron sword on his waist on his left side.

The man began to grin after hearing Todd's answer. "Yes, that is me, I am the son of Zeus and my name is Hercules. I was instructed to help you throughout your journey to Troy and back. What might be your names, warriors of the gods?"

Todd was shocked to be meeting Hercules, since he thought he never actually lived in real life. He believed Hercules was only a myth. Todd, still awestruck, said to Hercules, "My name is Todd and this is my wife Natilia. We are grateful for your offer of a tent for tonight."

Hercules replied, "That is a strange name and I would say that name means Toddacis. Your wife looks as beautiful as a goddess in her golden armor. I would also say she is a graceful warrior willing to die to protect her love."

Natilia was impressed that Hercules understood what she was willing to do for Todd. She said, "Thank you, Hercules. Yes, I would die for Todd, for I love him very much."

Hercules was heartened to see their love for one another and was moved by it. "I see and understand that very well. Come, I have a tent made for you two for the night."

Todd and Natilia followed Hercules. He brought them to the campsite he'd setup. There was a small campfire with two tents nearby. As they approached the campfire,

Hercules said, "You are fortunate to arrive when you did, for I have just finished cooking some fresh deer meat if you would like some to eat along with clear water from the stream."

Todd and Natilia were very hungry since they had not eaten in a while. They sat down next to each other at the campfire. Todd replied, "Thank you for the meal, Hercules. I was starting to wonder if we would get any food tonight."

Hercules appreciated Todd's thanks. He said, "Worry no more since you are now here with me. Eat, drink and rest. We will set out for Sparta in the morning and make it there by the afternoon."

Todd was very grateful to Hercules for providing them with food and shelter. He said, "We are much obliged. Thank you again, Hercules, for all you have done for us."

After they all finished their meals, Todd and Natilia said goodnight to Hercules and went into their tent. They took off all their armor and got into the bed.

Natilia wrapped her arms around Todd and said to reassure him, "We will find out the reason for all of this, Todd. And soon be back home in Rome where we belong."

Natilia's comment made him think about his family back in his time and his new family and life in Roman Times. Todd missed them all and hoped he would one day be back home with one of his families. He replied, "Yes, we will find out why and then get back home. Don't worry, Natilia." He kissed her goodnight and gently rubbed her back.

As Todd was rubbing her back, Natilia said "I know we will, Todd. I am just glad to have you here with me and that I am not alone."

Todd was comforted by Natilia and was glad that she was there as well. He said, "Me too, Natilia, me too. I'm happy you are with me and that I am not alone." They fell asleep in each other's arms.

Todd and Natilia awoke the next morning to Hercules. He came into their tent and announced, "Wake up, you two. We need to get ready to leave now if we are to make it to Sparta by the afternoon this day."

Hercules left their tent and Todd and Natilia got out of bed. They gathered up their belongings and exited the tent. Once outside, they both put on all of their armor. Once they were fully armored, Todd helped Hercules take down the tents. After the tents were packed, Hercules put them on his back to carry them all the way to Sparta.

When everything was packed up and ready to go, the group headed out. As they traveled towards Sparta, the day got very hot. Todd spoke out with enthusiasm, "Well, at least it's the middle of the summer, and not winter and cold out."

Hercules laughed when he heard this and replied, "I like you, Toddacis. You think of the good things and not the bad."

Todd was pleased to see Hercules was taking a liking to him. He said, "Well, after all we've been through it's best to look for the positive, Hercules."

Hercules, who thought he was a warrior of the gods, said, "I can only begin to imagine all the things you both have gone through for the gods. I say we rest for the midday meal if you wish to, Toddacis, for it is about midday."

Todd was ready to take a break. They had been walking all morning. He said, "Sure, let's rest and have our midday meal." Natilia was tired and glad they would be stopping. She wondered what food Hercules might have and asked, "Hercules, what will we have for this meal today?"

Hercules felt bad for not having a lot of food. He answered, "It is not as good as our evening meal was yesterday. All we have is some bread, cheese, grapes, and water."

Natilia thought it would be plenty. She said, "Those are very good foods. I am sure we will enjoy them."

Todd was very hungry as they had traveled a long way. He said, "Yes, let's eat up."

As they sat and ate their midday meal, Todd thought about this amazing journey and meeting two famous people from Ancient Greece's history. He was presently having lunch with the legendary Hercules and just the other day he'd had a dialogue with Homer, the great philosopher and poet of Greece.

Once they were finished with their meal, Hercules, Todd and Natilia packed up and started towards Sparta once again.

Later in the day, the small group was pleased to see the city of Sparta in the distance. They stopped to take in a quick view of the city and immediately noticed scores of Greek soldiers gathered down near the harbor. There were many galley ships there also. So many that they stretched from the harbor all the way out to sea as far as the eye could see.

Hercules looked around, took in a deep breath and let it out. He said, "Yes, this is where we need to be."

Todd was amazed by the multitude of Greek soldiers gathered in the city. He asked, "So where to now, Hercules?"

Hercules sought Todd's approval suggesting, "I would like you to meet my good friend Odysseus. He may know where we are to go and what we are to do."

Todd agreed with Hercules' suggestion. He said, "Alright, that sounds like a good plan. Let's go find your friend."

Hercules nodded his head in acknowledgement. Todd took Natilia by the hand and they all headed toward the city gates.

As the party neared the city gates, the roadway became crowded with groups of soldiers. Todd felt like he was caught up in a whole army unit. They entered the city of Sparta in a wave of soldiers.

Once Todd, Natilia, and Hercules entered through the large gates, they moved to the side as the soldiers continued on. Todd looked around at the huge crowds of people in the city. He asked Hercules, "So where do you think would be the best place to find Odysseus in the city?"

Hercules thought for a second and answered, "I believe we should try the harbor first. He may be making ready his ship."

Todd thought this was a good idea. In a city this crowded, it would be difficult to locate someone. He said, "Sounds good to me. If he's not there, then I guess we could go to the palace and check there."

Todd and Natilia followed Hercules through the large crowds as he made his way to the harbor of Sparta. The streets were very crowded and difficult to maneuver through. It seemed like every step they took they would bump into someone by mistake.

When they finally arrived at the harbor, Hercules spotted Odysseus right away. He pointed to a man on a galley ship and said, "There he is. I knew he would be down here. Let's go meet him and see what he thinks we should do." They continued to move through the large groups of people milling about to get to Odysseus' ship.

Odysseus was standing aboard his ship busily giving orders to his men. Once they reached Odysseus' galley ship, Hercules ran up the ramp and greeted him. He asked, "Odysseus, my friend! It is good to see you! Are you well?"

Odysseus was surprised but happy to see Hercules in Sparta. He answered, "Hercules, son of Zeus! I am glad to see you! Yes, I am well. But why are you here?"

Hercules laughed vigorously after surprising Odysseus. He responded, "I have come with two others, Odysseus. One is a warrior of the gods who has come to take back the bow of Apollo from the city Troy. His name is Todd but I call him Toddacis. He is right here behind me."

Todd, still holding Natilia's hand, made his way up the ship's ramp. Hercules had just stepped aside, so Todd could meet Odysseus. He introduced himself saying, "Hi, I'm Todd. It's nice to meet you, Odysseus."

Odysseus eyed Todd and seemed to be sizing him up. He replied, "It is my honor to meet you, Toddacis. By the look of you, I would say you are a warrior from the gods, for your armor is rather strange. If I may ask, is this your wife in the golden armor?"

Todd looked at Natilia who stood beside him and answered, "Yes, this is my wife. Why do you ask?"

Odysseus said, "I thought she must be your wife, since she is equipped with stunning gold armor and she is lovelier than any of the most beautiful girls in all of Greece, if I may say. What is your name, enchanting lady?"

Natilia knew very well Odysseus was attempting to charm her. She answered confidently, "My name is Natilia. And you do not need to praise me, Odysseus, for I am only for my husband. If he found out that anyone touched me, by the gods, he would kill them very swiftly. Odysseus, sir, I would recommend you watch yourself in speaking with too much flattery towards me."

Odysseus laughed at Natilia's bold statement. He admired her honesty and loyalty to her husband. He responded, "I see. Beauty so soft and sweet, yet as hard and sharp as a blade, Toddacis, does she speak the truth?"

Todd fearlessly stated with a glare, "Yes, what she says is true. I will strike down anyone who touches her."

Hercules saw that things were starting to heat up. He quickly stepped in between them and said, "Come now, Odysseus. She is a woman of the gods and married. Let us discuss why we have come. We are here to seek your help in getting us to Troy. Can you assist us? The gods wish it to be so."

Odysseus laughed again realizing his friend was keen to change the conversation. He replied, "Of course, Hercules. I can help you get to Troy. Come, I will take you before King Agamemnon and see what he can do for you."

Hercules was relieved to hear that Odysseus was willing to help them. He said, "Very well, let us go to Agamemnon and see if he can help us with this goal that the gods have laid before us."

The group walked down the ships' ramp and made their way through the crowds until they arrived at the palace gates. The guards at the gates let them through without question, since Odysseus was with them. They proceeded into the palace.

As the visitors progressed through the palace, Todd noticed there was a long row of columns along their left and right sides. Odysseus led the way and they advanced all the way up to where King Agamemnon was sitting on his throne.

Agamemnon watched the small group as they approached. As they neared, he asked, "Odysseus, what brings you here? I was not expecting you yet. Unless you have come to tell me the ships are made ready and we can now make way to Troy to burn it to the ground."

Odysseus spoke carefully so he would not upset Agamemnon. He answered, "King Agamemnon, we are still preparing the ships and should be able to make way in short time. I have come to speak with you about another important matter."

Agamemnon was indignant to hear of 'another important matter.' He asked angrily, "What matter could be more important than getting our ships ready for war?!"

Now Odysseus was angered. He responded boldly, "A matter of the gods! The son of Zeus, Hercules, has come here with this warrior of the gods, Toddacis and his beautiful wife, Natilia to go to Troy with you and take back the bow of Apollo for the gods."

Agamemnon laughed at Odysseus' incredulous statement. He leaned forward from where he sat on his throne and said, "Odysseus, am I to believe you?! These three people here are from the gods themselves?! Incredible!" He thought for a moment, then stated further, "I will need a demonstration."

Odysseus knew that Hercules was of the gods. He answered with confidence, "Very well. Test them, but might I say if you test them, you are also testing the gods."

Agamemnon thought the whole thing was a charade anyway. He replied, "I will take my chances, Odysseus. You, there, Hercules, lift up that big stone chest filled with gold. This will be your test." Hercules grinned at Agamemnon and said, "As you wish, Agamemnon."

Hercules walked over to the large stone chest filled to the top with gold. He bent down and picked it up easily. He lifted it up over his head and then dropped it down on the ground. It hit the ground with such force that the lid popped open and gold coins went flying across the floor.

Hercules walked back over to the others standing in front of Agamemnon and stated, "I am the son of Zeus. Have I passed your test, Agamemnon?"

Agamemnon was surprised by Hercules' feat of might. He replied, "Yes, I trust in your power and strength. Now for you, warrior of the gods, I must say your armor is very odd. You will fight my two bodyguards here by my side. They are the very best besides that fool, Achilles. You will be tested by them. If you fail, you will be killed for your traitorous lie about being a warrior of the gods. Go now, fight!"

Todd tried to plead with Agamemnon, so he would not have to fight his bodyguards and kill innocent men. He said, "Don't do this, sir. It will not be a good outcome for your men. I will try not to kill them for their sake, but not for yours."

Agamemnon laughed at Todd's appeal as though it were futile. He answered, "We will see. Proceed!"

Todd shook his head in disappointment. He looked at the two guards who had edged closer and now seemed prepared to attack. He quickly observed their appearance and noted bronze shin guards, bronze body plates, and leather bracers on their wrists. He also noticed they carried bronze round shields and each had a spear in their hand with a short sword sheathed at their hip for backup.

Both of the guards charged him at the same time. They had their shields held up in front of them and their spears pointed at Todd.

Todd stood his ground and raised up his shield. When the two guards crashed into Todd's shield with their spears, one spear tip shattered and the other spear broke in half.

Now that their spears were destroyed, Todd drew out his sword. The two guards quickly recovered from the recoil of hitting Todd's shield and drew out their bronze short swords. They charged at Todd again with their swords ready to strike.

As they collided, Todd blocked one guard's sword with his shield and the sword bent on impact. At the same time, he blocked the other guard's sword with his own sword. Again the guard's sword bent on impact. Todd's equipment was much denser and stronger.

Todd quickly slashed at the second guard's shield and sliced the top part off. The blow also caught the guard's bronze chest plate and left a large gash in his armor. Todd then kicked the guard knocking him away.

The first guard came at Todd again, while he had his back turned. Since Todd couldn't see him coming, the guard thought he had the advantage and swiftly stabbed Todd in the back. The bent bronze sword was no match for Todd's steel body plate, so it did no damage.

Todd quickly spun around having felt the blow from behind. He stopped with his sword right against the guard's neck. The guard dropped his sword as he stared at Todd in terror through the bronze helmet he was wearing. Todd shoved him away and turned to Agamemnon angrily. He said, "There! Your guards have been defeated. Now do you believe Odysseus?"

Agamemnon stood up from his throne and said, "Well, well, Odysseus! It would seem the gods have come to my aid and would like to see Troy burned to the ground as well."

Odysseus tried to remind Agamemnon of their true mission. He advised, "They have come only to go to Troy and take back the bow of Apollo for the gods. Not to fight for you and destroy Troy. That is your undertaking, Agamemnon."

Agamemnon refused to listen to Odysseus. He said, "You may believe that, Odysseus. But I know they were truly sent here to help me crush Troy and see it burnt to the ground."

Odysseus decided it was no use trying to argue with Agamemnon. He asked, "You will help them in what it is they seek?"

Agamemnon sat back down on his throne and looked at Todd, Natilia, and Hercules. He answered with great joy, "Yes, I will help them. And Achilles will be the one they sail with to Troy. Tell him they are sent from me to aid him."

Odysseus knew very well why Agamemnon wanted Todd and the others to travel with Achilles. He said, "As you desire. I will take them to Achilles and share your message with him."

Agamemnon replied with a devious smile, "Good! Now go at once and then finish making ready the galleys for the war."

Odysseus gave a curt nod and turned away. He headed out of the palace followed by Todd, Natilia, and Hercules. They made their way back down towards the harbor.

As they proceeded through the crowded streets, Odysseus shared his thoughts. "I do not understand why Agamemnon and Achilles have such discord. Agamemnon is well aware Achilles hates the gods. I know that is why he has directed me to take you to him."

Hercules hoped to make the best of the situation. He stated, "We must do as Agamemnon has instructed. We will sail with Achilles. I believe I have heard tales of him. Is he a great warrior from the gods?"

Odysseus was good friends with Achilles and knew him quite well. He answered, "Yes, he is, but he dislikes the gods very much. I do not think he will mind taking you with him if I ask it as a courtesy for me."

Todd thought he knew what Agamemnon was trying to achieve. He said, "I guess Agamemnon is trying to make Achilles angry."

Odysseus confirmed Todd's suspicions. He replied, "Yes, I believe that is Agamemnon's purpose for sending you three to sail with Achilles."

Hercules tried to assure Odysseus that everything would be fine. He said, "I do not think Achilles will mind having us aboard if we keep to ourselves."

Todd knew from history and mythology that Achilles was wrathful and a great warrior. He stated, "I hope so. I know I'm going to try my best to stay on his good side. I don't need to fight anyone else today."

Odysseus was still unsure how Achilles would take the news, but he knew there would be no real fighting, since Agamemnon's guests were with him. He said, "Achilles would only engage you for training. We shall see how well he welcomes you three as we will reach his ship presently."

The group traveled back to the harbor through the busy city streets as they had their conversation. They continued on and made their way down the harbor walkway.

As they neared the end of the harbor, Odysseus stopped at the only galley ship with black sails. He hoped Achilles was in good spirits. Odysseus announced, "This is Achilles' ship. We shall see what he thinks of our unexpected visit."

The group proceeded up the ramp of Achilles' ship. As they made their way onboard, Achilles spotted Odysseus leading the small party and came over to greet him. He asked with a smile, "Odysseus, my friend! What brings you to my ship?"

Odysseus tried not to reveal too much too soon. He answered, "Achilles, I have come to bring these three people to you. They will be traveling with you to Troy."

Achilles knew Agamemnon must be behind this scheme. He asked, "And why would I be taking these three on my ship to Troy?"

Odysseus could tell Achilles already knew what must be going on. He answered truthfully, "King Agamemnon ordered me to bring them to you for travel on your ship to Troy. But I am asking you as my friend to do this kindness for me. Let me introduce you. This is my friend Hercules, the son of Zeus. He is traveling with the warrior of the gods, Toddacis and his lovely wife, Natilia in her beautiful golden armor. I only took them before Agamemnon to request they accompany us on this journey.

Achilles replied irritably, "And is this why they cannot travel with you to Troy? Agamemnon saw fit to put them with me and try to madden and provoke me. Is it not so?"

Odysseus knew Achilles recognized Agamemnon's plan. He answered, "Yes, I believe it is so. But I ask this of you, my friend. Please let them travel with you."

Achilles was frustrated by the situation. He growled, "Very well! I will do this for you, Odysseus. Not for that pig Agamemnon. And I will not let him treat me like a dog he can control for much longer!"

Odysseus understood Achilles' anger towards Agamemnon. He said, "Yes, I know very well he has no control over you. And I appreciate you doing this favor for me, Achilles."

Achilles was adamant that Agamemnon know he had no control over him. He responded, "Good! Be sure to tell Agamemnon that I am obliging your request and not submitting to his orders. My actions are for you, not for him."

Odysseus agreed saying, "I will let Agamemnon know. And please do take good care of my friend, Hercules and his companions, Toddacis and Natilia. They are all from the gods and dear to me."

Achilles laughed at Odysseus' concern. He said, "Odysseus, you and the gods are very amusing. Have no fear, for I will take good care of these passengers."

Odysseus was grateful for Achilles' reassurance. He replied, "Thank you, Achilles. I will take my leave." Odysseus turned away and started to make his way off the ship. He turned back and called out, "Journey well, my friends."

Odysseus headed down the ship's ramp leaving Hercules, Todd, and Natilia standing with Achilles. Todd hoped to stay on Achilles' good side. He said, "Thank you for taking us with you, Achilles."

Achilles replied crossly as if Todd had said something wrong. "Do not thank me for taking you. Odysseus deserves the thanks for asking me."

Todd persisted hoping to make it clear that they were grateful to Achilles. He stated, "Well, you had the option to say no to Odysseus' request, so please know we appreciate what you're doing for us."

Achilles thought about what Todd said and then replied more calmly, "Yes, that is true. Now I must tell you, there are no rooms for you to sleep inside of my ship. You must stay on the deck with my crew."

Todd could tell Achilles meant what he said. He replied, "That will be fine. Thanks, Achilles."

Achilles scoffed at Todd's continued thanks. He said, "Go find an area to keep yourselves out of the way and to sleep for the journey, for we should be departing soon."

Todd and Natilia walked away and headed to the very back of the ship. They made a bed for themselves out of the supplies Hercules had given them.

Hercules had followed them to the rear of the ship. He also made up a bed beside them. They sat down to rest once their area had been arranged.

A short time later, the bell of Sparta was rung. Achilles yelled, "Finally. Alright men, we make for Troy and immortality! Let us go and not waste another hour here!"

At once Achilles' men started rowing hard and fast. The ship began to move away from the harbor out into the sea.

Todd, Natilia, and Hercules stood up to watch their departure. They saw all the galley ships leaving port heading in the same direction towards Troy. Agamemnon's ship was at the head of the fleet.

As they reached the open sea, the fleet of ships no longer had to have the men row. This was because the wind was very strong that day. It blew intensely, as if the wind itself wanted them to make it to Troy quickly. With this advantage they made it very far in a matter of hours instead of days.

As dusk came, the fleet of galley ships did not rest. They all proceeded to sail forward under Agamemnon's orders.

Once it was completely dark out, Todd and Natilia decided to try and get some sleep. They stayed in their armor, since they had no privacy. They untied their swords and kept them by their sides along with their helmets.

As they tried to get comfortable for the night, Todd started to think again about why all this was happening to him. He told Natilia what was on his mind. "I don't know if all of these things happening to us are the actions of the gods, Natilia."

Natilia looked at him confused and asked, "What do you mean, Todd?" Todd recalled what he had found when they were in Feudal Japan. He answered, "Well, the sword we took from Hojo is not from that time or your time or from my time either."

Natilia thought it still must be the gods' will. She said, "It is not from any of our places or times. It is from the gods and of the gods. That is why you have never seen it before, Todd."

Todd thought she could be right, but then he remembered what he'd seen on the bottom – UGA. What did UGA stand for? Perhaps it could be United Gods Alliance or United G... It was yet another mystery to try and figure out. Todd decided he was too tired to dwell on it tonight. He said, "You may be right, Natilia. But let's not worry about it tonight."

Natilia saw that he was troubled thinking about it. She gave him a kiss and said, "Todd, do not concern yourself over it. Let's just sleep and see what the next day brings us."

Todd agreed and kissed her goodnight. He fell asleep with his hand clasped in Natilia's.

In the morning, Todd awoke to Hercules saying, "Come Toddacis. It is morning and we will arrive at Troy very soon. But for now we are going to eat our morning meal."

Todd woke Natilia who was still at his side. He said, "Good morning, dear. Time to get up, they have breakfast ready for us." She rubbed her eyes and asked, "How much longer until we are at Troy, Todd?"

Todd stood up. He looked out to sea and at the sun low in the sky. He answered, "My guess is by midday. But I don't know for sure."

Todd tied his sword around his waist. Natilia stood up and tied on her sword as well. They went over to Hercules, who was already eating his breakfast.

When Hercules noticed them approaching, he said, "It is about time you two joined me. We have a number of fresh fish that were caught last night, bread and cheese. As for drinks, we have some good Spartan wine. Not nearly as fine as the wine of the gods, but it should satisfy."

Todd was hungry and looked forward to a good meal. He replied, "That sounds great, Hercules, but I don't drink wine, only water. Do you have any water? And how much food is there, enough for everyone?"

Hercules was shocked to learn that Todd did not drink wine. He responded, "You do not drink wine?! Well, that is fine, I suppose. Yes, we do have water. And there is plenty of food for all the men, Toddacis."

Todd was glad to hear there was ample food for everyone to eat. He said looking around the ship deck, "Good. Thank you, Hercules. Have you seen Achilles? Do you know where he is?"

Hercules pointed towards the hull of the ship and mumbled with a mouthful of bread, "He is in the storage area of the ship. You will find him there."

Todd hoped to meet with Achilles to try and get on better terms with him. He replied, "Very well. I will go see him after our meal." Todd sat down beside Natilia, who had already taken a seat near Hercules, and they enjoyed a good breakfast.

When Todd finished eating, he got up and picked up his helmet and shield. Natilia asked quickly, "Todd, where are you going?"

Todd answered, "I'm going to talk to Achilles. Are you coming with me?" Natilia was relieved he asked her to come. She replied, "Yes, for a moment I thought you were going to leave me here alone."

Todd was surprised by Natilia's comment. He said, "Well, I thought you would know to follow me. You can't think I would ever leave you alone here."

Natilia got up and took hold of Todd's hand. She replied with a smile, "Good. Do not ever leave me alone. And do not forget you still need to continue with my training."

Todd said, "Yes, I know I promised. We will take it up again soon."

Todd and Natilia walked hand in hand down to the storage area of the ship. When they entered the storage area, Todd saw Achilles engaged in training.

Todd didn't really know what to say, but thought he'd start with a greeting. He called out, "Hey, Achilles! How are you today?"

Achilles suddenly stopped training and looked at Todd annoyed. He answered gruffly, "I was doing very well until I was interrupted."

Todd realized Achilles was dead set on training and thought maybe that is how he could break the ice. He said, "I'm sorry, Achilles. I was just going to ask if you would like to train with me."

Achilles was surprised by Todd's suggestion. He replied, "Truly? Well...yes, let us train together. Do you have your sword?"

Todd was glad to see he might be getting on Achilles' good side. He answered, "Yes, I do. It's right here. Are you ready to duel now?"

Natilia was still standing with Todd holding his hand. Achilles looked at her and asked, "What of your wife, is she going to be leaving us now?"

Todd knew Achilles probably didn't want Natilia to stay but he did. He answered, "No, she will watch to learn more of the way of the sword."

Achilles was surprised by this but didn't really care either way. He simply replied, "Very well. We can start."

Todd was thrilled to think he was about to be dueling with the famous Achilles from Greek mythology. He said with a look of glee on his face, "This should be fun!" Todd studied Achilles, noticing his all black body plate, shin guards and arm guards.

Achilles put on his black Greek helmet. In his left hand, he held his black round shield and in his right, his iron short sword.

Todd was already dressed in all of his armor. Now that they were both ready, Todd let go of Natilia's hand and they began to fight.

Todd raised his shield as did Achilles. They both charged at one another, slamming into each other's shields. After rebounding, Todd quickly raised his sword.

Achilles matched his movement, raising his own sword. They both swung at each other at the same time and hit their swords together. Both of them pushed hard against one another's swords.

When Todd's and Achilles' arms grew tired from holding each other back with their swords, they pushed off one another and continued to duel. They battled on for a while and Natilia watched quietly from the side. Todd won all the duels, except once or twice Achilles came very close to beating him.

They grew fatigued from their many rounds of dueling and decided to stop. Achilles, Todd, and Natilia went back up to the ship's deck to get some fresh air and rest.

Todd stood near the railing of the ship with Natilia by his side. He took off his helmet and set it against his shield that was leaning against the ship deck's side wall. Todd stood gazing out to sea and took a deep breath. He knew he needed to relax and get in the right frame of mind to do battle once they arrived at Troy.

Achilles came over and stood beside Todd. He asked, "Where did you learn to fight so well, Toddacis? I have never seen fighting such as that in my life."

Todd recalled all the great people he'd met that had trained him to be an even better fighter. He answered, "Well, I was trained by many good people, but I have not seen them in a long time. Hopefully I will be able to see them again soon."

Achilles didn't know Todd was referring to people from his travels in time. He stated, "They must be great warriors, Toddacis." Todd thought of Quintius and Julius and replied a little sadly, "Yes, they are very great warriors and have kind hearts as well."

Natilia had heard Todd's and Achilles' conversation and knew Todd was talking about her father and Julius. She suddenly felt deeply homesick. She put her hand on top of Todd's resting on the ship's edge and said, "We will see them again soon, Todd. Do not worry, for I know somehow it will be so."

Todd placed his other hand over top of Natilia's and looked into her eyes. He saw a tear run down her cheek. Todd wiped away her tear and said, "We will see them again, Natilia. We will."

Todd wrapped an arm around Natilia's shoulder to comfort her. Achilles wondered about their sadness and asked "Are they lost to you, Toddacis?"

Todd was not really sure how to reply. He answered, "Yes and no. They are where we cannot reach them, but they are still in our hearts, so not completely lost to us."

Achilles thought perhaps Todd meant they had passed away or disappeared. He stated, "You are a brave man, Toddacis, for you go on without them. I can tell it is in hope of finding them, if I am correct."

Todd replied, "Yes, that is right and we will find them again soon." He squeezed Natilia's shoulder and gave her a reassuring smile.

Achilles also encouraged them to keep up their faith saying, "I am sure you will." He turned at hearing commotion at the head of the boat. He was excited to see the beaches of Troy.

Achilles quickly ran to the head of the ship and yelled to the men, "Every man row, and row fast! We are taking the beaches of Troy and we will become immortals for it! You are all lions! Let us go and take the beaches of Troy and make them ours!"

Todd and Natilia hurriedly put on their helmets and picked up their shields. Now fully armored, they moved to the front of the ship and found Achilles standing with Hercules.

Their ship was ahead of the whole Greek fleet. A soldier came up to Achilles and asked, "My Lord, are we not going to wait for Agamemnon?"

Achilles turned to the soldier and said with a malicious smile, "You serve me, not Agamemnon, am I right?" The soldier realized his mistake and immediately replied, "Yes, my Lord. I am sorry."

Achilles said, "It is fine. Now gear up and be ready for our arrival!" He yelled out to all his men, "Everyone, stop rowing and gear up now!"

The men stopped rowing and Todd noticed the galley continued to move forward towards the shore at good speed with the wind from the sails.

As the ship was about to hit the shore, all the soldiers were geared up and ready to disembark. As they neared the beach, Achilles boosted their moral by yelling, "Go men! Let us take our immortality for ourselves!" The ship hit hard on the shores of Troy and the soldiers quickly jumped out.

As they came ashore, some of the soldiers got hit by arrows and were killed on the spot. Todd and Natilia jumped off the ship together and landed in the sand softly. They both held their shields up and walked slowly forward side by side. The archers continued shooting at the landing army.

Hercules jumped out of the ship after Todd and Natilia. Once he hit the sand, he ran up behind them to take cover as they moved forward towards the archers.

Todd looked over at Achilles and his group of men. He saw they had made a boxlike shape out of their shields and were all connected together as one. He noticed they were also moving forward at a similar pace, slowly heading towards the Trojan archers.

As Todd advanced forward with Natilia and Hercules, he could feel the arrows impacting his shield even harder. He knew they were very close to the archers now.

Hercules also sensed they were nearing the archers. He swiftly darted around Todd and Natilia, drawing out his short sword. Hercules immediately started slashing down the archers, before they could even draw their swords in defense.

After Hercules took off, Todd and Natilia both drew out their swords and ran after him. They sprinted to the top of a small sand hill and attacked the archers alongside of Hercules. Many archers perished at their hands.

Meanwhile, Achilles and his men assaulted another group of archers down the beach. As the Trojan archers dropped one after another, the remainder began to flee toward the temple of Apollo.

When the attackers noticed the archers were escaping, they pursued them towards the temple of Apollo. Some of the archers took shelter in the temple, while the others retreated to the city of Troy.

Achilles reached the doorway to the temple first and struck down the temple guards unassisted. His men arrived and sought out the archers hiding inside.

Todd, Natilia, and Hercules followed Achilles and his men to the temple of Apollo. When they reached the temple, they found Achilles' men looting the gold and silver icons and furnishings. Todd, with Natilia close by, stepped out of the temple doorway and looked toward the city of Troy.

They saw a group of horsemen riding towards them. Todd and Natilia quickly reentered the temple to join the others. Natilia said, "That was a lot of horsemen, Todd. Will we be able to hold them off?"

Todd answered confidently, "Yes, we will, Natilia. Just be prepared when they arrive, ok?"

Natilia knew she could trust in him. She replied boldly, "I am ready. I will stay with you and fight by your side."

Todd smiled and said, "Good! I'll be right back."

Todd hastily sought out Achilles. He found him and announced, "Achilles, there is a large group of horsemen riding towards the temple."

Achilles was undisturbed by this news and eager to fight. He said, "Good, let them come. We will kill them all here and now."

As they heard the horsemen arrive outside, Achilles' men hid in the dark corners of the temple and laid in wait to ambush the Trojan horsemen. Todd and Natilia were standing side by side in their own dark corner waiting to strike the Trojans. Hercules did the same in the shadows of an alcove across from Todd and Natilia.

The Trojan horseman entered the temple slowly. Achilles' men waited patiently for all the Trojans to enter. Once the Trojans were all inside the temple, the soldiers jumped out of their dark hiding places and attacked.

Achilles' men took out most of the Trojans. Todd killed many himself quickly with his katana and Natilia did the same with her gladius.

When all the Trojans were slain, Achilles' men let out a cheer of victory. Todd noticed Achilles was nowhere in sight. He grabbed Natilia's hand and said, "Let's find Achilles."

When they came upon Achilles near the temple entrance, they found him standing face to face, talking with a Trojan soldier.

Achilles' men had the two of them surrounded. Achilles said, "Go home, Hector, Prince of Troy. Be with your wife before we do war. It is not time for your death this day but later you will die."

Hector replied angrily, "You killed innocent people today. I will remember that when the time comes, Achilles."

Hector turned and exited the temple. He jumped up onto his horse and rode off into the distance back toward the city of Troy.

After seeing Achilles let Hector go, one of his soldiers confused by his actions asked, "My Lord, you let...you let him go?!" Achilles didn't look at the soldier. He continued watching Hector ride off and answered, "It is too soon for his death."

Achilles turned and headed back into the recesses of the temple to look for the bow of Apollo. After a short time, Achilles came back to the entrance and over to Todd. He said "I am sorry, Toddacis. The bow of Apollo is not in this temple. It must be somewhere inside the city of Troy."

Todd knew they would make it into the city of Troy. He answered positively, "No problem, Achilles. We will get it when we get into the city."

Achilles was surprised by Todd's conviction. He said, "You seem to have great faith that we will make it into the city of Troy, even with their large walls."

Todd knew how they would breach the city walls. He answered with a smile, "Let's just say I have a good feeling it will happen."

The other ships started to arrive on the beach so Todd, Natilia, and the rest of the first landing party headed back to the shoreline. Todd found Odysseus and his ship landed. He went up to him and said, "Well, we have taken the beach in a matter of minutes. And we took the temple of Apollo as well. But the bow of Apollo was not there."

Odysseus was surprised to hear that the bow was not in the temple. He said, "That is very strange, for the bow is normally in the temple. Perhaps the Trojans are using it for some purpose, but I do not know what that might be."

Achilles walked by and called out, "Odysseus, if you sailed any slower, you would have missed the war." Odysseus chuckled at Achilles' good-natured mocking. He yelled back as Achilles continued walking, "Ah! I do not mind missing the start! So long as I am here for the end, that is what really matters, Achilles!" By the time he'd finished his reply, Achilles had already disappeared into a crowd of soldiers.

Odysseus returned to unloading his ship and Todd and Natilia went to find Achilles' campsite. They would be staying with Achilles and his men during the siege of Troy. They found Achilles had chosen a spot that was far away from the rest of the army of Greeks.

Todd and Natilia were also pleased to learn a large tent had already been put up for them. They entered the tent and found Hercules seated inside.

Hercules stood and said, "You two have finally come. Do not worry, for I am only here to share a meal of victory with you both, as we all did fight very greatly today."

Todd was glad to see Hercules and appreciated his kind gesture. He replied, "Yes, we did fight well today. It would be our pleasure to have you join us for the midday meal."

Natilia was also happy to see Hercules. She said, "Yes, of course, we greatly enjoy your company, Hercules."

Hercules smiled and responded, "Ah. You are both too kind. Come and sit, let us eat this great food as a celebration for our triumph this day. We have fresh fish, salted pork, and some good cheese, almost a whole wheel this time, as well as some sweet grapes and soft bread. And I took the honor of getting you some good milk and fresh water, Toddacis, just for you and your lovely wife."

Todd was impressed by the feast Hercules had put together for them. He and Natilia sat down and Hercules took his seat again. Todd said, "Thank you, Hercules. This is amazing."

They started to dig in, piling food on their plates. Natilia laughed at Hercules' over eagerness and said, "Hercules, be sure to save some for us." They all laughed and enjoyed a delicious meal.

Shortly after they finished their midday meal, Achilles came storming back into the camp. Seeing how mad he was, Todd knew right away it was King Agamemnon that must have angered him so much.

Todd and Natilia made their way over to Achilles to find out what was troubling him and what might be their next plan of action. Achilles had come out of his tent and saw them approaching. He said, "We are not going to help Agamemnon take the gates of Troy. He can do that himself, Toddacis. I am sorry but he has gone too far this time, even for me."

Todd understood Achilles' resentment. He replied, "That's fine, Achilles, I understand. But we should at least go watch and see how badly he fails."

Achilles was gratified by Todd's comment. He invited Todd and Natilia into his tent.

Achilles offered them a seat and asked, "You would still wish to see the battle then?" Todd was glad to see he had made Achilles feel a little better about the situation. He answered, "Yes, of course, I would."

Natilia thought of a useful battle strategy and said, "And we can look for any weaknesses the Trojans may have as Agamemnon attacks the gates." Todd smiled broadly at her for making this excellent suggestion.

Achilles also liked the sound of this plan. He said, "Very well. It is settled. We will go and see if the Trojans have any disadvantages that we can use against them."

Todd agreed and said, "Sounds good. So when Agamemnon sets out, we will only go to watch and see how they do."

Achilles confirmed that they would not provide any assistance. He replied, "Yes, as you stated, for I will not help him after what he has done to me this day."

Todd asked, "If I may ask, what did Agamemnon do to you, Achilles?" Achilles hesitated, looking both angry and sad. He answered, "He took a beautiful woman from me. She was one of the Apollo maidens from the temple we seized this morning. The men gave her to me as a prize from the plundering of the temple. Her beauty is without equal and her charm and intelligence is enchanting. I adore her, Toddacis."

Todd thought about how he felt when he first laid eyes on his wife, Natilia. He said, "To find an amazing woman is a great thing and even better if the right one marries you."

Achilles replied with sadness, "She is the most magnificent woman I ever met in my life. I fear I may never see her again."

Todd went over to Achilles and placed a hand on his shoulder. He said, "Don't say that Achilles. I think you will see her again and get to be together as you desire."

Achilles smiled at Todd's reassurance. He replied, "I must believe I will see her once more, for a warrior of the gods has told me it is so."

Todd disregarded his 'warrior of the gods' comment and simply said, "Yes, you will see her again, Achilles. Don't worry. Right now we need to be ready to depart to go watch the battle at Troy's front walls."

Achilles nodded in agreement, jumped up, and headed out of the tent. Todd got up to leave as well, but Natilia grabbed his arm stopping him. She pulled him close to her, hugging him tightly and gave him a kiss. Natilia said "Todd, your words to Achilles were so thoughtful. And what you said about finding the right person to marry was touching." She smiled and gave him another kiss.

Todd was pleased to make Natilia happy. He said, "I was only telling him the truth, Natilia. I am very fortunate to be married to you and love you so very much, my dear." He softly touched her face and gave her a gentle kiss.

Natilia cherished Todd's love and tenderness. She replied, "I love you too, Todd. I could not have picked a better man than you to spend my life with."

Todd smiled at her and said, "Me too, Natilia. Now let's go prepare to depart for Troy. I guess we'll need to figure out a way to get into the city and take the bow of Apollo from the Trojans. At least, I think that's our reason for being here…"

Natilia replied, "That sounds like a good plan to me. Let us go." Todd and Natilia exited the tent and saw Achilles standing nearby. His soldiers were hurrying around preparing for battle, even though they were just going to observe the fight.

Achilles motioned to Todd and Natilia to come over. They approached him and he advised, "The Greeks are heading to the city wall now, Toddacis. You and your wife should get your helmets and shields, just in case."

Todd knew all too well they might need their full protection. He responded, "We were just headed for them now. Thanks, Achilles."

Todd and Natilia hurried back to their tent and retrieved their shields and helmets. Now that they were fully armored, they headed back over to Achilles and waited for the group's departure.

Hercules joined the waiting group as well. After a few minutes, Hercules asked impatiently, "Are we going to go see this fight or just stand around all day?"

Achilles laughed then called out to his troops, "Alright men! Let's head to the hill, where we can watch the battle from a good vantage point!"

Hercules was pleased to be moving out. He stated loudly, "Alright! I have been waiting for something fun all afternoon." Achilles smiled and shook his head at Hercules' enthusiasm.

When Achilles' party reached the hill top, they could see the Greek army moving towards the city wall. They also saw a large group of Trojan soldiers waiting to defend the city. Todd was shocked by the enormous height of the walls of Troy.

Natilia stared at the city and softly said to Todd, "This city was never here during the Roman Republic." Todd knew the fate of Troy. He whispered to her so the others nearby could not hear him, "That's because this place is going to be burned down and totally destroyed by the Greek army."

Natilia was surprised to hear this outcome. She asked, "Are they going to break down the walls, Todd?" He answered, "No, they will not be attacking the walls. They get in a different way with the help of Odysseus. His cunning mind comes up with a trick and the Trojans let the Greeks into Troy."

Now Natilia was shocked. She asked, "But how? How could he trick them into letting their enemy in?"

Todd didn't want to ruin the surprise for her. He smiled and said quietly, "You will see very soon, Natilia. For now, let's just watch this fight the Greeks are going to lose." Natilia nodded in agreement.

Todd and Natilia watched as the two armies stood facing each other with a large gap between them. Two soldiers met in the middle of the gap and started to combat each other. Todd couldn't make out who they were or if he knew them.

As the two men continued to clash, one of them fell but was not killed by the other fighter. The fallen man, a Trojan, started to crawl toward another Trojan soldier standing nearby. The Greek fighter pursued the crawling man but was quickly killed by the standing Trojan soldier as he neared the crawling Trojan.

Agamemnon yelled out 'Charge!!!!' after the Greek fighter was killed. The two Trojans hurried back into the army of Trojan soldiers as the Greek forces charged at them.

After the Greeks started to charge, they heard Hector shout, 'Fire the Bow of Apollo!!' A moment later, they saw a thin blue blast come from the top of the wall and blow away a large group of Greek soldiers. The soldiers seemed to disintegrate when they were hit by the blue flash.

Todd immediately thought it must be some kind of plasma gun or cannon. This was very strange, and made the situation extremely difficult and dangerous. Todd knew he needed to figure out something and quick. He grabbed Natilia's hand and quietly led her away from the rest of the group watching the battle. They slipped away unseen. The Trojans fired the gun five more times at the Greeks until they started to retreat.

During the fighting, Todd and Natilia stealthily made their way around to the side of the city wall unobserved. They searched along the wall for a possible way in and discovered a hole dug in the ground. It was right at a small broken section of the wall and looked big enough to crawl through.

Todd decided to give it a try and made his way into Troy. He waved his hand under the wall and Natilia crawled through as well. They entered the city unnoticed by the Trojans.

Todd and Natilia tried to stay out of sight by standing behind an archway near where they had entered the city. Todd knew they had to figure out a plan to steal the Bow of Apollo, as the Trojans called it, but he was pretty sure it was really some type of plasma cannon.

Todd whispered to Natilia, "We need to come up with some way of taking the Bow of Apollo without the Trojans finding out." Natilia had been peeking out from behind the archway to scrutinize the city. She replied, "I think that will be very hard, for I am sure they guard it well, since it is a weapon of the gods."

Todd asked, "I know but we still have to come up with something since we've made it into the city. When do you think would be the best time to try and take it?"

Natilia thought for a moment then responded, "I do not know how, but I would say in the darkness at night would be the best time to try."

Todd smiled and said, "Yes, very smart. We'll wait for nightfall and can figure out a plan in the meantime. But for now we need to come up with a place to hide or some way to blend in."

Natilia had spotted somewhere they could keep out of sight. She advised, "I don't think we'll blend in very well in our armor, but I think I have a place for us to hide."

Todd asked, "Great! What do you have in mind?"

Natilia replied pointing, "Those bushes over there can conceal us until nightfall comes. Then under cover of night we can steal the Bow of Apollo and make our escape."

Todd was impressed by her idea. He replied, "That is why I love you so much, Natilia. You are very clever, and beautiful too. Now let's go get behind those bushes, before we are seen standing here."

Todd and Natilia cautiously made their way over to the large bushes and took cover behind them. Then they waited patiently for nightfall.

It was starting to grow dark so Natilia asked quietly, "Have you decided on a plan, Todd?" Todd whispered his reply, "I think our best bet is to simply sneak up to the city wall, take out the guards, and swipe the Bow of Apollo. Once we have it, we'll rush back here and sneak out the way we came in...under the wall. Then we'll need to hurry back to camp in case we need any support from Achilles or Hercules."

Natilia agreed with Todd's scheme. She said "Yes, that does sound like a good option. We will need to be quick and do our best to go unnoticed."

It was now dark out except for some dim light from the full moon and torches that lit the streets of Troy. Todd whispered, "Ok, let's go get the Bow of Apollo."

Natilia nodded her head in confirmation. Todd made sure there was no one nearby and he and Natilia came out from behind the bushes.

Todd and Natilia moved ahead toward the front wall. They had seen the plasma cannon up on the front wall near the main gate and needed to find an access door that would lead them up top. As they advanced along the wall, they tried their best to stay in the shadows of the buildings and houses.

As they grew near to the main gate, Todd spotted a single guard standing at a doorway. He knew this must be the way up onto the top of the wall. The guard had on a helmet, body plate, and shin guards all in silver. He held a square silver shield that had a yellow sun painted in its middle, and a silver sword strapped on his waist.

Todd whispered to Natilia, "Watch closely. I'm going to act quickly and take out this Trojan guard."

Natilia was always worried for Todd's safety. She said, "Ok, but please be careful, Todd."

Todd smiled and replied, "Hey, it's me, of course I'll be careful." Natilia said to herself as Todd moved away, 'And that is what worries me.'

Todd moved towards the guard slowly, making his way along the wall. He stopped and soundlessly placed his shield on the ground. He drew out his sword and stealthily snuck up behind the guard.

Todd grabbed the Trojan guard around the head, covering his mouth, and cut his throat in one swift motion. Then he quietly laid his lifeless body down on the ground.

Todd signaled for Natilia to come over to him. When she reached him he asked, "Did you see what I did and how I did it?"

Natilia was surprised and impressed by how quickly he had dispatched the guard. She advised, "Yes, I saw it. That was very skillful, Todd."

Todd replied, "Unfortunately, we needed him out of the way, so I wanted to be sure you saw this deadly move in case you every need it in the future. Now let's move quickly before the next watch comes by and finds this guard dead."

Todd picked up his shield. He and Natilia advanced through the doorway to go up on top of the wall. They went up the stairs and came to a landing and a doorway. Todd glanced out and didn't see the Bow of Apollo. He knew they hadn't yet reached the area where they'd seen the Trojans firing the weapon.

Todd and Natilia continued up and came to another landing and doorway. They hid in the dark corners of the landing and Todd took a quick look out to the wall. He saw four guards protecting the plasma cannon. Todd whispered to Natilia, "I see only four Trojan guards protecting the Bow of Apollo. You take the two on the right and I'll take the two on the left, alright?"

Natilia replied, "Yes, the two on the right. I will not let you down, Todd."

Todd looked at Natilia with a smile and said, "I know you will do very well, Natilia." They both quietly drew out their swords and were ready to attack. Todd whispered, "Now" and they rushed at the four guards.

Todd reached the first guard who had his back to him and used the same deadly move as he used before on the guard below. He grabbed him around the head, covering his mouth, and slashed his throat. The guard fell to the ground and landed on his back.

The other guard near Todd saw the first guard fall and started to raise the alarm. He drew his silver sword and lunged at Todd. Todd blocked the guard's sword strike with his shield. As the guard recoiled from hitting Todd's shield, Todd swung his sword over the guard's square silver shield and cut off his arm. The guard's dismembered arm dropped to the ground with his shield still attached to it. Todd swung another fierce blow and cut off the Trojan's head to quiet his screams.

At the same time, Natilia charged at the two guards she was to handle. She brutally stabbed her sword into the neck of one guard with his back to her. She quickly drew out her sword and the guard dropped to the ground.

The other guard turned on Natilia and swung his sword at her. She swiftly blocked his blow with her own sword and held him back with all her might. Natilia felt him starting to overpower her, so she shoved her shield at him knocking him back. As the guard fell back, he lost his footing and tumbled over the wall. He fell into the city, screaming until he slammed into the ground.

Now that all four guards were dead, Todd and Natilia stood alone with the plasma gun. Todd said, "Since the whole city has heard we're here, we need to grab the Bow of Apollo and get the heck out of Troy! We'll probably run into trouble getting back to our way out under the wall. You'll need to be ready for anything and ready to fight, ok?"

Natilia understood it was urgent they leave Troy and knew it would be difficult. She replied, "Yes, I'm ready to fight. Let's go."

Todd quickly sheathed his sword back in its holder around his waist and picked up the plasma gun. The gun was the shape of a rifle and as long as his arm. It looked like a crossbow down at the end of the barrel. They sprinted back to the doorway and down the stairs. They exited the ground level door where the Trojan guard lay dead.

Todd and Natilia quickly retreated back along the wall. They could hear the Trojan soldiers coming their way in pursuit. Natilia led the way and Todd kept checking behind for their pursuers. Natilia saw they were nearing their hiding place and advised, "Todd, I see the bushes up ahead!" Todd replied, "Good, now let's get to the hole!"

Just then an arrow struck the wall right behind Todd's head. Trojan archers on the wall had spotted them trying to escape with the Bow of Apollo and were taking aim.

Todd yelled, "Get your shield up! Keep moving! We're almost there!" The archers opened fire with several arrows hitting Todd's and Natilia's shields.

Todd and Natilia reached their escape hole out of the city. Todd told her, "I'll cover you. Tie your shield on your back and go through now!" Natilia tied her shield to her back and started crawling through the hole, as Todd used his shield to cover both of them.

The archers continued to rain arrows down on the intruders. Several were stuck in Todd's shield, while many bounced off. Todd crouched down, dropped the gun, and maneuvered getting his shield tied to his back, all while keeping the shield up to cover himself. He grabbed the gun and started to climb through the hole.

As Todd advanced into the hole, he could hear the Trojan soldiers getting close. The archers continued to fire on him. One of the archer's arrows met its mark and caught him in the left calf muscle as he moved forward. Todd continued to crawl through to the other side of the wall.

As Todd came out from under the wall, Natilia was there holding up her shield to cover them. She called out, "Hurry, Todd!! More archers have arrived on the wall!"

Todd scrambled out under Natilia's shield. He said, "We need to start running. I want you in front of me. Keep your shield up and once we get some distance. keep it tied to your back so it will block most of the arrows." Natilia quickly agreed, "Ok, let's go or we will die here!"

Todd and Natilia took off running away from the city walls. A barrage of arrows assailed them. Many went whizzing by and several struck their shields and armor.

As Todd and Natilia got further away from the walls, the arrows were no longer coming close to them. They continued to run until they reached the hill, where they had watched the battle with Achilles and Hercules.

They stopped at the hill to rest for a minute and catch their breath. The arrow in Todd's calf muscle also needed some attention. Natilia could tell it was bothering him and wanted to get it out. She said, "Todd, please let me take a quick look at your leg."

Todd sat down and replied, "It's not so bad. It just started to ache a little since we were running."

Natilia was concerned for his welfare. She insisted, "I still want to look at it now and make sure you are well, Todd."

Todd agreed, "Okay, check it fast. Then we need to get moving."

Natilia dislodged the arrow and pushed up Todd's green jade armor to his knee. She was thankful to see he was only bleeding slightly. There was a small cut and a reddish-purple mark from the impact.

Natilia advised, "You were very lucky this time. The arrow only gave you a small cut, but you will have a big bruise."

Todd said, "So it was just getting difficult to run, because the muscle's badly bruised. That's a relief."

Natilia asked, "Yes, I am grateful it is not a bad injury. Now should we make our way back to the camp?"

Todd looked back at the city of Troy. He saw a large group of soldiers exiting through the gates. He replied, "Uh...yeah, time to go now!"

Natilia heard the urgency in his voice. She asked, "What is it, Todd?" Todd, still watching the army headed towards them, answered, "Umm...the whole Trojan army."

Natilia now looked back at the city of Troy and saw the sizable army moving their way. She was shocked to think this large number of Trojans was coming after them. Natilia stated, "Yes, we must get back to the Greek camp as quickly as we can."

Todd rapidly pushed his leg jade armor back into place and jumped up. He said, "I couldn't agree more. Let's go!" They speedily ran all the way back to the camp.

Todd and Natilia entered their tent winded and breathing heavily from the long run. Hercules, who was laying down sleeping, awoke from their noisy entrance and jumped up. He asked, "Where have you two been, Toddacis? We wondered where you might have gone. We thought perhaps you fled from the field of battle. But look, I see you have brought back something that appears to be the Bow of Apollo."

Todd explained where they had been. He said, "Hercules, we would never run from the battlefield. What we did was find a way into the city of Troy by going through a hole under the wall. Yes, this is the Bow of Apollo. We stole it. Then escaped from the city the way we came in, after being chased down. But now they know about the hole, so I'm sure it will be closed up."

Natilia shared more of the story. She added, "Yes, they chased us down and many archers fired endless arrows upon us in the city and outside of the walls. We only just made it out of there alive. But we have the Bow of Apollo."

Hercules was impressed by their plan and actions. He said, "That was a very clever idea. While everyone was busy watching the battle, and it was a fierce one, you two found a way into the city unnoticed. Well done!"

Todd, still trying to catch his breath, said, "Yes, that's what we did. Thanks, Hercules."

Suddenly the alarm was raised down near all the Greek camps. The Trojans were attacking. Hercules reacted immediately and took off to join the fight.

Todd and Natilia stayed behind to rest. They were exhausted after their frenzied getaway.

Todd rested for a short while, then decided to join the conflict. He hid the plasma gun under the bed in the tent and asked Natilia to keep watch over it. When he reached the battle site, both the Greeks and the Trojans were fighting fiercely.

Todd spotted Hercules in the raging battle and rushed over to fight with him. Hercules was surprised to see Todd beside him. He stated, "I did not think you were coming to join this fight, since you were tired from your exploits in Troy." Todd smiled and said, "I can't just sit by and let you fight by yourself."

Rapidly a Trojan soldier came charging up behind Todd. He heard the soldier's approach and turned just in time to block the attack with his shield.

The Trojan was stunned from the impact with Todd's shield and stood still for a moment. Todd took advantage of this error and hit the Trojan with his shield. The soldier fell back and hit the ground hard. Todd quickly lunged and stabbed his sword into the soldier.

Todd pulled his sword out of the dead Trojan on the ground and noticed the armies had stopped fighting one another. Todd was confused as he looked around. All the men seemed to be gathering around two people fighting. Todd made his way through the groups of Trojans and Greeks until he was right in front of the fight.

Todd could tell from their armor that the two fighters were Hector and Achilles. He understood why everyone had stopped fighting to watch these two clash.

Suddenly Hector cut the throat of Achilles and he fell to the ground choking on his own blood. Hector bent down and pulled off his helmet. But it wasn't Achilles. It was a young man who looked to be only about 16 years old.

Hector was upset to see this youth mortally wounded. He sadly used his sword to end the boy's slow death. Hector then stood up and walked over to Odysseus. He stated, "There has been enough killing this day."

Odysseus nodded in agreement and replied, "Yes, there has been enough death for today."

Hector turned to his men and ordered, "Back to Troy!" Odysseus in turn commanded, "Back to the ships, men, to your campsites!"

Todd was relieved the fighting was over. He made his way back to Achilles' campsite and his tent, where Natilia was waiting for him. When he entered the tent, he noticed Natilia had already taken off all her armor and gotten into their bed. She asked, "Are you well? Will you come to bed and rest, Todd?"

Todd told her he was fine and took off all his armor. He set it beside Natilia's armor. Todd said, "I'm not getting in bed just yet. I want to have a closer look at the Bow of Apollo. I won't be long." Todd took the plasma gun out from under the bed and started to examine it.

Natilia replied, "Do as you must. I will be waiting for you to join me in bed."

Todd looked up at Natilia and noticed how tired she seemed. He smiled at her and said, "I'll just be a few minutes, Natilia, I promise." She smiled back at him and watched as he continued studying the plasma gun.

Todd closely inspected the plasma gun, or as everyone called it, the "Bow of Apollo." After a short time, he found what he'd been looking for...a small engraving that read "MADE IN THE UGA".

Todd recalled the light saber that had the same inscription on it. He thought about why he kept traveling through time and was now sure there was more to all this than just the gods having willed it.

Todd put the plasma gun back under the bed and got into it with Natilia. She asked, "Did you find what you were looking for, Todd?"

He answered, "Yes, I did. And I think I'm starting to better understand things about our traveling to different time periods. But I haven't figured everything out just yet. There are still a lot of questions unanswered."

Natilia wrapped her arms around Todd and gave him a kiss. She wished she could ease his troubles. She said, "Let us rest for now, so we can regain our strength. We can think on this more tomorrow and hope to find our answers."

Todd held Natilia close and gave her a tender kiss. She was warm in his arms and he started to relax. He said, "I hope we find some answers soon. I'd really like to understand what's going on."

Natilia reassured him saying, "You will solve this mystery. I love and trust in you, Todd. You will figure it out. I know you will do so."

Todd closed his eyes and they both drifted off to sleep in each other's arms. They slept well into the morning. They awoke with a start, when Achilles barged into their tent and shouted, "Toddacis, wake up! Come with me now!"

Todd jumped out of bed startled. He saw Achilles had tears streaming down his face. Todd grabbed his armor and started putting it on quickly. Natilia also got up and hurriedly started to dress in her armor.

While dressing, Todd asked, "What has happened, Achilles?" Achilles wiped at his eyes and answered, "When the Trojans attacked the Greek camp, my young cousin put on my armor and led my men into battle. My men thought it was me, so they did not question the orders. Hector murdered my cousin."

Achilles continued angrily, "I am going to kill Hector! I want you there to make sure there is no trickery. He must fight me himself with no assistance from his men. The brute will die today by my hand!"

Todd understood Achilles' pain at losing his cousin and would support him in avenging his death. Todd replied, "Of course, I will come help you. Natilia will come too."

Achilles was anxious to depart. He stated, "We go at once. I will kill that damn Prince!! And send him straight to Hades!"

Todd and Natilia had finished dressing in their armor and followed Achilles out of the tent. Achilles climbed into a chariot and motioned for Todd to join him.

Achilles noticed Natilia had climbed aboard too. He said, "No, Toddacis. Your wife may not come."

Natilia assumed Achilles didn't want her to come, because she was a woman. She asked angrily, "Why not?!"

Achilles didn't answer her directly. He faced forward, grabbing the reins of the chariot, and said, "Have her stay here and protect my woman."

Todd didn't know why Achilles would not want Natilia to come, but he wasn't going to argue with him now. He said, "I'm sorry, Natilia. Would you please stay here and look after the woman in his tent? Keep her safe. Please do this for me."

Natilia was upset at being uninvited. She answered, "I will do this for you, Todd. Not for anyone else." Natilia stepped off the chariot. Todd jumped off, gave her a quick kiss, and whispered, "Thank you Natilia, I love you."

Todd climbed back on the chariot and Achilles immediately rode off towards the city of Troy. Achilles drove the chariot fast all the way to the gates of Troy.

Once they reached the city gates, Achilles started yelling for Hector to come out. He kept screaming out Hector's name, slandering and taunting him.

After a little while, the gates opened. Achilles jumped off of his chariot, grabbed his shield, and drew out his sword.

Hector walked out through the gates dressed in his silver armor. His square shield had a golden sun in the center of it like the rest of the Trojan soldiers. His short sword was drawn and he was ready to fight.

Todd waited in the chariot while Achilles approached Hector. He saw them exchange a few words but could not hear what they said. After their brief exchange, Achilles and Hector started to battle one another.

Achilles moved quicker and struck first, hitting Hector's shield. As a result, Achilles backed up a little bit, catching himself from the recoil. Achilles came at Hector again swiftly with another strike.

Hector stopped the deadly blow with his sword this time. While he blocked Achilles' sword with his own, he hit Achilles' shield with his shield and forced Achilles to back off.

As Achilles backed away from having their shields clash together, Hector swung his sword a few times as Achilles dodged the strikes. Countering Hector's swings, Achilles slashed at him trying to land a blow.

While they were throwing swings at one another, Achilles managed to block one of Hector's strikes and quickly lunged at him. Achilles' sword stabbed Hector in the right leg. After being stabbed, Hector dropped his shield and backed away from Achilles.

Achilles threw his own shield on the ground to keep the fight even. He charged at Hector and jumped into the air attacking Hector's left side.

As Achilles tried to land a strike in Hector's neck, Hector turned and blocked Achilles' sword. As Achilles was landing on the ground, Hector slashed out and cut Achilles across his body plate along the chest.

Achilles tucked and rolled away from Hector. Hector pursued him and tried to stab him while he was on the ground. Hector missed and stabbed the ground instead as Achilles continued to roll out of the way.

Achilles jumped up and faced Hector. This time Todd heard what Hector said to Achilles. "I gave the boy the honor he deserved and let him have a proper burial." Achilles replied angrily, "You gave him the honor of your sword!"

Achilles rushed at Hector and swung his sword fiercely. He struck him in the chest and knocked him down. Achilles stood back and yelled at him, "Get up, Prince of Troy! I won't let your fall take my glory!"

Achilles moved closer to Hector and he started to get up. As Hector pulled himself up, he thrust his sword at Achilles. Achilles quickly moved out of the way of Hector's sword and grabbed the arm he'd thrust out.

Achilles took advantage of Hector's vulnerable position and stabbed clear through his silver body plate. Achilles pulled his sword out of Hector and he dropped to the ground.

Hector lay gasping for air until the life seeped out of him. Achilles turned towards the city of Troy. He looked up at the king and soldiers watching the fight from atop of the wall and yelled out, "I killed Hector!! Me, Achilles! Your Prince Hector is dead!!"

Achilles came over to Todd, who was still waiting in the chariot. He said, "Toddacis, give me the rope that is there in my chariot."

Todd noticed Achilles seemed pretty agitated. He thought he must be overexcited from the fight. Todd grabbed the rope. As he handed it to Achilles, he asked, "What do you need the rope for?" Achilles took the rope and said, "You will see, Toddacis."

Achilles went back over to Hector's body and tied the rope around his ankles. He then walked back to Todd and tied the other end of the rope to the back of the chariot. Achilles climbed into the chariot and said, "We return to the camp now."

Todd asked, "You have accomplished your task?" Achilles, still set on punishing Hector further even though he was dead, answered, "Yes, Hector deserved death. I have avenged my cousin."

Achilles snapped the horse's reigns and the chariot departed. He held his right hand up in the air in a fist as a sign of victory. He continued holding it up for all the Trojans to see until they were out of sight of the city. Achilles and Todd rode all the way back to the Greek camp with Hector's body dragging behind them.

Achilles and Todd rode through the Greek camp and the soldiers stared in amazement at Prince Hector's lifeless body. They continued through and didn't stop until they'd reached the camp with Achilles' men situated away from the others. When the chariot came to a stop, Todd jumped off the chariot and went looking for Natilia.

Todd made his way to Achilles' tent and went inside. He found Natilia sitting with Achilles' woman. He smiled at them and stated, "Achilles did it. He won the fight."

Natilia was happy to see Todd but sad about these circumstances. She approached him and said softly, "If Achilles has won, then this girl's cousin is now dead."

Todd suddenly realized the complexity of the situation. He replied, "I'm sorry for her loss, Natilia. We should go. I'm sure she and Achilles will want to be alone now."

Natilia agreed that they should give Achilles his privacy. She said, "Yes, let us leave. Maybe we could go continue my training."

Todd responded, "That sounds like a very good idea. Let's go find some space out of the way."

Natilia was excited to work on her training. She said eagerly, "Perhaps behind our tent? Let's go see."

They said their goodbyes to the young lady and moved towards the entrance of the tent. Suddenly Achilles walked through the opening before they could head out.

Todd saw in his face that he was full of sadness and anger. Todd felt it was best to leave Achilles to his thoughts. He and Natilia exited the tent.

Upon leaving Achilles' tent, Todd and Natilia headed back to theirs. They found the area behind their tent to be suitable and Todd began to train Natilia. They trained for the remainder of the afternoon, then went into their tent to rest and had their evening meal.

When night came, Todd and Natilia went down to the coastline and walked hand in hand along the shore. He looked at her beautiful face shining in the moonlight and said, "I thought it would be nice to do something peaceful and enjoyable with you tonight, Natilia. Before you know it, we'll be in another fight, or battle, or having to do something crazy again."

As they walked along the moonlit shore, Natilia felt relaxed and happy. She smiled at Todd and said, "This is very sweet of you, Todd. You make me feel so special and happy. I am a lucky woman to have a man like you in my life. You always show me how much you truly care."

Todd wrapped his arms around her and looked deep into her eyes. He replied, "I'm just glad I could make you happy, Natilia." They continued their walk further down the beach.

As they progressed along the shore, Todd thought he saw a shadow move out of the corner of his eye. He said to Natilia, "I think we should head back to the camp now."

Natilia was puzzled about why he was ending their evening so soon. She asked, "Why? Is there something wrong, Todd? It is very nice out. The night is calm."

Todd didn't want to alarm her. He answered, "Yes, it is nice out, but I'm getting a little tired. Hopefully, we can do this again sometime soon." Todd smiled at her and gave her a kiss. They held hands and walked back to the camp.

When they arrived at the camp, Todd noticed an old man standing on a chariot with Achilles' woman. Achilles stood nearby and Todd heard him say to the old man, "You will have your seven days of peace."

The old man had tears in his eyes. He replied, "Thank you, Achilles. You are an honorable man." The old man started to ride off and Todd saw that there was a cart attached with a body laid out in it. The chariot made its way through the Greek camps and headed for Troy.

Todd and Natilia walked over to Achilles. Todd asked, "Who was that, Achilles?"

Achilles continued watching the old man ride off as he answered Todd, "That was the King of Troy, Toddacis. He came to me in regards to his fallen son, Hector. He wished for his son's body. He asked to give him a proper burial and have seven days to honor his son's death. I gave him this honor and agreed that no Greek would attack Troy during this time period."

Todd knew this was a very noble deed. He said, "You are a good man, Achilles. That was both respectful and honorable. I know the gods are proud of you."

Achilles appreciated Todd's kind words. He was also tired and felt the weight of the day. He said, "Thank you, Toddacis. Now we must all take our leave. Go, be with your wife and rest. In seven days' time, we will attack the city of Troy and overpower her."

Todd was thankful for this reprieve. He could take a break and not have to think about attacks or fighting for seven days. He replied, "Very well. I will relax and spend this time with my wife." Todd and Natilia left Achilles and went into their tent.

Todd and Natilia took off all of their equipment and got into bed. Todd kissed Natilia goodnight and said, "I guess we'll have time for long walks on the shore now."

Natilia smiled at him and replied, "I would like that very much. Good night, Todd. I love you." He kissed her again and they fell asleep in each other's arms.

Four days passed and there was peace as Achilles had agreed with the King of Troy. Todd and Natilia spent time together, training, walking, talking, and laughing.

On the fifth day, Hercules invited Todd to have lunch with him and Odysseus. This was the day when Todd would hear about Odysseus' plan. He had figured out a way to get into the city of Troy without breaking down the walls.

As they sat eating their meal, Odysseus spoke up, "I think I have figured out how to get into that damned city."

Hercules laughed loudly and remarked, "Very funny, Odysseus! Have you come up with a way to tear down the walls?!"

Todd knew very well Odysseus' plan. He asked, "What's your plan, Odysseus? I'm guessing it's very good."

Odysseus was pleased to hear Todd's interest in his idea. He said, "Yes, it is good, Toddacis. I believe it will work, for we just need to make a giant horse for the Trojans. We can construct it from our galley ships and then leave a few dead bodies nearby. The Trojans will think we have left and made the horse a gift to them and their god.

We will hide a few select warriors in the giant horse. The Trojans will think we have sailed home, but we will really have our ships hidden over there behind those large cliffs. If they take our gift into the city of Troy, we will conquer them!"

Todd shared his encouragement for the idea. He said, "That's brilliant! It may very well work, Odysseus. I think you should go at once and tell Agamemnon your plan, so we can get started on it right away."

Hercules didn't really like the idea of hiding to attack someone. He would much rather face his enemy head-on. He said, "I am not so sure about men hiding in a giant horse. But if it is to be our plan, this hoax may be to our benefit."

Odysseus was pleased to have Todd's and Hercules' approval and support. He stated, "Very well. It is settled. I will go tell King Agamemnon about this great plan of ours and we will make our giant horse straightaway."

Odysseus got up and headed to Agamemnon's tent. He presented the plan to Agamemnon. Agamemnon thought it was ingenious and a cunning trick. He ordered them to get started on it immediately. The whole Greek army began taking apart a few galley ships and rebuilding them into the giant horse.

Todd went back to his tent to find Natilia and tell her the exciting news. When he entered the tent, he found her sitting and eating a meal.

Todd was eager to tell Natilia about the plan. He announced loudly, "Natilia! We have found a way to breach the walls and get into the city of Troy!"

Natilia was stunned and a little skeptical about this news. She asked, "And how are they going to do that, Todd?"

Todd had run to the tent and was still trying to catch his breath. He replied, "Well, we are going to build a giant horse as a gift for the Trojans. But a few Greek soldiers along with us, Achilles, Hercules, and Odysseus will be concealed inside it. Meanwhile the rest of the Greek army will be hidden at sea behind the cliffs. If the Trojans believe this gift is in honor of our defeat and departure, they will take it into the city."

Todd continued, "Then in the middle of the night while the city sleeps, we will slip out of the giant horse. From inside the city walls, we will take the gates and open the city to the rest of the Greek army."

Natilia thought about the daring plot Todd had just described. After a brief silence, she said enthusiastically, "This might just work, Todd! When are we going to start making the giant horse?"

Todd was pleased to see her keen interest. He replied, "The construction has already begun. They are dismantling some galley ships to build it. I believe the "Trojan Horse" will be finished by the last day of peace."

Natilia decided she wanted more training time with Todd. She asked, "Do you have time to train with me, so we are ready when that day comes."

Todd was happy to hear Natilia wanted to be ready for the coming action. He responded, "Of course. Let's make the most of these two days, so we are prepared for the surprise attack."

As discussed, Todd and Natilia trained hard for the next two days. On the eighth day, when the peace was to end, Todd buried the plasma gun before they left to fight in Troy. Todd, Natilia, Odysseus, Hercules, Achilles, and a few other Greek soldiers got into the belly of the giant horse.

Todd was sitting next to Achilles. He asked, "Achilles, I heard you order all your men home instead of waiting behind the cliffs. Why did you do this?"

Achilles had decided this plan would succeed and he didn't want any more of his men to die. He simply answered, "So they could be with their wives and families."

Todd guessed that Achilles had suffered enough loss. He replied, "Oh, I see."

Hercules was restless. He would rather just attack the Trojans directly. He said, "Odysseus, I do not much like this hiding and waiting to strike. We could just take the city by storming it with our sheer power."

Odysseus understood Hercules' feelings but knew there would be great costs. He replied, "Hercules, I understand. But this way we will not suffer great losses of good men. And we will still be storming the city. Just differently, from the inside and with the gates open for the entire army."

Natilia was starting to feel very anxious. She whispered to Todd, "Are you sure we will be safe in this giant horse, Todd? What if they are able to tell we are hiding in here?"

Todd was well aware that they would not be discovered. He smiled at her and answered, "I know we will be fine. Do not worry, Natilia."

Natilia was doubtful but tried to feel more confident. "Ok Todd. I trust in you. I just do not want anything bad to come of this."

Odysseus had been keeping watch through the small cracks in the horse. He hissed at them softly, "Shhhhh! Be quiet, the patrol is coming."

The Trojan patrol rode nearby to check on the Greek camps. They were surprised to see camps and ships gone and a large strange object. They approached and found no signs of the Greeks, just a few dead bodies and a giant wooden horse. The Trojan patrol rode away quickly, headed back toward the city of Troy.

A short time later, a small group of Trojans rode up quickly and went straight to the horse. They dismounted and stood silently studying it. They started to move around and Todd heard one of the Trojans say, "Be careful, my Lord, they died of the plague!"

The King of Troy stopped moving and spoke to the man beside him as he looked up at the horse. "What do you make of this, priest?"

The priest thought for a moment then answered, "It is a gift my Lord. An offering to the gods for their safe trip home and to us to make amends for all the dead."

Hector's younger brother knew the Greeks would not give up so easily. "No father! Do not take this gift. It is a trap! Burn it here and now, for nothing good will come of it!"

The priest looked at the prince scornfully. He knew better than to incur the wrath of the gods. He said to him, "My prince, it is a gift for the gods. We must take it for their honor. To leave it would offend."

The King of Troy agreed they must revere the gods. He said, "Very well, we will take this gift for the gods and celebrate with it in Troy." The King ordered his men to move the giant horse.

By midday, the Trojans had relocated the giant horse to the city of Troy. The people of Troy rejoiced for their triumph. A large feast was set up and musicians played lively music. The Trojans ate there fill, drank lots of wine, and danced around the giant horse.

As the Trojans celebrated their false victory, Odysseus opened up a sack of food that was stored inside the horse. He passed around the food and the secret guests ate their midday meal, while all of Troy celebrated around them.

When nightfall came, all of the Trojan people were passed out on the ground. Most had had too much drink, but some were just exhausted by their revelry.

Odysseus decided the coast was clear and opened the small door under the giant horse's belly. He let down a long rope that softly hit the ground. He signaled for everyone to go and they all climbed down the rope.

Todd and Natilia descended the rope and reached the ground. Odysseus was headed for the gates, so they followed him.

As Odysseus proceeded, he was silently killing the sleeping Trojan soldiers. The Greek soldiers that had been in the horse with them were also slaying the Trojan soldiers passed out around the horse.

Hercules had immediately proceeded to the top of the wall, right above the gates, and waved a torch high in the air. While down below Odysseus, Todd, and Natilia opened the gates to the city. Seeing Hercules' signal and the gates being opened, the Greek army positioned outside of the city advanced as quickly as possible.

When Achilles left the belly of the horse, he ran directly toward the palace.

As the Greek army charged the gates of Troy, Todd and Natilia ran for the palace in hopes of finding Achilles. Natilia asked, "Are you sure Achilles went this way, Todd?"

Todd had recalled what would happen to Achilles. He hoped he could change it. He answered, "Yes, I'm sure. We must get up there quickly if we are going to save him."

There was a large crashing noise behind them. Natilia looked back and saw the city starting to go up in flames. She said, "Yes, we better hurry before this city is burned to the ground!" They sprinted to the palace but found both Trojan soldiers and palace guards protecting the entrance gates.

Todd and Natilia quickly moved along the palace wall, looking for a possible way in. Todd found a small foothold and tried climbing up. He made his way and Natilia followed right behind him.

When Todd and Natilia got over the wall, they discovered two dead Trojans. Todd knew Achilles had been this way. He said, "Achilles was here. We need to hurry or he is going to die!"

Natilia wondered what Todd was going to do to try and help Achilles. As they moved forward, she asked, "How are we going to save him, Todd?"

Todd hadn't figured out a plan yet. He answered, "I'm not sure but we have to at least try."

Todd and Natilia reached an intersection in the palace hallways. Natilia asked "Which way should we go?"

Todd didn't want to risk making the wrong choice. He answered, "Umm...I think we should just go straight and see where that leads us."

Natilia was feeling the urgency of the situation. She replied, "Ok, let us hurry."

Todd and Natilia continued to run straight ahead down the hallway. They passed another corridor but proceeded straight forward.

When Todd and Natilia reached the end of the hallway, they found the entrance to the king's throne room. They entered the throne room where two Trojan guards were posted. The guards spotted them immediately and ran at them.

Todd quickly raised his shield and blocked one of the Trojan's swords. He used his shield to shove the Trojan away and swiftly slashed at him with his own sword. Todd cut off the Trojan's right arm and head with two swings and the Trojan's body collapsed to the ground.

The second Trojan guard had come at Natilia. She quickly ducked down and cut the Trojan's knee caps with her gladius. He crumpled to the floor and she stabbed him in the throat.

After defeating the guards, Todd and Natilia continued through to the other side of the throne room and went out a doorway. They proceeded for a short distance and arrived at a pavilion area. They saw four Trojan soldiers dead on the ground and Achilles standing with the same girl that had departed with the King of Troy the night he'd taken back Hector's body.

Todd called out, "Come on, Achilles! Take her with you, but we have to get out of here now!"

Achilles grabbed the girl's hand and they started towards Todd and Natilia. They had moved only a few steps, when Achilles suddenly fell to the ground with an arrow stuck in his heel. Achilles tried to get up, but was immediately shot by two arrows in his chest. He dropped again, falling on his back, and the life went out of his eyes.

Agamemnon came up the steps from the other side of the pavilion and headed straight for the girl. He grabbed her by the throat and said viciously, "You almost cost me this war! And now with no Achilles to save you, your death will be nice and slow!"

Agamemnon drew out his short sword. Before he could stab the girl, Todd rushed at him and slashed both of his back calf muscles.

Agamemnon collapsed to the ground. Todd stabbed him through the chest then withdrew his sword. Agamemnon tried to speak but just gurgled up blood. He died slowly, staring up at the sky.

Agamemnon's guards arrived and saw him on the ground. They came charging at Todd and Natilia. The guards hoped to help Agamemnon, but they didn't know it was already too late.

Natilia spotted them first and blocked them with her shield. She shoved them back with all of her might. She quickly swung her sword at one of the guards and hit his shield, backing him up even further. She was about to swing again, when he suddenly fell face first to the ground.

Natilia looked down and saw he had an arrow stuck in his back. The other guard came at her and she quickly ducked away. She faced the guard and he charged at her. When he got close, she smacked him with her shield. He took the hard blow to the face and was knocked down. As soon as the guard hit the ground, Natilia stabbed him clean through his chest and left him for dead.

Todd came over to Natilia and asked if she saw the archer that took down the guard. They both looked around and saw the girl crying over Achilles' body. The Trojan archer ran over to the girl, grabbed her by the arm, and ran away with her.

Todd noticed the archer was Hector's little brother, who had most likely avenged his brother's death by killing Achilles. Todd and Natilia would not see the girl or archer again.

Once the Prince of Troy was gone, Odysseus and Hercules ran up to Todd and Natilia with a large group of Greek soldiers. Odysseus was stunned to see Agamemnon and Achilles dead on the ground. He asked, "What has happened?!"

Todd knew he had to tell the right story. He answered "The King was killed by Achilles. Then an archer took down Achilles and ran off."

Natilia knew how the Greeks would feel about losing Achilles. She said, "Achilles had great courage and bravery, and he died with great honor. The gods will be happy to have him by their sides."

Hercules picked up and carried Achilles' body to the gates of Troy. Meanwhile, the palace was sacked of all its goods and the city of Troy continued to burn.

All the Greeks gathered outside the city gates as Troy went up in flames. Odysseus had had constructed a large platform. Hercules carried Achilles' body up and placed it on the top of the platform. He then placed two gold coins over his eyes for the boat man. He said, "Go, be with the gods and my father now, Achilles." Hercules climbed down from the platform and Odysseus lit it on fire. Todd, Natilia,

Odysseus, Hercules, and the Greek soldiers all stood solemnly in honor of Achilles' memory.

When there was nothing left but a pile of ashes, they all departed. Todd told Odysseus and Hercules that they would be down to the ships shortly.

Todd and Natilia headed back to where their tent had been. Todd looked around a little bit, trying to find the right spot. As he looked, Natilia asked, "Todd, why don't you leave the Bow of Apollo here hidden in the ground by the beach?"

Todd recalled that this place had been discovered and dug up by archeologists, so he knew he couldn't leave the plasma gun here to be found. He answered, "We need to be sure that no one finds it here, so we must take it with us."

Natilia thought that made sense. She agreed, "I understand. It is a very powerful weapon created by the gods. It should not be left unaccounted for here in the sand, for someone may find it in the future."

Todd smiled at Natilia and said, "You're exactly right. That's why we must take it back with us." Todd located the plasma gun and unburied it. He and Natilia headed to the galley ships that were loading for the return trip to Sparta or their own homelands.

As Todd and Natilia reached the ships, Odysseus saw them coming. He approached Todd and said, "Toddacis, I have news for you. Agamemnon has no one to take his place as king upon his death. We, the council, have decided to appoint you as the new King of Sparta, for we are grateful for all you have done for us."

Todd was shocked by this pronouncement. He thought to himself, 'What would I do as king?' He replied, "No, Odysseus! You don't have to do this for me. I can't accept this privilege."

Odysseus insisted the council's decision was twofold. He said, "We are not doing this just to honor you, Toddacis, but for the benefit of all the people of Greece and Sparta. We believe you to be the best for this position."

Todd was flattered that the council chose him, because they thought he'd be a good leader. He stated, "Since you put it that way, Odysseus. Very well, I will accept the job and do my best for the people."

Odysseus was thrilled that Todd had agreed. He asked, "Good, then it is settled! Will you join me in my galley for the journey back to Sparta, Toddacis?"

Todd knew Odysseus would not get lost in his travels to Sparta. He responded "Yes, we would be glad to travel with you, Odysseus. Could you please locate a large cloth or canvas in which I can wrap the Bow of Apollo?"

Odysseus went onto the ship and came back with a large cloth. "Here, Toddacis. Will this work to cover the Bow of Apollo?"

Todd took the cloth and wrapped up the plasma gun. He replied, "Yes, this is fine. Thank you, Odysseus."

Odysseus was now eager to depart. He said, "Now, let us board and leave this place. We head to Sparta. And after I take you there, I am happy to journey home to my very lovely land, Ithaca."

Todd knew the difficulty that lay ahead for Odysseus in his travels home. He stated, "I hope your journey home will be swift, Odysseus."

Odysseus was confident that it would be. He replied, "I believe it shall, Toddacis." Odysseus turned and headed up the ramp onto his galley ship. Todd and Natilia started to follow him up the ramp but stopped when they heard Hercules calling out to them.

Hercules came to tell them goodbye. He said, "I am sorry but I cannot journey back with you. There are things I must attend to now. I must go a different way and take a different ship. I am very glad to have met both of you."

Todd responded, "It was very nice to meet you too, Hercules. Thank you for everything you did for us. We certainly understand if something else needs your attention."

Hercules smiled at them both and felt humbled by Todd's appreciation. He said "Thank you, Toddacis and Natilia, for understanding my needs."

Natilia hugged him and said, "Of course, we understand but you will be missed, Hercules. Have a safe journey. Now go before the ships leave you behind." Hercules took off and started running back to the other ship but turned to wave goodbye.

Todd and Natilia boarded Odysseus' galley ship and picked a spot for their two day journey back to Sparta. When the ship was ready, Odysseus yelled, "Men! We make for our return to Sparta!" Immediately all the men started to row and the ship set out for the city of Sparta.

As their first day at sea was coming to an end, Todd and Natilia went to lie down in their spot for the night. Todd took off all of his armor and put it with his shield nearby. He kept his sword next to his side for the night. Natilia also removed all of her armor and placed her sword down by her side.

Todd said to her as she lay down next to him, "I don't know if we will ever get back to Rome, Natilia." Natilia was surprised by this comment. She had tried to remain hopeful. She replied, "I believe we will see Rome again, Todd. Perhaps the gods will bring us back to Rome, so we can live in peace and have a family."

Todd was glad to see she still had hope of returning to her time and home. He said, "That would be wonderful, Natilia. I do wish that it will happen. But I just don't know what to make of all this time travel and strange weapons. It doesn't make any sense."

Todd thought about his discoveries in feudal Japan and ancient Greece. But he hadn't found anything like that in Roman times. And he had no idea what UGA might mean. He didn't know if it had anything to do with the gods or not. He was no closer to answers, just more confused.

Natilia thought about it as well. She stated, "It is all very odd, but the gods do many things beyond our understanding. We must live our lives in honor of the gods and hope they will grant us peace and happiness." She wrapped her arms around Todd and continued, "Do not let it worry you, Todd. The gods will do their will. We may not know their reasons, but what comes of it is as they wish. I do know that I am very glad to have you by my side through all of this."

Todd considered her view and said, "I'm happy you are here with me too, Natilia. But I need to understand the purpose for what's been happening to us and I intend to find out."

Natilia saw how determined he was to get some answers. She said, "I do hope you discover the purpose and soon, for I do not want to travel again unless it is home to Rome so we can live in peace."

Todd reassured her saying, "I will figure this out, Natilia. Don't worry. We'll get answers to this mystery." She kissed him good night and fell asleep in his arms.

The next day, Todd and Natilia had a quiet morning and then trained until about midday. They had just sat down to begin their midday meal when one of Odysseus' men called out, "Sparta! We have arrived at Sparta!"

Odysseus moved to the head of the ship and confirmed the sighting. He announced, "We dock at once for King Toddacis of Sparta!"

Odysseus approached Todd and Natilia and said, "This is where we will go our separate ways, Toddacis and Natilia. It was very good to meet the two of you. Once we land, only the three of us will go ashore. I will come with you to establish you as the King of Sparta as the council wills. Then I must set sail at once to return to my dear Ithaca and my beloved wife."

Todd felt bad knowing what Odysseus would go through on his journey home. He replied, "Thank you for all you have done for us, Odysseus. We wish you safe travels home. Once I'm established King of Sparta, I'll have your ship restocked and quickly supplied for your journey."

Odysseus was pleased by Todd's offer. He said, "Thank you, Toddacis. That would be most helpful."

As they approached the harbor of Sparta, Natilia, looked at Todd and said, "I do hope everything goes well for us once we get to Sparta, Todd." He wrapped his arm around her and gave her a kiss on the forehead. He hoped for the same good fortune. He replied, "I'm sure it will be fine, Natilia. You know I won't ever let anything bad happen to you." Natilia smiled and rested her head on Todd's chest as they pulled into the harbor.

Once the ship was docked, Odysseus said to them both, "Now that we are safely in port, let us proceed to the palace and make you the new King of Sparta." Todd and Natilia, still hoping for the best, followed Odysseus to the palace.

At the palace, Odysseus declared Todd as the new King of Sparta. Once the council's pronouncement was accepted and Todd was named King, Odysseus returned to his ship along with the goods Todd supplied him for his long journey home to Ithaca.

Odysseus set sail shortly before the city of Sparta held a great celebration. A large feast was served that night at the palace in honor of the new King of Sparta, and his wife, the Queen. Todd and Natilia enjoyed a wonderful, festive evening.

Later that night, Todd made a list of things to change and improve in the city of Sparta. He also made a short list of people to rule after him in case they should suddenly go through time again. When Todd finished his lists, he got ready for bed.

Natilia was already lying down in the bed. She smiled up at him and said, "Todd, I think this may be what the gods wanted for us, to be King and Queen of this city."

Todd appreciated that Natilia was happy and still optimistic. He smiled and replied, "Perhaps it is."

Natilia thought of the Bow of Apollo and asked, "Have you decided what to do with the Bow of Apollo, Todd?" Todd got into bed and answered, "No. I haven't yet. It's under the bed right now. I need to come up with a good place to hide it, so it will never be found."

Natilia snuggled up to Todd and tried to think of a good hiding place. She suggested, "What about burying it under the palace?"

Todd thought for a moment and answered, "That might be a good place, but I was thinking it really needs to be away from people and buildings, so it hopefully wouldn't be found for a very long time." Natilia gave it further consideration and suggested, "Then maybe you should bury it deep in the woods or wilderness somewhere."

Todd knew that cities expanded and woods were often cut down to accommodate new development, so he worried it would be discovered in the future. He was tired and thought he'd give it some fresh thought in the morning. He replied, "Let's get some sleep and we can think about it some more tomorrow."

Natilia was also very tired. She agreed, "Yes, let us get some rest and not worry about anything until tomorrow." Natilia gave him a kiss goodnight and started to drift off to sleep.

Todd listened to Natilia's steady breathing, but he wasn't getting sleepy yet. He had a strange feeling. He tried to dismiss it, thinking he was just exhausted from all the excitement of the day. He had a lot to adjust to in a new city and sleeping in its palace as king. The night still felt a little off to him. Maybe strange like the other nights before he traveled through time. But now he was feeling drowsy and too tired to think about it anymore and was soon fast asleep.

THE TIME THAT TRAVELED PART IV THE FUTURE

When Todd woke, opening his eyes, he found himself in a very bright, all white room. He sat up, but his eyes had to adjust to the intense light. Once his eyes had fully adjusted, he saw he was still lying in his bed from the night before. He looked down by his side and realized Natilia was no longer in the bed with him.

Todd was anxious to find her. He jumped out of bed and quickly grabbed his sword. He tied it to his waist around his shorts on his left side as usual. He picked up his shirt that was still sitting on the end of the bed and put it on. He found his shoes sitting on the floor near the end of the bed and put them on. He looked around for his armor, but it was nowhere in sight.

Todd looked under the bed for the plasma gun and found that it was still there. He pulled it out from under the bed and placed it on top.

Suddenly Todd heard a girl's voice say, "Todd, you will not need your sword here. There will be no harm done to you. Please relax and take your sword off." He immediately drew out his sword and yelled, "Where am I? And what have you done with Natilia?!"

The girl's voice responded, "Todd, please put your sword away and lay it down on the bed. I'll answer every question you have."

Todd was not yet ready to lower his guard but was curious to find out what questions she could answer. He asked, "How do I know I can trust you if you won't show yourself to me?"

The girl was silent for a moment then responded, "Very well. If it will help you relax and put down your sword, I will show myself."

Suddenly a girl came out of the wall in front of him. She had brown hair and eyes, a young, healthy body, and was nicely tanned. She was dressed in an all-white, skintight jumpsuit.

The girl made eye contact with Todd and asked, "There, is this better for you? Would you please put your sword on the bed?"

Todd was glad to be able to see who he was talking to but stayed defensive. He answered, "I'll put it away but not on the bed."

The girl sighed and replied, "Fine. That will be good for now. I see you have gotten the last item of the wrongly placed. You did very well in accomplishing all of your tasks that were set before you."

Todd was surprised to hear her speak to him like he had completed a mission. He asked, "What?! What do you mean, the last of the wrongly placed? And how do you know my name? I don't even know who you are, where I am, or when I am!"

The girl apologized, "Oh, I am sorry. I should start at the beginning and in doing so, I will probably answer many of the questions you may have wished to ask. First, my name is Ashiea and you are in the year 5452AD of your eras' time count. You are on the planet Earth in what used to be the United States of America. I believe you would have known it as the state of Florida. So now I will start at the beginning, since you know my name, where you are, and how you said it, 'when' you are."

Todd was shocked by what little he'd heard so far. He burst out, "This is crazy! How has this happened? Why me? What could I do any better than one of your people? Why not just send one of them through time?" Ashiea appreciated Todd's intelligent questions. She smiled and answered. "Be patient, Todd. I will share our purpose and explain everything in detail."

Todd was a little disappointed he would have to wait for his answers. He said, "Alright, let's hear it then."

Ashiea smiled and gathered her thoughts. She began, "You are very brave, Todd. That is why my people love you. But now where to start..."

Ashiea continued, "My people have had the ability to go back through time for a great many millennia. We only allow certain people to travel through time in the past to learn more about our history and to see how people and cultures existed. A few months ago, we started to notice small changes in our time period. Things that hadn't been there before were and some things started to vanish right before peoples' eyes, never to come back.

Our leading scientists came together to discuss the matter and try to resolve it. In a short time, they figured out the problem.

They discovered that from us traveling back in time, we had started to change the future of our world and galaxy."

Todd astutely realized why he had found the two futuristic weapons in the past. "So it was your people that left the light saber and this plasma gun behind in the past."

Ashiea was remorseful about this costly error. She answered, "Yes, it was our fault. But we hurriedly attempted to correct the problem. We sent people from our era back in time to where these items were left but, unfortunately, our people kept failing at the task. It was taking too long to rectify the error and our time period was beginning to change drastically."

We had to come up with another option. We decided to search through the timeline of history from our beginnings to find the right person to send back in time. Someone we would guide to the right places and events in those times."

Todd was now angry to learn he'd been used and manipulated. He stated "So you sent me back in time to clean up the mess your people created!"

Ashiea knew he was upset. She responded "Yes, we did but it was for a very good reason."

"We determined you were the only one perfectly suited for the mission. You had a very good knowledge of history in those times. You were well-fit physically and had some defensive and sword training. And the most important attributes you had, that many others did not, were bravery, heart, and hope."

"We ran you, and a number of possible candidates, through our computer projection model. We looked to see how each of you would perform with the time travel and the necessary tasks to be accomplished. You achieved the highest possible percentage of completing the tasks successfully. But there was one thing that occurred on your journey that we did not anticipate."

"The love and relationship that you developed with Natilia was unexpected. We could not just bring you back to your era or hers. You would not be able to live in Ancient Rome. You might change history or your own future. But that is another topic I will cover later. For now let's talk about the two items you discovered back in time, the light saber and the plasma gun."

Todd was interested to learn more about the weapons. He asked, "Yes, they were very strange things to find in those time periods. How did they end up there? And UGA is stamped on each of them. What does that mean?"

Ashiea was impressed that he'd noticed the markings on the two objects. She answered, "Ah! We wondered if you would find the etchings on the weapons. As to how they came to be there, well, that's quite easy to explain. They were accidentally left behind by some of our groups of early time explorers. We should have been more careful when we went back in time and visited the past. As for the UGA, that answer is simple. It stands for the United Galaxy Alliance."

Todd was glad to finally be getting some answers, but he was still concerned about Natilia. He asked, "Ok. Now please tell me what's happened to Natilia? Where is she?" Ashiea reassured him that Natilia was alright. She replied, "Oh. You don't need to worry for her. She is very safe and right in the next room." Ashiea pointed behind her and continued, "The room I just came from through this back wall."

Todd thought he could trust what Ashiea was telling him about Natilia, but now he wondered why he traveled back to Ancient Rome since there was no weapon to recover. He asked, "Well, I'd like to see her soon. But tell me why did I go back to Roman Times? There was no UGA item to locate."

Ashiea was silent for a moment and looked like she was trying to figure out how best to answer Todd. She stated, "That is a little more complicated to explain. You see, we realized after running our time projection model that our era would still be breaking down, or disappearing I should say, and that was even when we had successfully retrieved the two items left behind.

We quickly began to realize that the time machine we'd created was meant for a broader purpose. We thought it was only to study and learn from the past, but we were wrong. It was theorized that it could also serve as a tool to change past events that would lead to this very advanced age we live in now. So we studied the past even more closely and used many different variables and events in the time projection models. We finally narrowed it down to the Roman Times.

We determined we were destined to use the time machine to go back and save scrolls from the Great Library before it was burned down by the illustrious Julius Caesar. The scrolls in the Great Library contained thousands of years of science, technology, and knowledge. That is why we sent you to Roman Times. And you had to go there first, otherwise none of this could be as it is."

Todd was shocked to hear this explanation. He said "I thought if you change the past, you would change the future."

Ashiea appreciated his perceptiveness. She smiled and said, "Todd, you are correct. You see, you were changing the future to this future or, at least, making it stay the same future it should turn out to be."

Todd was very surprised to figure out that his actions had adjusted the future for the better. He stated, "Wow, so I was chosen to go back in time and complete these tasks to make sure the future would turn out the same."

Todd still had questions about other experiences from his travels. He asked "So what was the Tree of Healing about?" Ashiea looked perplexed and asked, "What tree?"

Todd realized she had no knowledge of the Tree of Healing, so he decided to keep this information to himself. "Oh, nothing, umm... What will happen to me now? And Natilia? Will you send us back to our own times?"

Ashiea felt bad for Todd. She knew he and Natilia both wanted to go home, but at the same time, did not want to be separated. "We had planned to send you both back to your own times. But since you have developed a strong relationship and are married, we won't do this. Unfortunately, you will both have to stay here in our era to be together. It is a sad price to pay for love."

Ashiea sighed and continued, "We are sorry, Todd. You are a very good person and we regret having to put you through all of this. Many of our people thought it was too much to ask of one person. But our time was deteriorating and all the greatness of our future would have been lost now if not for you."

Todd thought about their loved ones and asked, "What about our families? Will Natilia never see her father, Quintius again? Or me, my mom, dad or sister?"

Ashiea smiled and replied happily, "We have brought them here to this era to be with you. You can all live in peace together. We confirmed that taking them out of history wouldn't change the future. And it actually helps make our time more stable having you, Natilia, and your families here. So Todd, you can now live here in the year 5452AD and in the safe protection of the UGA here on Earth."

Todd was thrilled to hear that both of his families were there with him. He stated eagerly, "I would like to see everyone now, please."

Ashiea was pleased to see he was adjusting well to all this new information. She responded, "You will have to wait just a little while for that, Todd. I first need to know what type of house you would like to live in, as well as a location for it to be built. You have accomplished extraordinary deeds for us. This is a well-deserved honor, so please tell us of your greatest wish for a home."

Todd was a little taken aback by this offer but started to think about it. He recalled one of the things he'd dreamed about growing up and answered, "Could you build me a Disney Castle? I always wished I could live there when I was a kid."

Ashiea smiled at the thought of it. She responded, "Well now, that is something I did not expect? So where would you like us to build a Disney Castle for you?"

Todd thought Florida might be nice but then had a better idea. He suggested, "How about Hawaii or what used to be Hawaii in my time period? Is that a possibility?"

Ashiea liked his imagination. She answered, "That will be fine. We will have your new home built in one day's time. Now I guess we should let you see everyone. Let's go into the next room."

Todd put his hand on the hilt of his sword and followed Ashiea out of the large white room. A white doorway in the wall slid open silently and they entered the next room.

As Todd walked through the doorway, he was pleased to see Natilia, Quintius, his mom, dad and sister. They were sitting together, talking quietly and all getting along beautifully.

Natilia was the first to see Todd come into the room. She immediately jumped up, yelled, "Todd!!!" and ran over to him. She hugged him tightly and said "I was so worried about you, for when I woke you were not by my side. I was fearful as to what may have happened to you. But this woman came to me and said not to worry, that you would be here very soon. I am so happy to have you back in my arms once more, Todd." She gave him a kiss and reluctantly let go of him but kept a hold of his arm.

Quintius had gotten up as well and came over to Todd. He slapped him on the back and said, "It is good to see you, Toddacis. After you both disappeared, I had come to believe that I would never see either of you again. Now I understand why you were brought here by these people."

Todd was overjoyed to see everyone. He replied, "I'm just happy to have Natilia back by my side where she belongs and to be with all of you, my family.

Todd's mom, dad, and sister had joined the reunion gathered around Todd. They each embraced him briefly. His dad said good-humoredly, "Well, this isn't college, but at least you did very well for yourself and your life. I would have never guessed my son would be a hero time traveler of the future."

Todd's mom said happily, but teary-eyed, "Todd, we are so very proud of you and what you have achieved for these people and yourself. You have shown everyone what we already knew you to be, a truly remarkable person."

Todd replied, "Thank you, mom and dad. I've missed you all and wondered if I would ever get to see you again." Todd had taken Natilia's hand after hugging his family. He wanted to keep her close by.

Todd's sister looked at Todd and Natilia hand in hand and said, "You two make a cute couple. And I think Natilia is really nice, Todd."

Todd was a little embarrassed but proud of his intelligent, talented, and beautiful wife. He replied, "I do too. Thank you, Jordan. Did you hear we are married?" Jordan answered, "Yes, and I wish I could have been there to celebrate with you."

Todd's mom spoke up, "Yes, Todd, I'm very disappointed that we weren't able to be a part of your wedding. My only son vanishes, saves the future, gets married, and we don't get to see any of it."

Todd smiled at his mother and replied, "I'm sorry, mom. At least we are all together now and you have been able to meet Natilia. We can have our own celebration soon."

Ashiea interrupted, "I see you are all very happy to be together, but there will be more time later for everyone to catch up. Right now, I need Todd and Natilia to come with me to meet the leader of our galaxy. He wishes to thank the very person himself who saved our time."

Todd was surprised to hear this exciting news. He agreed saying, "Okay, let's go." Todd told his family, "We'll see you all again shortly."

Ashiea was pleased that Todd seemed interested in meeting their leader. She started to head for the doorway and said, "Right this way. I must tell you that you are both heroes of the entire galaxy now. You are loved by everyone." Todd and Natilia followed her in stunned silence.

Ashiea, Todd, and Natilia exited the room and proceeded down a light blue-colored, long hallway. At the end of the hall, they continued out onto a large balcony which overlooked an enormous crowd of people. On the balcony stood a tall man who looked to be in his early twenties. He was wearing an all-gold jumpsuit.

Todd and Natilia approached the man who stood near the balcony railing. Natilia squeezed Todd's hand nervously. She was a little anxious about meeting the leader of the entire galaxy, as well as being in front of the massive crowd of people that stretched as far as the eye could see.

The man greeted them in a deep voice, "My name is Zixyon. I am the ruler of the United Galaxy Alliance. Let me be the first to say thank you for saving our time period, Todd and Natilia."

Todd replied humbly, "Thank you for selecting me and entrusting me with your important mission of protecting the future and its people. It is a great honor."

Zixyon was gratified by Todd's response. He shouted out, "We will now celebrate for what has been successful this day!"

Suddenly twenty starships flew overhead and fireworks went off in the air all around them. The crowd cheered as Zixyon placed platinum medals with gold and silver trim around Todd's and Natilia's necks.

Todd decided to make the most of this exhilarating moment. He drew out his katana and raised it high in the air in salute to all the people. The crowd went wild.

Natilia resolved to enjoy the experience too. She smiled and waved to the cheering people.

After the commemoration, Ashiea led Todd and Natilia back to the room where their family was waiting. She said, "I hope all of you enjoy your stay here, while Todd and Natilia's house is being built. It should be finished tomorrow morning. I am also very pleased to tell you that Zixyon has awarded them a very large amount of UGA credits, so none of you will ever have to work a day of your lives here in our era."

Todd was very grateful to the people of the UGA and Ashiea for their gifts and recognition. He thanked her and asked her to share his gratitude with her people.

Todd and Natilia spent the rest of the day with their family telling them all about their adventures. The group enjoyed a great feast that evening and they all spent the night together in one large room. The couples shared a bed. The beds were spread out in the four corners of the room and enclosed with silvery curtains.

After everyone had said their good nights, Todd and Natilia got into bed. Natilia snuggled up to him and said, "I am so happy that all of this is over and we can now think about starting a family together."

Todd was relieved to have answers and to know that they didn't have to worry about moving through time anymore. He replied, "Me too, Natilia. And I can't wait to see our new home."

Natilia smiled and said, "I know it will be a great home, for we are with the people of the gods now." Todd knew better than to try to dissuade her from her beliefs. He responded, "Yes, I'm sure it will. And I picked a very nice castle for us."

Todd kissed Natilia then continued, "Did you notice that everyone here is very young?" Natilia answered, "Yes, I did see this. It is probably because the gods gave them immortality that will keep them young forever. I believe they have done this for us as well."

Todd supposed this could very well be true. Anything seemed possible now. He said, "That would be amazing. Now let's get some sleep. I love you. Good night."

Natilia replied, "I love you too." A short time later, they fell asleep holding one another.

In the morning, Ashiea woke all of them and escorted them to a shuttle ship bound for Hawaii. They ate a light breakfast on the shuttle and arrived in Hawaii in only thirty minutes. The shuttle touched down right in front of their new home and it looked exactly like the Disney Castle from all the movies.

The party exited the shuttle and made their way towards the castle. Before Todd entered with everyone else, he stopped and asked Ashiea, "Before you go, I have one last question for you, Ashiea."

She replied smiling, "Yes, Todd. What is your question?"

Todd hesitated for a moment, staring at Ashiea's face. He asked, "How old are you? You look to be very young, like maybe only eighteen years old, but you give the impression of someone more mature and experienced."

Ashiea laughed at Todd's question. She advised, "I am seventy-five years old, and our time counting is still the same as when you lived in your era. Because of our advances in medicine, we enjoy healthier lives that keep us young."

Ashiea had her own query for Todd. She asked, "I have been wondering how is it you were able to push yourself forward and have the courage to continue when you did not understand how or why time was traveling?" Todd answered honestly, "I believed I would find the answers. I tried to stay prepared for the worst while hoping for the best."

Ashiea nodded in agreement. She said good-bye, walked back to the shuttle, and flew away. Todd went inside to join his family in their brand new, very big, and luxurious castle.

Todd lived happily with Natilia and his family, until a few months later. Late one night when he was recalling his time travel adventures, he suddenly realized the night did not feel quite right.

Fic Todd
Todd, Kyle.
The time that traveled

REMOVED FROM COLLECTION
OF
PRINCE WILLIAM PUBLIC LIBRARIES

1 2   2 1   1

Made in the USA
Monee, IL
31 October 2021

80828055R00104